D1553105

The Peerless Seer

By B.S. Gibbs

Creative Assistants:

S.R. Gibbs & A.R. Gibbs

Edited By:

Stephanie L. Ryan

Cover Design By:

Anca Gabriela Marginean

The Emaleen Andarsan Series is a trademark of B.S. Gibbs.

Printed in the United States of America

First Printing, 2015

ISBN 978-0-9969509-0-9

www.Emaleen.com

This is a work of fiction. Names, characters, places, and incidents are the products of the author's imagination or are used fictitiously. Any resemblance to actual events, locales, or persons, living or dead, is entirely coincidental.

This work does not express any views or opinions. And, thus, it does not reflect any views of any organization, including any governmental organization.

In Loving Memory of my Mother.

Special thanks to A.R. and S.R. Gibbs for providing creative assistance, and to Stephanie Ryan for her expert editing assistance and advice.

Special thanks also to my Father for teaching me to follow my dreams, and my Husband for his support while I was writing.

Chapter 1

It was the end of a school day in early June, in a small town in the New York Adirondacks. Eleven-year-old Emaleen Barsan was waiting impatiently for the instruction from her teacher to pack her backpack and for the ring of the school bell so that she could go home. Emaleen, who had light brown hair and green eyes that slightly gave off a mysterious sparkle, barely contained her impatience. She couldn't wait for the school day to end. It always made her heart race with excitement and joy.

As dismissal time came near, she usually felt an increasing eagerness for the freedom that she experienced when she left school for the day. It meant she was free to explore her own interests, which were many and varied. She would also no longer be confined to a classroom filled with about a dozen students, who were all expected to sit quietly in chairs arranged in neat rows, for an hour or more at a time, listening to the teacher lecture.

"Class, please copy your homework down from the board," directed Ms. Perch, the teacher. "When you are done with that, please pack your backpacks."

Emaleen did not stop to copy down the homework as her teacher instructed. Instead, she started packing her backpack. As she put her books in her backpack, her mind was filled with anticipation over what she could possibly do after school. She was already considering several possibilities to choose between and couldn't wait to discuss them with her friend, Skye Stewart, who was often her companion in her many adventures.

The two girls frequently enjoyed going on treasure hunts through the woods and around the lakeshore near Emaleen's home. Sometimes, Emaleen would find small animals that were hiding in the bushes.

She also couldn't wait to feel the warm sun and breathe the fresh air. Outside in the warm sun, surrounded by plants, trees, and animals, she would feel a surge of energy and sense of wellbeing that she didn't

1

feel while inside, especially not in the small, gray school building. Also, outside of the school, she felt free and confident while inside the school she felt trapped and restricted. Inside the school, she also felt very restless and had a difficult time containing and controlling her energy.

"Emaleen!" called out Ms. Perch in a stern voice. "Did you copy your homework down from the board yet?"

Emaleen wasn't listening, so she didn't respond to her teacher's question. Although she was a quick learner, Emaleen didn't like school very much. She often failed to pay attention to her teacher. She would rather hear a quick explanation and get to the work right away so that she could get it done quickly. She wasn't interested in listening to what seemed to her to be long, drawn-out instructions that she didn't feel she needed. To her, extensive instructions were unnecessary and boring. This attitude contributed to her inattentiveness.

Also, she didn't have the patience to spend much time on her work. She would usually finish her work early and then offer to help other students in the room. Many of the other students looked forward to working with Emaleen because she had an ability to explain the lessons so that it was easy for them to understand. And, she enjoyed helping her classmates because she liked being active and busy.

Although Emaleen had great potential for learning, her teacher wasn't impressed. It was clear to Ms. Perch that Emaleen did not put all of her effort into her work. Some things had just come easy for the girl and, as a result, she had developed a habit of only putting enough of herself into her work to just get by. It was as if she was using only a part of her brain and not fully applying all of her abilities. Unfortunately, she didn't realize she was doing that and the consequences that were connected. Instead, she believed her teacher was unfairly hard on her. She also thought that the teacher was demanding more effort than was necessary.

Just one more minute, thought Emaleen, and the bell will ring. One more minute, she thought, and she would be heading home. She thought about walking through the woods, across the bridge over the river, and down the dusty, stone covered road to the home that she lived in with her aunt and uncle.

"Emaleen, are you listening?" asked Ms. Perch sternly, trying to break into the girl's thoughts. "Emaleen!"

The girl did not respond. She was deeply lost in her own thoughts. But this was not a new occurrence for her. She had a habit of wandering off into her own thoughts. Sometimes it was during a lesson when she already understood the materials being covered. Other times, it was because she would just rather be somewhere else, and she imagined herself in those places.

The teacher seemed to understand these reasons. She would often gently remind Emaleen to come out of her thoughts and put her mind back into her schoolwork. But Ms. Perch also frequently seemed exasperated at her student's frequent lack of attention.

Emaleen just couldn't direct her mind fully to her studies. Although she generally realized that an education was important, the manner in which it was delivered was, in her opinion odd and dull.

As she sat deep her in her own thoughts and not hearing her teacher, a quick thought flashed through Emaleen's mind, and she responded by looking over at the windows. There, she saw a robin sitting on the window sill. The robin had a white, crescent moon shaped spot on one of its wings.

Emaleen had seen this bird many times before. But today, it seemed to her as if the robin was watching her. She shook her head and laughed to herself. It was ridiculous to think the bird was watching her. But the coincidence of the bird appearing around her so many times, with such an unusual marking, must mean something, she thought.

As Emaleen continued to watch the bird, she thought about how on her walks she would often imagine the various animals that must be nearby as if she could see them in her mind. She would often think of a kind of animal only to find the animal along her journey. She would also point out to her friend, Skye, numerous animals that were hiding in bushes and deep grass, and sometimes she would move a rock to reveal a hidden frog or snake or other animal to show her friend.

Discovering an animal never surprised Emaleen. She thought it was normal and that it happened to everyone. But she had never discussed her ability with other people, and so her belief that it was normal remained unaltered. She also never wondered at the surprise that her friend, Skye, always expressed when they were walking together and Emaleen found a hidden animal. Nor did she question why her friend never demonstrated the ability by discovering animals to point out. She simply assumed that her friend had the same ability but had chosen not to use it.

Suddenly, her thoughts were interrupted by a loud, irritated voice. "Emaleen Barsan!" It was her teacher, Ms. Perch, who frequently called out her name during the school day to get her attention.

"Emaleen! How many times do we have to do this? Emaleen?" stressed Ms. Perch. The teacher then loudly clapped her hands three times to get her student's attention.

Ms. Perch, a thirty-five-year-old woman, had taught at the school for the past ten years. The teacher appeared stern and severe with her black hair pulled back tightly into a bun on the top of her head. Emaleen often wondered if Ms. Perch's hair would come out of her head if the bun were pulled just a little tighter. Ms. Perch also had dark brown eyes that expressed an intense understanding as if she could read people's thoughts. At that moment, the teacher's deep eyes were gazing intently at Emaleen, sternly demanding a response from her student, who was now finally paying attention.

"Ms. Perch," replied Emaleen softly and nervously. "What is it?"

Emaleen looked at her teacher with a pained look on her face. She was sure that Ms. Perch was annoyed and that she would not like what her teacher would say next.

"Did you copy your homework down from the board, Emaleen?" asked Ms. Perch for the second time.

4

"No, Ms. Perch," answered Emaleen in a guilty sounding voice. "But I will do it now."

Emaleen reached into her backpack to retrieve her assignment book. She quickly copied the assignment down and put the book back in her backpack. She looked up at her teacher with a slight smile.

Ms. Perch then said, "Since you daydreamed half of this day, you will stay and stack the chairs. I also want you to put all of the books away. You will need to alphabetize each shelf, too." Then the teacher added, "Skye can stay and help you if she wants."

When she was finished giving this command, Ms. Perch turned away from Emaleen to face the rest of the class and said, "Class, I have an additional assignment, which is inspired by your classmate, Emaleen. I would like everyone to write an essay tonight, which will be due tomorrow. For your essay, you will pick a career that requires attention to detail. You will explain how the career requires attention and what would happen if the person didn't pay attention. One example is a brain surgeon. Could you imagine a doctor doing brain surgery and not paying careful attention to what he or she is doing? That would be very scary, wouldn't it? Now, don't use my brain surgeon example. You must come up with your own idea."

Suddenly, the bell rang, and the students instantly started moving toward the door. They lined up in front of the door and turned to Ms. Perch, eagerly awaiting permission to leave. Ms. Perch often told them, "The bell doesn't dismiss you from class. I do." So, the students knew that they must patiently wait.

"Class dismissed," called out Ms. Perch after they had all lined up. Then she turned to Emaleen and said sternly, "You may leave when you have finished your duties."

As her classmates walked out the door, some turned to give Emaleen a quick, resentful look, likely because of the extra homework assignment. But some of her classmates gave Emaleen a small smile, even though they knew they would be writing an essay, which the teacher had blamed on her.

Emaleen sighed as she watched the class and the teacher exit. At times, it was hard enough for her to fit in without her teacher helping to make enemies for her, she thought. She was just different enough, with different interests and viewpoints, that it was difficult for her to find friends with any interests in common with hers. And, some of the activities that the girls at school found so interesting were boring and pointless in her view. For instance, she didn't like to play dress-up with dolls. She thought it was boring to dress a doll, only to change the clothes again and again. She also was not interested in using the dolls to stage pretend drama scenes such as dates with boys.

Another difference was that she wasn't interested in the latest fashions and trends like the other girls. She had her own unique sense of fashion. In fact, because she found it interesting to wade in the creek behind her house, climb trees, and collect and study leaves and rocks, she preferred functional clothes over binding ones. She preferred to be comfortable so that she could be free to explore. She particularly liked crop pants and t-shirts when she was active. And, when she wasn't wading in creeks, climbing trees, or exploring the woods, Emaleen liked to wear long flowing skirts and sometimes dresses that swirled around her when she twirled.

They should get to work immediately, thought Emaleen, so that they could finish and leave shortly. She turned to look at Skye, who was already stacking the chairs in the corner of the room. Then Emaleen picked up two chairs at one time and carried them over to the corner to stack them.

"Thanks," Emaleen said to Skye as she stacked chairs. She was so pleased that her friend had stayed behind to help her. The work would go quickly now and then they could walk home together.

As she stacked chair after chair, Emaleen thought about how silly it was for the students to have to stack the chairs every night and then put them back every morning. She had heard that this was so that it would be easier for the school custodian to sweep and mop the floors. But, she wasn't quite sure why Ms. Perch made *them* do this, or why she had made Emaleen do this when usually each student had to stack his or her own chair before leaving. It seemed unfair to her. But she worked hard to get the job done quickly.

After they were done with the chairs, she and Skye turned their attention to the bookshelf to sort and put away the books. They worked as quickly as possible. Both were eager to finish and leave.

Skye, a blonde-haired, amber-eyed girl, was just a few months younger than Emaleen. She was pretty but had a toughness and an inner strength that gave her courage. She was also Emaleen's closest friend and often looked out for her. But she had a different style of dress than Emaleen. Because she was a tomboy, she never wore dresses but was always in jeans or shorts and a t-shirt. Her hair was also always neatly combed and tied back into a ponytail.

The girls had known each other since they were babies and had play dates arranged by their families. They also were in the same classes in school each year since kindergarten. So, they had essentially grown up together and knew each other better than anyone else did.

The two girls continued to work quickly to put the books back on the shelf in alphabetical order. But their interest in getting out of the school motivated less care in ensuring perfect alphabetic order. At this point, Emaleen really didn't care about accuracy, particularly as there were only two weeks left before summer vacation and she doubted Ms. Perch would check the book order herself. And, Skye couldn't wait to start her afternoon adventures with her friend. Also, Ms. Perch had left as soon as the other students had filed out, leaving the two girls alone in the classroom. As there was no one there to check their work, it was less than perfect.

When they were finished, Emaleen gave her friend, Skye, a big hug and a warm smile. Then the two girls walked out of the classroom together, down the long, dark, and dreary hallway, toward the main entrance of the building. As they approached the main entrance, Emaleen could see the sunlight shining through the doors, lighting up the last few feet of the hallway.

Once outside, Emaleen stopped, took a deep breath and tilted her face up toward the sun to feel its warmth. After a brief moment, she continued her walk away from the school. She began to feel a sense of peace and relief with each breath, and with each step she took as she walked away from the building.

As Skye walked with her friend down the sidewalk leading away from the school, she half-skipped, half-walked, in a meandering fashion, almost knocking into Emaleen a few times. It looked to Emaleen as if Skye, too, was feeling the same peace and joy that Emaleen was feeling because they were leaving the school building. But school didn't bother Skye as much as it did Emaleen. Skye was more patient, adaptable and easy-going, and less restless than her friend. She also liked school.

Skye was the first to break the silence as she stated, "I don't know why Ms. Perch gives you such a hard time. She doesn't seem to like you very much." Skye looked at her friend with compassion and sadness. She didn't like that Ms. Perch made her friend unhappy, and she wished the teacher would stop.

"I know," agreed Emaleen. "I don't know what I did to make her not like me." After a pause, she added, "I just can't wait for summer."

"It's almost over," said Skye. "You can make it. I'll help you."

"Thanks," said Emaleen. Then after another short pause that resulted from Emaleen stopping to think, she asked, "Do you want to come over to my house for a little while?"

"Sure," answered Skye. "But I have to call my mom."

"Good. Let's race to my house," Emaleen said as she began to run.

Skye bounded quickly after her friend but was unable to catch up despite putting all of her energy into the competition. But after several minutes, Emaleen slowed to allow her friend to catch up and then Skye closed the gap between them. After Skye caught up, Emaleen giggled and then sped back up. Emaleen reached the front porch of her house before Skye. When Skye arrived on the porch, the two stopped for a moment to catch their breath before going inside.

Chapter 2

The house was a large, two-story, dark-stained wood structure that almost blended into the trees surrounding it. It was old, dating back to the late 1800s. The front of the house had a large railed porch that stretched across the front of the house and down the sides.

Sitting on the porch were several wooden Adirondack chairs. These chairs had seats that slanted downward toward the back and backs that also slanted backward from the base. They were so comfortable that sitting in one could result in the occupant taking a nap.

After Emaleen entered the house, she walked through a sitting room and into the family room, which was an interior room without windows. As she walked into the family room, she saw her aunt, who was sitting on the couch, waiting for Emaleen to return from school.

Emaleen had been adopted by her aunt, Zeraida, when she was only a few weeks old. But even though her aunt was legally her mother, Zeraida preferred for Emaleen to refer to her as an aunt. She had explained to her niece that she did not want to replace Emaleen's birth mother. She knew, but did not share with her niece, the possibility that birth mother and daughter might be reunited someday. So, she wanted to keep the natural birth relationships as they were. But Zeraida, having raised her niece from birth, loved the girl dearly, and if circumstances were different she would have wanted to be called mother.

Zeraida had promised Emaleen that when the time was right and the girl was old enough to understand, she would tell her niece all about her birth parents. In the meantime, Zeraida had shown her niece the original birth certificate, which stated that Emaleen's mother was named Seanna Andarsan and her father was named Mannix Andarsan. She also showed Emaleen the adoption papers from the court.

Zeraida Barsan was a forty-two-year-old woman with brown hair that fell far down her back and light gray eyes that captured and reflected back the colors around her. There was also a slight sparkle in her eyes that was so faint it could almost be missed without close observation.

9

Zeraida was ten years older than her sister, Seanna. She had a mind that was very sharp, and she was in great physical shape. Emaleen was often shocked at how much energy her aunt had at her age. Her aunt seemed to have limitless energy and seemed more like a girl in her twenties than a mature woman in her forties. Of course, Emaleen was just eleven years old, so Aunt Zeraida seemed old to her.

"Come with me into the kitchen for a moment, Emaleen," requested Aunt Zeraida when she noticed her niece.

"Skye, can you stay here?" Aunt Zeraida asked pleasantly as she started to walk away. Emaleen followed her aunt through a doorway in the family room that led to the kitchen. When they arrived in the kitchen, Aunt Zeraida pointed to a chair and motioned for her niece to sit.

"How was your day? Did you meet anyone new? Did anything unusual happen?" asked Aunt Zeraida, mysteriously. Every school day, her aunt pestered Emaleen with the same three questions when she arrived home. Emaleen didn't know why her aunt asked the questions, but it was always easier to answer them than to quiz her aunt.

"Aunt Zeraida," said Emaleen with a sigh. "I didn't meet anyone new today and nothing unusual happened. It was like every other day, and Ms. Perch was her usual self. I have extra homework tonight because Ms. Perch decided that I wasn't paying attention enough. And, I don't know why she is so mean to me. I get pretty good grades." As she finished speaking, Emaleen looked sad and irritated.

Zeraida looked at her niece sympathetically and commented, "I don't always agree with your teacher. But I believe that she is trying to help you learn all that you are capable of. She is trying to push you to work hard so that you can learn more than you realize that you can."

In response, Emaleen rolled her eyes. It was frustrating to hear her aunt supporting her teacher's actions. But she also knew that her aunt had her best interests at heart. So, she tried not to get too mad at her aunt.

Aunt Zeraida continued, "Anyway, I can't explain it to you now, but a really good education is so much more important for you than it might be for the other kids in your class. Your mind will be your most powerful tool, and you need it to be well-educated. And, paying attention and using your senses to gather information even when you think you don't need to pay attention or when something is boring will allow you to *see* more, so much more, than you can imagine. You would be surprised at the important things that people miss because they are not using all of their senses and all of their minds. If you learn nothing else but to be able to carefully observe your surroundings and listen to others, you will have learned some incredibly powerful lessons. It's also important when someone speaks to you that you can interpret what the person means, what the person is not telling you, and what everyone else thinks the person is saying. I know you probably won't really believe me until you *see* for yourself, but you'll just have to trust me for now."

"I suppose I will have to *see* for myself," replied Emaleen thoughtfully and with a slow sigh. "But why are you always asking me if I have met someone new or if something unusual happened?"

"Because, as I said, it's important to pay attention to what is going on around you. Everything has a meaning and a purpose, even if it seems unimportant at the time. But if you can't *see* the signs, you won't be able to *see*. And you must do everything you do with very careful attention to what you are doing," Aunt Zeraida advised softly and gently. She was worried that her talk might sound like a lecture to her niece.

"I don't think I'll ever *see* whatever it is that you think I will *see* someday," grumbled Emaleen doubtfully.

"You will," Aunt Zeraida assured Emaleen. "And you will be surprised by what you *see* when you finally do. You have special gifts that you have yet to discover, and you have a lot to learn about the world."

"But for now," Aunt Zeraida added, "until you do *see* for yourself, you must be patient and learn from those who will teach you. You must also pay attention to the detail in every lesson. It's the only way that you will become prepared to *see*."

Aunt Zeraida's facial expression changed suddenly as if she wished to change the subject. She then stated softly, "Would Skye like to stay for dinner and then work on homework with you?"

"I'll ask," Emaleen said as she stood up from her chair and started to walk away. As she did so, she thought about her aunt's words. It was upsetting that her aunt appeared to have taken the teacher's side. It didn't seem to her that her aunt understood her concerns. But she also knew that her aunt loved her very much and that she meant well. And, although she didn't fully understand, she could sense that there was at least some wisdom behind her aunt's statements.

Emaleen walked out of the kitchen and back into the living room and found her friend sprawled out on the couch. Skye had her head on one end and her feet up on the other end. She looked so content and relaxed that Emaleen thought the girl might be asleep. Skye had a way of making herself instantly comfortable in whatever surroundings she found herself in. It was one of the many things that Emaleen liked about Skye and one way in which Emaleen wished she could be more like her friend.

"Do you want to stay for dinner?" Emaleen proposed to her friend hopefully.

"I can't," replied Skye in a disappointed voice. "My mother is making a special dinner tonight. She told me not to be late for dinner. But I can stay for a little while, and we can do something fun."

"What do you want to do?" asked Emaleen. Then, she had an idea. "Do you want to play in the creek?" asked Emaleen hopefully.

"Yes!" exclaimed Skye, jumping up and down with excitement.

"Cool! Let's go!" Emaleen exclaimed.

So, instead of doing homework, the two friends went outside to explore the shallow creek that ran behind Emaleen's house. The creek connected to the lake that was down the hill from Emaleen's house.

The girls liked to gather clay from the banks of the creek. They would often use the clay to make figurines that they would dry on a rock in the hot sun. They loved to make models of the animals that they saw in the woods. Lately, they had been making deer and moose figures. A moose sighting was infrequent near their actual homes, but they were fairly common around the area.

The two friends also liked to wade into the creek with bare feet and their pants rolled up. They would then dredge rocks from the bottom of the creek and wash them. They imagined themselves searching for jewels and gold in the creek. But despite their many efforts, Emaleen and Skye had never found any jewels or gold. Most of the rocks they found were usually either a dull gray or black color. But the lack of success did not deter them from continuing their searches. They started every search with excitement and joy, hoping for a great find. And even though they had not yet found any treasure, they still had great hope of doing so.

Now, the girls headed to the creek, for the first time this season while chattering excitedly about what they hoped to find. After they took off their shoes and socks and laid them on a large rock on the bank, they rolled up their pant legs. Emaleen was the first to walk out into the cold water of the creek. She let out a slight squeal because the water seemed chillier today than it normally did at this time of year.

"It's really freezing in here," Emaleen complained to her friend while shivering loudly.

After seeing Emaleen's reaction to the water, Skye took a deep breath and walked into the water behind her friend. But she paused as the cold water hit her shins. Then she started to shiver loudly.

Skye smiled and then laughed as she shouted loudly, "Argh! Let's find some treasure." Emaleen laughed in response. Skye could be so silly sometimes, thought Emaleen.

The cold water didn't stop either girl. The girls walked across the creek to a large rock on the other side with Emaleen in the lead. On the rock were a couple of sand sifters, the kind used in a sandbox or on a beach. They had left these on the rock last fall.

The girls used the sifters to dredge the bottom to gather up some dirt and rocks from the creek bed. They would then shake the silt and sand through the holes of the sifters, leaving behind the rocks, which they would sort through eagerly, hoping to find gold and jewels. Once each girl had a sifter, they each wandered off to separate areas in the creek, their feet sinking slightly into the muddy bottom.

Today, Emaleen picked a new location that she had never tried before. The location was just below a small waterfall, caused by the creek flowing down a small hill and the water tumbling over the rocks. The water falling over the rocks was crystal clear. It reflected the sunlight.

As she stood in her new location, in the cold water, Emaleen surveyed the area immediately surrounding her. She was looking for a good place to dredge with her sand sifter.

Although the water cascading over the rocks was sending ripples through the water, the water was still clear enough for the bottom below to be visible. Looking down through the water, Emaleen saw something small that glittered, sending off flickers of light. It was so small and so faint that she might have missed it if she hadn't been looking so intently at the bottom.

"Skye, I think I found something!" shouted Emaleen with excitement.

"I'll come over in a second," replied Skye, who was holding a sifter, which she shook from side to side to remove the dirt.

Emaleen reached down with her hand and tried to grab the object. But when her hand returned to the surface, and she opened it, she found nothing but a large gray rock.

"It's gone!" shouted Emaleen in disappointment.

"Are you sure?" asked Skye in a hopeful voice. "Why don't you keep looking? You might find it again."

When Emaleen looked down into the water again, she couldn't see anything glittering. The object that she thought she had seen had disappeared from view. She stopped to think for a moment. There was a chance, she thought, that her attempt to retrieve the object might have loosened it and sent it into motion in the flowing water, sending it down the creek. But it was also possible that the glittering that she saw was an illusion or it could have been just a chip or a shaving of metal. It could also still be there, she mused, but it might be covered further by dirt that had moved when she reached down for it.

Emaleen looked over at her friend, who had a pile of brown and gray rocks on the bank next to her, and who was panning with her sand sifter.

She wondered for a moment whether she should go over and work with Skye. But instead, she reached down into the water with her sand sifter and pulled up the dirt where she had thought she had seen the glittering object. She sifted the dirt around until she had just a few pebbles. All of the pebbles she found were pretty routine and boring, so she dumped them back into the water, throwing them out a distance so that they would not fall back into her work area.

Then, Emaleen reached into the water again and pulled up more dirt. She swirled the dirt around in her sand sifter until the dirt was all gone, leaving behind a few dark gray pebbles. She started to pick them up to throw them back into the water, but as she lifted the largest one, she saw a bright red-orange object underneath it. She called out to Skye as she picked it up and discovered that it was a crystal gem about two inches in size. It was red-orange in color and translucent instead of perfectly clear.

As the light hit the gem, it reflected, casting a rainbow from the gem to the water at Emaleen's feet. She gasped in surprise and wonder. Skye, who had just appeared from the other side of the creek to join her friend, also gasped in surprise. The two stood there in silence, amazed at Emaleen's find and the rainbow that it had created.

Emaleen whispered quietly to her friend as if someone might hear, although she wasn't sure why. "Skye, please don't tell anyone about this gem. Can we keep this a secret?"

Skye nodded in agreement. Emaleen wiped the gemstone dry on her pants and put it in her pocket. Then Skye looked at her watch and realized that it was almost time for dinner.

"I have to go home now," said Skye sadly. "It's getting late. But I'll see you tomorrow at school."

Skye turned to gather her things and leave, waving fondly as she walked back toward the house. Emaleen followed behind her, thinking that she should probably return to her house to eat dinner and do her homework too. When Skye reached the Barsan house, she turned to walk back down the driveway and started on her way to her own house.

Chapter 3

As she walked back to the house, Emaleen thought about the red-orange gem. She wondered what it was and why it had been in her creek. She had been searching the creek bed from time to time over a year or two without a find. And, although she had long dreamed of finding treasure, she hadn't fully believed that she would ever find any.

She had liked the strange sense of power she felt when she had first held the gem in her hand. She wanted to take it out of her pocket and examine it closely. But she also wanted to keep the gem a secret, so she resisted the powerful urge to hold it. Instead, she kept the gem in her pocket.

When she reached the house, her aunt was on the porch waiting for her. "Your pant legs are wet," scolded Aunt Zeraida softly.

Aunt Zeraida added, "You must have been in the creek searching for treasure again. Did you find anything interesting?" She looked at her niece's face closely, searching for a reaction.

"Umm — no," Emaleen lied, feeling instantly guilty. She didn't like lying to her aunt, and she did it very rarely — almost never. She knew that her aunt trusted her because of her honesty, and she didn't want to violate that trust. But she also wanted to keep the discovery of her prized treasure to herself for a little while longer.

"Are you sure?" asked Aunt Zeraida doubtfully.

She knows I'm not telling her the truth, Emaleen thought. That made her worry. But still she had this strong feeling that she needed to keep her gem a secret from everyone, including her aunt.

"Yes," answered Emaleen, biting her lip as soon as the word came out of her mouth. Again, she felt very guilty, but she wasn't yet ready to tell her aunt about the red-orange gem.

"Okay then," said Aunt Zeraida while looking carefully at her niece as if she wasn't sure that she believed her. "Dinner is on the table. It will be just the two of us tonight. Your uncle had to go on another trip. He won't be gone long, though," Aunt Zeraida promised.

"Where did he go?" asked Emaleen. "And, when will he be back?" She hated when her uncle went on trips. She loved spending time with her uncle, and she would miss him.

"He went to visit your grandma," answered Aunt Zeraida. "She needs help around the house. But he will only be away for a few days."

Emaleen looked at her aunt for a moment and wondered whether she should point out that she had never met her grandmother. She really wanted to know why that was the case. But she thought that her aunt and uncle must have their reasons. One day, she thought, she would ask them. But right now she was thinking more about her gem and how badly she wanted to go upstairs and get a good look at it.

"Okay," stated Emaleen, relieved that he would not be gone long.

"Now, let's eat dinner," suggested Aunt Zeraida.

"Can I go upstairs and change first?" asked Emaleen hopefully.

Aunt Zeraida nodded. Emaleen ran up the stairs excitedly. She couldn't wait to get to her room so that she could take the gem out and examine it alone. She ran up two steps at a time and reached her room, which was immediately opposite the top of the stairs. She opened her door and almost threw herself into her room. She shut the door quickly behind her and turned on her light.

Emaleen then pulled the gem out of her pants' pocket and held it in the palm of her hand. She sat on her bed and reached her hand out under the lamp on her bedside table. She leaned forward to take a close look at the gem under the light. It looked clearer than it had at the creek, and she could now see all the way through it.

As she examined the gem, she thought she saw something move inside the stone. It was a quick, small movement but Emaleen couldn't tell what it was. Was it reflecting light inside the gem? She didn't know, but she continued to watch the stone intently, hoping to see the movement again so that she could figure out what it was. But after several minutes of waiting, she gave up and put the gem down on her bedside table. She then quickly changed her clothes, put the gem in the pocket of her pants, and went downstairs for dinner.

When Emaleen walked into the kitchen, she saw a pizza and place settings for two at the table. She sighed. She didn't want to disappoint her aunt, but she wanted to examine her new gem alone in her room.

"Aunt Zeraida?" Emaleen asked tentatively as she approached the kitchen table where her aunt was sitting. "Can I eat upstairs in my room? I have to write a paper tonight. It's due tomorrow."

"Yes, you may," answered Aunt Zeraida. "And, I don't want to lecture you, but you really should have started the paper earlier. It's getting late."

Emaleen nodded and promised, "I will get the essay done quickly. But I will also do a good job." She knew her aunt appreciated efficiency. But her aunt valued quality even more.

Emaleen put a couple of slices of pizza with pepperoni and mushrooms on a plate and walked back to her room. Once in her room, she turned on her light and computer, and sat at her computer. She reached into her backpack and took out her assignment agenda. Looking at the homework, Emaleen sighed as she suddenly wished the work would magically disappear. But she knew it wouldn't.

Oh well, she thought, it's best just to get it done. Maybe if she hurried, she would have some time to go out onto the balcony and gaze up at the stars before going to bed.

Emaleen finished her vocabulary, spelling, and math homework first. Then she turned to the paper she needed to write about a career that requires focus and attention. She thought for a few minutes and concluded that she did not want to pick a profession that was obvious, such as a doctor, lawyer, or engineer. She wanted to write about a unique career — one that the other students would not think about. She liked to think creatively and differently.

Eventually, Emaleen decided to write about the importance of attention to detail as a petrologist, a scientist who studies rocks. She was particularly inspired by that career, given her recent find in the creek and her collection of gray rocks with mineral flakes that she had found in the water over the years. Many of her discoveries were displayed on a shelf over her bed. She also wished that she knew more about rocks and minerals so that she could identify her new rock.

As Emaleen worked on the essay, she was surprised to find that she really enjoyed herself. The writing became easier the longer she worked, until her words almost seemed to flow from her fingers as she typed her essay on the computer. She easily completed the minimum size of the assignment in a short amount of time and continued on to write a much longer piece. While writing the essay and researching the career of a petrologist, Emaleen started to wonder what kind of rock her red-orange gem was. But she put her thoughts aside and finished her essay first.

After she had finished her essay, she started to research her stone on the Internet. Initially, she couldn't determine what kind of gem she had. But, there were a few possibilities. It could be a tangerine quartz, citrine, andesine, fire opal, imperial topaz, or an orange garnet. She even found a picture of a red-orange sapphire, which looked a lot like her stone, and it surprised her because she had thought all sapphires were blue.

Despite her research, Emaleen couldn't figure out which of these her gem was. Many of them were not very common and some of them were found outside New York, in other parts of the world, or in another state in this country. Sapphires, for instance, can be found in other countries and in Montana, in the United States. She needed to make sure that she narrowed the choices down to a type of gem that could be found where she lived, which was in the Adirondacks in upstate New York. But she wasn't sure which of the gems she found in her research could be found in the Adirondacks. And, stranger yet, many of the gems in their natural form did not look like Emaleen's gem. They only looked like the gem when polished.

If she were to guess, based upon the pictures she found, she would guess that the rock was a red-orange sapphire. But sapphires weren't found in the Adirondacks. If the gem was a sapphire, then Emaleen wondered how it would have come to rest in the bed of the creek in her backyard. It just did not seem realistic that it could be a sapphire. But the rock really did look like a red-orange sapphire. It also seemed strange to her that she would find an already polished gem in the creek. The only explanation Emaleen could come up with was that someone must have lost the gem, and it made its way downstream to the creek behind her house.

Emaleen then looked over at her clock on the table next to her bed. It was getting late. She realized that she should print out her essay and pack her homework in her backpack. She would have to figure out what her gem was another time. It was now time for her to go to sleep.

She then carefully placed the gem on the shelf over her bed that she used to store her clay figures and other treasures. When the gem caught the light, it twinkled briefly as if it were winking at her. Emaleen stared at the gem for a few minutes, awed by its beauty. A feeling of calm and serenity overcame her as she gazed at it. Then, suddenly, she felt the urge to hold the rock in her hand. She reached up to the shelf and retrieved it. She placed it in the palm of her hand and rolled it around in her hand. As it rolled in her hand, Emaleen felt more and more relaxed and then happy. She also felt that sense of power she had felt before. But, after a few minutes, Emaleen put the rock back down on her shelf.

Suddenly, Emaleen started to feel guilty about the lie that she had told her aunt. Her aunt had asked her if she had found anything unusual while she was out at the creek, and she had denied it. If she had only found the types of common stones that she usually found, she would have been telling the truth. But this red-orange stone was unusual, and it seemed to have a strange effect on her. Maybe she should tell her aunt about the stone, she thought.

Immediately after that thought, her aunt knocked at her door. Aunt Zeraida called out from the other side of the door, "It's time to wrap everything up and go to bed."

Emaleen replied in a nervous-sounding voice. "Can I talk to you for a minute?"

"Of course," said Aunt Zeraida, opening the door as she answered. "What's on your mind?"

"You asked me today if I found anything unusual while I was at the creek. Well, I did find something, and I'm not sure what it is exactly." Emaleen took the gem from her rock shelf, placed it in her palm and reached her hand out toward Aunt Zeraida. Emaleen watched Aunt Zeraida's face carefully as she held out the gem. She noticed her aunt straighten a little as she glanced at the gem. Then Aunt Zeraida breathed in slightly as she stared intently at it. A few moments went by before Aunt Zeraida spoke.

"Yes, you do have something unusual here," commented Aunt Zeraida. "I haven't seen anything quite like it. But I have read about a gem like this. I'll look into what this might mean. In the meantime, I think your instinct to keep this stone a secret is correct. Don't tell anyone about this." Then she asked, "Does Skye know about it?"

"Yes, she does," agreed Emaleen, "but she promised to keep it a secret. She always keeps her word, so I know I can count on her."

"Thank you for letting me know about this gem. It's very important that you tell me about anything usual that happens to you or that you find," Aunt Zeraida said with a smile.

"Emaleen, on another note, I hope you understand what I was saying about your teacher today," implored Aunt Zeraida. "I hope you don't think I'm picking sides between you and your teacher, and choosing your teacher. I am choosing your side, and I will always choose your side, even when it doesn't seem like that to you, and even when I have to point out to you that you made some bad choices. But I'm hoping to help you understand that it doesn't matter who your teacher is and whether she is extra picky or extremely nice. It's your education that is the most important. To get that education, you need to figure out how to get along with your teacher. Also, I am always here for you, and I am willing to help you figure it out along the way and to help you determine the right choices to make. I will also not allow anyone to mistreat you. So, please always come talk to me."

Emaleen listened carefully to her aunt. She knew that her aunt didn't intend to lecture her, and she knew that her aunt cared for her very much and only wanted the best for her. At the same time, it was hard for her to listen when her aunt seemed to support her teacher's actions.

She thought her teacher had actually acted like a bully today. They had been teaching them at school about bullies, but sometimes it seemed that they forgot that adults can be bullies too.

Aunt Zeraida continued, "You should also know that I have some very important lessons that I am going to be teaching you when you are ready. You can think of it now as the passing down of your family's tradition and birthright. But in the meantime, you will need to work on building a very good base of knowledge in math and science. So, it's important for you to work hard at school. And, it's not just for good grades, but it's critical for you to become what you are destined to be."

Her aunt was often telling her about her destiny as if there was some grand plan for Emaleen to do something great. But she did not feel all that special and actually thought her aunt seemed a little crazy when she talked this way.

Zeraida suddenly realized that she had said enough and that it was likely that Emaleen was losing interest or that she was feeling lectured to. So, Aunt Zeraida sighed and decided to stop the talk. She really wished her niece would understand why her education was so important. But she couldn't make her niece understand by wishing. Emaleen would have to *see* for herself.

"Now it's time to go to bed," Aunt Zeraida said gently as she moved toward the door. "Leave the rock here on your shelf for now. And, don't take it out of the house." Aunt Zeraida closed the door behind her. Emaleen could then hear the sound of her aunt's footsteps as she walked down the stairs.

After Emaleen had dressed for bed in shorts and a t-shirt, she turned toward her windows, noticing the full moon in the night sky. She opened her windows and walked out onto her balcony, which hung off of the back side of the house. The balcony overlooked a hill leading down away from the house and toward the lake, which was several hundred feet from the house.

As Emaleen looked down at the water, she noticed that the moonlight shone brightly on the surface of the water. She also looked up and saw that the sky was clear and the stars were twinkling.

Emaleen took in a deep breath slowly and let it out slowly. She often walked out onto her balcony to enjoy the view and the outside air before going to bed. She loved the smell of the woods and the nearby lakes in the air. After several minutes of enjoying the view and the air, she turned and walked back into her room, closing the windows behind her.

She then turned off the light and climbed into bed. She looked over to her shelf and noticed that the gem was glowing, giving off a gentle scarlet light. She smiled and turned over to her side and fell into a deep, relaxing sleep. She felt better after having told her aunt about the peculiar red-orange gem. She didn't like to go to sleep with something on her mind, especially something that troubled her.

That night she dreamed of finding a clear, crystal-like rock with many smooth sides on it in the creek, in a place farther down the creek than she had ever panned before. The crystal looked very much like a diamond, but it was slightly long, with points on each end. Emaleen couldn't remember ever seeing a diamond like that in the jewelry catalogs that came in the newspaper every Sunday. She smiled in her sleep, thinking of the riches that she would find the next time she went into the creek to pan for treasure. If she were to find a real diamond, Emaleen, her aunt and her uncle would be rich. Then maybe she wouldn't have to go to school anymore. Maybe then she could get a tutor and be homeschooled.

Chapter 4

The next day at school was mostly uneventful and peaceful. Emaleen did her best to pay attention and she put extra effort into her work. Ms. Perch was pleased and gave Emaleen some compliments for her attention to the lessons. Ms. Perch also allowed her to go to recess a few minutes before the other kids in the class as a reward for her efforts.

After lunch, which was right after recess, Ms. Perch pulled Emaleen aside and handed her the essay on petrologists, which Ms. Perch had graded and marked with an "A." Ms. Perch smiled at Emaleen when she saw the girl's surprise upon seeing the grade.

Ms. Perch then said, "Emaleen, I owe you an apology. I should not have acted the way I did yesterday. It was unfair for me to give your classmates homework and then blame it on you. That was very wrong. But I was frustrated because I know you have tremendous gifts, and I also know that you don't use them. I've been trying to encourage you to work harder. But I was wrong to do what I did yesterday. I hope you can remember that teachers are human too, and that we, too, can make mistakes."

Emaleen nodded and smiled. But she did not say anything. She knew that teachers were human, but she had never heard one apologize before. She thought maybe Ms. Perch wasn't so bad after all. Maybe Ms. Perch did care about her and wanted the best for her.

"Emaleen," whispered Ms. Perch quietly so that only Emaleen could hear her. "You are a very smart girl. I know that you learn things quickly when you put your mind to it. You have an intellectual talent that you often don't use fully. I just know that you have great potential to do extraordinary things during your life. I'd hate to see you waste that by not working hard enough to match your talents. I'd really like to see you put yourself fully into your education. If you were to do that, I believe you could do anything you want later in life. So, I hope you prepare assignments of this quality for your teacher next year."

"Yes, Ms. Perch," responded Emaleen as she walked back to her desk. She was pleased by the compliment that she received from her teacher and also the apology. But she wasn't really sure what to think about Ms. Perch's speech about her talents and need to work hard. She sounded just like her aunt. Even so, she decided that she would try her best to work harder as Ms. Perch suggested. So, she did so for the rest of the school day.

At the end of the day, Emaleen skipped happily out of the classroom and out of the school. There was no homework that night since it was so close to the end of the school year. She was pleased with the prospect of more free time that afternoon to explore the woods and creek with Skye. But when they searched the creek for treasure later that day, the girls did not find anything unusual.

The next couple of weeks of school went by quickly for Emaleen. Because it was almost the end of the school year, the class watched some educational movies and played educational games. They also had a field day with competitions between the classes in each grade level. They also had more recess time.

But it was not all fun and games. There was also a final review of the year's school lessons and an introduction to some new skills that they would be learning the next year. Emaleen continued to work hard, but she could not wait for the school year to end. The last week of school went fast and before she knew it, the school year was over, and it was finally summer vacation.

At the end of the last day of school, the girls walked together through the woods down the path to Emaleen's house. They stopped along the way to pick wildflowers and watch a bunny rabbit that Emaleen had discovered hiding in a bush.

The bunny thought he was hidden pretty well, but the girls could see him sitting in the bush eating and wiggling his little nose. When he caught Emaleen's eye and realized he was visible, he turned quickly and scampered off farther into the bush. The girls then continued on their way.

When they arrived at Emaleen's house, they went into the kitchen for some food and found Aunt Zeraida there. They were hardly able to contain their excitement about the end of the school year and were jumping up and down, and all around, recklessly.

"Girls," said Aunt Zeraida. "I know you are both excited, but you really do need to calm down. It wouldn't be good for you to jump around like wild children and fall and break something, particularly at the beginning of the summer. Swimming and casts don't mix very well."

The girls calmed down and stopped jumping. Aunt Zeraida had a point, Emaleen thought. It would ruin their fun if either of them had a cast, she realized.

"Now that you have calmed down, we can celebrate," announced Aunt Zeraida with a big smile on her face. "I made you girls a special snack to celebrate your completion of the fifth grade and the start of summer break."

Aunt Zeraida led the girls outside. She had set the celebration up at the picnic table on the left side of the house, near a very tall and wide, old oak tree. She had even laid out a floral-themed tablecloth and napkins and had tied red and blue balloons at the corners of the table. There was also sparkling confetti around the top of the table.

The snack consisted of several different types of sandwiches, including peanut butter and jelly, tuna fish and pickle, and banana and chocolate spread. The sandwiches were cut into funny shapes such as moons, stars, and diamonds. For the drink, she had made frozen smoothies from fresh strawberries, blueberries, and blackberries that she had picked from the garden in their yard, crushed ice, and vanilla ice cream.

Aunt Zeraida smiled as the girls devoured the sandwiches and then took sips of the drinks. She had a joy for life that she loved sharing with others, particularly with her niece, Emaleen. Aunt Zeraida also remembered how excited she used to be as a girl on the last day of school each year. She was excited herself that it was the beginning of the summer vacation because she looked forward to the extra time with her niece.

This year, summer was especially important because Aunt Zeraida had plans to begin her niece's education in the skills and arts that Emaleen could be expected to inherit from her family, which were unique and rare gifts. Aunt Zeraida knew that she was not ready to share all of the family secrets with Emaleen, but she knew she must begin to prepare her niece. She didn't show it, but she often worried that her niece would not be trained in time — that Emaleen would find herself suddenly unprepared for what might come to be.

Despite her worries, Aunt Zeraida also knew that she had to be patient and give Emaleen some time to adjust to what Aunt Zeraida expected to come as a great shock to her niece. But with proper and careful guidance, Zeraida believed that Emaleen would be just fine and would learn what she needed.

With a smile, Aunt Zeraida stated, "Emaleen, I have a special present for you." She then went into the house and came back with a flat box wrapped in pink foil paper. She handed it to her niece, who opened it quickly, tearing the paper eagerly.

When Emaleen was finished pulling off the wrapping paper, she opened the box to find a large garment that looked a little to her like a robe. But it looked different than a robe. She held it up looking at it and trying to figure out exactly what the garment was. It had a hood and a tie-string at the neck and slits in the sides.

"It's a cloak," Aunt Zeraida informed Emaleen. "I thought you might enjoy wearing it. It's made completely out of cotton so it won't get too hot in the summer."

"It's really beautiful!" exclaimed Emaleen as she looked it over and noticed the lines on the front of the cloak that twisted around into a complicated pattern.

The pattern was about four inches wide, with thick black lines intertwining with each other and making a complicated design that looked like roads wrapping around each other. The pattern went along the edges of the opening of the cloak, up one side over the top of the head on the hood and down the other side.

"I'll help you," offered Aunt Zeraida holding her hands out for her niece to hand her the cloak. Emaleen handed her aunt the cloak and her aunt helped her put it on. Aunt Zeraida untied the ties at the bottom of the sides of the hood and then placed the hood on Emaleen's head and showed her how to put her arms through the slits on the side. Then Aunt Zeraida retied the ties. The cloak was long on Emaleen and just touched the ground. Emaleen swirled around in the cloak and the cloak billowed out as it caught the air.

"I love it," beamed Emaleen. Then she asked, "What are the designs on this cloak?"

"The patterns are called Celtic knots," explained Aunt Zeraida. "The Celtic knot is a part of our family heritage. The cloak is symbolic of our family's past. Our ancestors used to wear cloaks like this out in public, but in modern times, we don't. I will explain it all to you more someday when we have time, but today is a day of celebration. You should eat, drink, and play today."

"I've seen this pattern on other things around our house," commented Emaleen. She was curious about the meanings, but she knew her aunt was right. This was a day to play and have fun. They needed to celebrate the ending of the school year. So, she took the cloak off, folded it, neatly placed it back into the box, and set it on the table for the time being. She looked forward to wearing it again.

Aunt Zeraida then said, "Emaleen, I don't want you to be bored this summer, so I will have a series of challenges for you to complete over the summer. There will be at least one each week. Some weeks there may be more than one challenge. Some tasks may seem easy. But some tasks will challenge your mind in ways you never have experienced before."

Aunt Zeraida paused for a moment and then continued, "You will be rewarded for completing each challenge. But the greatest reward will be the knowledge that you gain and the feeling of achievement that you will feel. But I will also provide you with some other rewards. Some of these rewards may be items and some may be special outings with Skye. I will reveal each challenge to you as I am about to give it to you."

"Some of these challenges you must do on your own. But for some of the challenges, you may have help from Skye if she wants to participate too." Aunt Zeraida looked at Skye with a smile when she made the last statement. Skye nodded quietly in response.

"Do you have any questions, Emaleen?" asked Aunt Zeraida.

"No," Emaleen answered slowly.

Emaleen still didn't know what to think. But she didn't feel like getting into a discussion with her aunt just now. She just wanted to enjoy her first day off from school.

"All right," said Aunt Zeraida. "Well, we'll start after you've had a few days off from school. I'll let you know when it's time for the first challenge. In the meantime, please keep in mind what I told you a couple of weeks ago. You need to pay attention to everything around you. Each detail and happening has potential meaning. You need to be observant to *see*. But for now, enjoy your snacks and have fun."

Aunt Zeraida smiled and turned to walk back toward the house, leaving the girls to enjoy their meal alone. After she had left, the girls looked at each other quietly for a few moments, eating their food.

Emaleen was the first to speak, and she asked, "Skye, do you want to help with some of the tasks?" She hoped her friend would want to help so that she would not have to do the challenges alone.

"Yes, I do," Skye agreed immediately with eagerness. Skye was intensely curious about what the tasks could be, and knowing Aunt Zeraida, she was pretty sure that the tasks would not be boring. It also meant to Skye that she could spend more time with her friend.

Emaleen felt more confident about being able to accomplish the tasks knowing that Skye would be there to help her for at least some of them. She was also very curious about what her aunt might have in mind and couldn't wait for the challenges to begin.

Chapter 5

The two girls finished their sandwiches and drinks and started to clear the table, bringing the empty dishes and leftover food into the house. Then they ran up to Emaleen's room. They turned on the radio and turned up the volume so loud that the music blasted through the room and made the floors vibrate.

The girls danced energetically, making the floor shake as they did so. They sang along with the music loudly, holding hair brushes in their hands as if they were microphones. After a few songs, they turned down the music and settled onto Emaleen's bed, kicking their feet up against the wall.

Emaleen rolled onto her back and looked up at the ceiling. She loved that she didn't have any homework or anything in particular that she had to do. At the same time, she wasn't entirely sure what to do with herself.

Emaleen sighed and said to Skye, "What should we do now?"

Skye rolled over and answered in a bored voice, which surprised her, "I don't know."

The two sighed with discontent. The excitement of school being over had just worn off, and the girls weren't sure what to do. Suddenly, Emaleen came up with an idea.

Emaleen suggested, "Why don't we hike down the trail to the lake." Skye agreed, and both girls bounced off the bed and headed down the stairs. They skipped some steps somewhat recklessly on the way down and were lucky they did not trip.

As she ran past Aunt Zeraida on her way out of the house, Emaleen yelled out, "We're taking the path down to the lake. We won't be gone long."

"Take the phone with you," Aunt Zeraida replied, "and some water."

"I'll be right back," Emaleen called out to Skye as she ran back into the house.

Emaleen grabbed the cell phone from one of the tables in the family room, and she ran into the kitchen. Then, she took two plastic refillable water bottles from one of the cupboard shelves and filled them with water and ice. She then opened the refrigerator and stared inside, wondering what they should bring for food. Even though they had just eaten, she was sure they would soon be hungry again while on their adventure. She did not see any food in the refrigerator suitable for a hike, but on top of it, there were cookies and bananas, which she took.

She also retrieved a lunch bag with a long strap from the small closet next to the refrigerator and filled the bag with the food she had found. After filling the bag with enough food for their hike, Emaleen rejoined Skye on the porch.

Emaleen loved to walk down the path on their property leading down to the lake. Around the lake were many trees, and in the distance, the girls could see mountains. The girls also liked to watch the ducks swim on the water and throw bread out to them. Sometimes, they would bring paper and draw pictures of what they saw around the lake.

The girls walked down the trail, carefully avoiding the rocks in the path and holding on to trees as they navigated the steep descent downward. The girls needed to hang on to the trees as they walked down the path to the lake because it was steep and rocky.

At the bottom was a long, wide dock upon which the girls liked to sit, putting their feet in the water as they stared out into the lake and around the shore. When they reached the dock, they kicked off their flip-flops, put down their supplies, and sat on one end of the dock and put their legs into the water.

They liked this end of the dock because it gave them a view of a long stretch of rocky beach. It was one of the few places along the lake that did not have a house built up against the shore. The owners of this particular property left the area wild and only rarely visited the area. Emaleen had seen them just once, and it appeared to her that they were walking the property quietly and carefully so as not to disturb the wildlife.

As the two sat and stared over at the shore of the wild area, Emaleen noticed a red robin fly in and perch itself on a nearby branch. The robin had the same white shape on one of its wings as the bird she saw at school and that she had seen many times before. It seemed to Emaleen as if the robin was looking at her. She chuckled to herself quietly. It was strange how often she kept seeing this bird.

Suddenly Emaleen gasped in surprise as another event caught her attention. Skye turned to look at her friend and then turned her eyes to the wild portion of the shore, searching for whatever could have caused Emaleen to gasp. Skye searched and searched but could not find anything that could have caused her friend's reaction.

"Emaleen," Skye whispered quietly. "What's up?"

"A moose is coming," informed Emaleen in a distant sounding voice as if she were distracted.

"Really? I don't see a moose," said Skye. "Where do you see him?" Skye searched all around for the moose.

"He's not here yet, but he's coming," stated Emaleen with certainty. In her mind, Emaleen could see the moose coming down the hill toward the girls.

"Why do you think so?" asked Skye. "Can you hear him?" Skye still did not see a moose. She also did not hear one coming. She would have thought that such a large animal as a moose would make a lot of noise if it were heading through the brush toward them.

"No, I just see him in my mind. Don't you?" Emaleen asked suspiciously.

"No, I don't." Skye looked carefully at her friend with concern, wondering why she would say something so strange, and asked, "Are you hot? Do you feel faint? Do you need some water? Are you okay?"

Suddenly, the two girls could hear the sounds of breaking branches, as if something heavy was walking through the woods, crushing branches on the ground in the brush. The two girls turned their heads at the same time and stared intently at the trees on the shore opposite them. As they stared, the noise became louder and louder. Eventually, they saw a large, brown moose with a large crown of antlers on his head break through the brush and walk toward the water.

The moose stopped at the water's edge and took a long drink. Then it raised its head and looked at the girls, standing there for several minutes. The girls sat very still, afraid to move or even breathe for fear of scaring away the moose. As they continued to stare at the moose, it seemed to Emaleen as if the moose had noticed them.

The moose stared at them and then snorted. The girls continued to sit as still as statues for several minutes as the moose continued to stare back at them. Then the moose bowed his head down and then lowered one of its knees down to lower his head farther.

Without thinking, Emaleen stood slowly and then she raised her arm, reached her hand out in front of her, and stroked downward as if she was petting the moose on the nose. The moose let out a long, low, whistling sound. Then he stepped forward and stomped his front feet into the water, splashing as he moved his feet up and down, alternating each foot as if he were dancing in the water.

Emaleen still stood on the dock, holding her hand up as if she still had her hand on the moose's nose. Skye looked back and forth at Emaleen and then the moose in amazement, not knowing what to think. Skye had never seen anything like this in her life or had even heard of such a thing happening. And, even though the moose was actually a great distance away from the girls, it seemed to Skye as if her friend really was petting the moose because of the way the animal was reacting to Emaleen's movements.

A few moments later, Emaleen lowered her hand slowly and started to sit back down. The moose stopped its dance and then turned and walked slowly away, pushing its way back into the brush, crushing the brush loudly. As the moose traveled away, the noise of the moose making its way through the brush became quieter and quieter until the sound was gone.

The girls sat there in silence for several minutes after they could no longer hear the moose. Skye had a lot of questions but wasn't sure what to do or what to say. She looked at Emaleen and opened her mouth to speak, but the words would not come out.

Emaleen, too, sat there not knowing what to do. She couldn't explain even to herself what made her stand and then hold her hand out to the moose, or even why the moose appeared to bow to her or anything else that the moose did. She also sensed that her friend, Skye, was bewildered and it wasn't just because of the moose bowing, but it was also because Emaleen knew the moose was coming and because of the petting.

Skye also sat there thinking about the events with the moose. She had always realized that Emaleen was different from the other kids. But if anyone would have asked Skye what was different about her friend, she wouldn't have been able to describe it. She had just known. But Skye had always liked that her friend was different and unique. She thought that it was interesting and she always really enjoyed the time she spent with her friend. And, now she had direct evidence that Emaleen was different.

"What just happened with that moose?" asked Skye in a friendly but curious tone.

"Honestly, I don't know," replied Emaleen. "I knew a moose was coming, but I don't know why I stood up, and I don't know why the moose did what he did."

Skye believed her friend, but she asked, "How did you know the moose was coming?"

Emaleen replied, "I can see in my head an animal that is nearby before it appears. I think that sometimes I can also see animals that are nearby that stay hidden. Don't you see them too?"

"No, I don't think anyone else does," Skye replied. There was a short silence as the two girls sat there thinking.

Then Emaleen commented, "I just always thought that everyone could do this. So, I never thought it was unusual. Can we keep this our secret? I don't want anyone at school to know about this. They already think I'm kind of strange, and I don't want to be picked on."

"I won't tell anyone," promised Skye. "And, so you know — I don't care. I like you just the way you are. And, I'd rather spend time with you than any of the other girls at school. But I think you should tell your aunt about this. I always hear her asking you if something unusual happened. I don't know why she asks you, but it's like she expects something to happen and she's just waiting. Seeing the animals in your mind before they appear and also what happened with the moose today are both unusual things to happen — very unusual."

Emaleen nodded, not knowing what to say. Then she playfully splashed water at Skye with her feet with the purpose of ending the uncomfortable conversation. Skye splashed water back. The splashing continued until both girls were soaking wet. The girls then decided to walk back to the house. They put their shoes on, took a drink of water and then headed back up the hill.

As they walked back up the hill toward the house, Emaleen wondered what Aunt Zeraida would say. Would her aunt believe her? Skye was also wondering what Zeraida would say, but she was pretty sure that she wouldn't be there to hear it. Skye thought Zeraida might want to have a private conversation with Emaleen, but her curiosity was nagging at her fiercely.

Skye also thought about the challenges that Zeraida had planned for her friend. Skye liked Zeraida. She thought that like Emaleen, Zeraida was different and unique, and in a good way. Zeraida's eyes, for instance, seemed wise, and it appeared to Skye that her friend's aunt understood a great deal more than she let people know about. Zeraida was also good at giving advice when Skye asked for it, but sometimes the answers that Zeraida gave were not direct, and it took some time for Skye to figure out the guidance. But once Skye understood the advice, it was always helpful.

It was also interesting to Skye that Zeraida walked barefoot more frequently than she wore shoes and that she wore dresses and long skirts that were sometimes more like multiple layers of wraps of cloth than dresses. Zeraida also wore the most beautiful and unique jewelry with stones of different colors, some of which changed colors with the light.

Zeraida also often smelled of flowers. Skye thought that this was probably from the amount of time that Zeraida tended the flower and herb gardens that surrounded the house. The woman also frequently made things in the kitchen, such as preserves and pickles, and other concoctions. But sometimes when Skye visited, she couldn't tell by the smell what Zeraida was actually making. At times, Skye could smell very strange, unappetizing smells coming from Zeraida's kitchen that smelled almost like medicine.

As they approached the house, Emaleen could see her aunt sitting on the porch waiting for her. She had an intense look on her face as she glanced over at Emaleen. She knows, thought Emaleen. She always knows when something has happened, she thought.

Chapter 6

When the girls had almost arrived at the porch, Aunt Zeraida asked, "Emaleen, did you have fun? And did anything unusual, or out of the ordinary happen?" Aunt Zeraida looked closely at her niece's face, watching her reaction carefully.

"Yes, I had fun," replied Emaleen almost sadly. "But, I really need to talk to you." She had a confused and worried look on her face that informed Zeraida that the matter was serious.

Zeraida turned to Skye and said sweetly, "I'm glad you were here to celebrate the last day of school and spend some time with Emaleen. You are a really good friend." After a pause, she added, "Maybe you can come back tomorrow. I might have a challenge for you to do with Emaleen if you are interested."

"Oh, I am definitely interested," Skye replied instantly.

And, just as Skye had predicted, Zeraida said firmly but kindly, "Now, I need to talk to Emaleen, and I'll need to do so privately. Would you mind going home now?"

"That's fine. I understand," Skye admitted knowingly and then she turned to leave.

Zeraida turned to Emaleen and then as if she had forgotten something, she abruptly turned back to Skye, who had started walking away from the porch, and called after her. "Skye, one more thing. Would you mind keeping whatever you saw today a secret? I can't explain it now, but it's very important that you don't discuss with anyone what you saw today, whatever it was. If you have questions, you can ask me tomorrow. You can also tell your parents."

"I won't tell anyone," Skye called back. Zeraida was relieved because she knew that Skye was the sort of girl who kept her promises.

After Skye was far down the road, Aunt Zeraida looked at her niece, waiting for her to explain what had happened. Emaleen was silent for a moment, trying to organize her thoughts about what had happened. She wasn't sure she could explain it.

Sensing that Emaleen was at a loss for words, Aunt Zeraida began, "Whatever it is, even if it doesn't make sense or it seems crazy, you can tell me. Just start wherever you can, and we'll figure it out together. And you don't need to worry about what I'll think. I promise that I won't think you are crazy."

Emaleen took a deep breath and confided, "I really don't know where to start. I did something that was strange, and I don't know why. It was like it was what I was supposed to be doing, but I don't understand it, and it scares me."

Zeraida placed her hand on Emaleen's shoulder in support and assured, "It's okay. I'll help you figure it out."

Emaleen began, "Well, we were down on the dock with our feet in the water, just relaxing and talking, and I saw in my mind this big moose coming through the woods to the lake shore. A few minutes later, the moose came crashing through the bush and took a drink of water."

"Then he looked up at me and stared at me, and after a couple of minutes of staring at me, the moose bent one of his knees down and seemed to bow to me," continued Emaleen. She also shared with her aunt the figurative petting that she had done and the animal's prancing in the water in response.

Emaleen, who hadn't been looking at her aunt while she spoke, stopped and looked at her aunt to observe her reaction. What she saw surprised her. Her aunt didn't look upset or disturbed. Her aunt's face was glowing with excitement and what seemed like pride. Emaleen was confused. She expected her aunt to tell her that she needed to sit down, rest, or see a doctor.

Zeraida then spoke calmly, "Emaleen, I know I haven't told you this before, and it's going to sound strange. Please listen carefully to all that I have to say before you react and say anything."

"That sounds kind of serious and scary," declared Emaleen with a tremble in her voice. She didn't think she could hear about anything scarier than what had happened with the moose.

"You shouldn't be scared. It will be all right," assured Aunt Zeraida. "But you should know that you were born into a family that has certain powers. Some people think of these powers as magic, but to me, they are so much more. They require more than just the waving of a wand."

Aunt Zeraida continued, "Our people are called *seers*. I will explain this more to you another time. I think you need to hear about this a little at a time. But for now, it's important that you don't talk about being a seer to anyone, not even Skye."

"Ummm…" murmured Emaleen. She was shocked and did not know what to say. She had believed in magic when she was a younger child, but she had grown to realize that there was no such thing as magic. At least, that's what she had thought. And, now she had magic?

"So, why then did the moose bow and prance at me?" asked Emaleen. "Were you playing a joke on me?" But she didn't really think her aunt would do that. Aunt Zeraida always seemed pretty serious. Emaleen just did not know what to think about what her aunt was telling her or what had happened with the moose. It didn't seem real.

"I'm not sure yet what your encounter with the moose means," admitted Zeraida. "But I do know that you must be starting to discover one of your gifts. It involves animals. But exactly what you will be able to do with that gift remains to be seen. We'll have to work together to figure that out. You may have other gifts too, but it is this one that has started to reveal itself now."

Emaleen looked surprised and excited at the same time. When her aunt had spoken many times in the past about the gifts that she might have some day, Emaleen thought she was talking about math, or science, or some career-related skills and abilities. She hadn't imagined that it would have anything to do with magic or animals prancing and bowing to her.

After a few moments of silence as she collected her thoughts, Emaleen asked, "So, I am a witch, then, right? Will I learn to fly on a broomstick or disappear in a cloud of smoke? Will I be able to turn people into toads?" She stared at her aunt intently, searching her aunt's face carefully for a reaction.

"No, you are not a witch," answered Aunt Zeraida. "You are also not a wizard or a magician. And, no you will not fly on a broomstick, disappear, or turn people into toads. You might, however, learn how to float through the air on your own, though. We will talk more about what seers are later on, and you will start to learn what a seer can do as you begin your training. In the meantime, please be patient."

"But what does it mean that the moose did that?" questioned Emaleen. "Am I a ruler of the moose or something?"

Zeraida thought quietly for a moment and answered, "I have never heard of anything like this happening before. It seems that this moose had some reason for greeting you. But I don't know why he would do that. Although some seers can have certain powers associated with animals, I have never heard of a wild animal taking such notice of a seer on its own."

"Was the moose the Moose King or something?" asked Emaleen. She was desperate for an explanation of the strange event.

"I don't think there is any such thing," said Aunt Zeraida chuckling. "I really don't know exactly what this means. I wish I knew everything. But I have to admit that there are some things about being a seer that I don't know. And there are things that happen from time to time that take me by surprise and that I don't know how or why they occurred. This moose situation just might be one of the mysteries of the seers that I haven't figured out yet. But maybe one day we will know what this means."

Her niece had so many questions that it was somewhat tiring. But at the same time, Aunt Zeraida was pleased that her niece was thinking critically about the situation and asking intelligent questions.

Emaleen had turned red when her aunt had started chuckling. It seemed to her that her aunt was laughing at her as if she was asking stupid questions. Aunt Zeraida smiled and reached out to hug her niece. The hug assured Emaleen that her aunt was not laughing at her.

"I'm sorry," apologized Aunt Zeraida in a soft, quiet voice. "I wasn't laughing at you. I was just picturing a moose as a king of some kind. The image of a moose with a crown on his head seemed funny to me."

Then Aunt Zeraida suddenly changed the subject, saying, "Emaleen, it would be helpful for us to figure out what talents and abilities you have with animals. I want you to decide upon a pet for us to get. We will use your relationship with your pet to figure out what it is that you can do." Zeraida looked at her niece waiting for a response.

Emaleen thought for a moment and then she decided, "I think we should get a cat."

Zeraida nodded but then she added, "We need another animal too, one that you can interact with more. You will have some interaction with the cat, but we need an animal that will work with you more than a cat will. Cats tend to be too independent, and they can also be fickle. That makes working with a cat difficult."

Emaleen thought for a few moments again, but it was not long before Zeraida interjected, "I have an idea. I have a friend who has the perfect animal. I'll call him and see if he's available to come visit us."

"What kind of animal is that?" asked Emaleen curiously.

Zeraida replied, "If I can get my friend to come, which I can't guarantee, then it will be a surprise. In the meantime, let's get your cat. Hopefully, we will find a kitten so that we can start fresh without the animal already having an attitude."

"We'll go tomorrow," continued Aunt Zeraida, "but I would like you to read a book about cats that I have in my library. It will be important for you to understand your animal fully. You will need to study lots of different animals from now on so that you learn how to use your gift and explore its full potential."

Emaleen smiled at her aunt. She wasn't surprised to hear her aunt mention a need to study.

Aunt Zeraida then went upstairs. Emaleen could hear her aunt's footsteps on the floor above. But she couldn't tell where her aunt was walking. She started to wonder where her aunt's library was located. There wasn't one upstairs. Also, Emaleen had been in Aunt Zeraida's room and had never noticed any books before. But Aunt Zeraida returned quickly with a book about cats, and to Emaleen's surprise, a book about moose. Where, thought Emaleen, does she keep her books?

"It's getting late," observed Aunt Zeraida. "I should make you a quick dinner. Then, you should probably start getting ready for bed. But you can read some tonight if you would like. You should also think about what kind of cat you would like to get. We'll go into town in the morning and find a kitten."

Emaleen and her aunt ate a quick dinner of leftover pizza that her aunt had reheated in the oven. After they had finished eating, Aunt Zeraida kissed Emaleen on the cheek, gave her a hug, and wished her a good night.

Emaleen went upstairs and prepared for bed. She crawled into bed with her cat book and started reading. She read the book late into the night, finishing it before she fell asleep. The book explained all about how to care for a cat and what a cat needs physically and emotionally to be happy and healthy. The book also provided information about the personality of cats in general and the pros and cons of the different breeds of cat. Emaleen couldn't wait to get her new kitten tomorrow. But she eventually fell asleep and dreamed of kittens.

Chapter 7

The next morning, Emaleen woke up early, looking forward to getting her new kitten. She had dreamed all night of different kinds of kittens and woke up still not sure what kind she would get. But the kind of kitten really didn't matter to her.

While still in her bed, Emaleen imagined snuggling with her new kitten on her bed while she read at night before going to sleep. She also imagined playing games with her cat, making it jump in the air and spin as she whipped a cat toy around on the floor and in the air. Maybe, she could get one of those laser pointers that shot out a spot of red light that the cat would chase if you moved it around, she thought.

Emaleen jumped out of bed and went downstairs to the kitchen still in her pajamas. Her aunt already had breakfast ready. Emaleen ate her food so quickly that she almost inhaled it. She could not wait to get her new kitten. She could hardly contain her excitement.

"Slow down," her aunt scolded her gently. "We're not leaving for a little while yet."

Although she had scolded her niece, Zeraida smiled. It made her happy that her niece was so excited.

"Okay," sighed Emaleen, slowing down only a little. "Where are we going to get the kitten from?"

"Well, first we're going to try the shelter, but it may be harder to find a kitten there," answered Aunt Zeraida. "I know last night I said that you should try to get a kitten. But so many animals need homes, and they aren't all kittens. So, I'd like you to consider an adult cat too. But the animal you choose is up to you. Please promise to keep an open mind, just in case."

"I will," promised Emaleen, looking at her aunt intently. She was so excited to get a pet that she didn't care whether it was a kitten or an adult cat.

After Emaleen had finished breakfast, Aunt Zeraida asked her to get ready. So, she ran upstairs and changed out of her pajamas quickly.

"I'm ready now," declared Emaleen running back down the stairs and rejoining her aunt.

"Before we go to the shelter," said Zeraida, "we need to go to the department store to pick up a couple of litter boxes, litter, cat toys, maybe a cat house and, of course, some food. It's important to make our new family member feel at home."

On their way to the shelter, Emaleen and her aunt stopped at the department store to get the items they would need. They also purchased cans of kitten food and cans of adult cat food so that they were ready for whatever age of cat they chose.

After finishing at the department store, the two continued on to the animal shelter. At the shelter, Aunt Zeraida filled out a form. Along with the form was an information page that explained that to adopt a pet it would be necessary to speak with a pet adoption counselor.

The form instructed that a pet adoption counselor was a person in charge of ensuring that the people who came to pick out an animal were prepared to care for an animal and could be trusted to take good care of the animal. After Aunt Zeraida had read the information to her niece, the two went over to the adoption desk to start the process.

At the desk was a young lady in her twenties. She introduced herself as Grace, a pet adoption counselor. Grace, asked Emaleen and Aunt Zeraida a lot of questions, hoping to be able to help them choose a cat who would be best suited to their interests and personalities and to determine whether they would be good owners.

Emaleen talked about how she was hoping to find a cat that was different from an ordinary, common cat. She felt that a unique, unusual cat would be more suited to her personality. But Emaleen could love any cat that was willing to be loved and returned some affection.

After speaking with Emaleen, Grace left the room saying that she would be back soon. The counselor then went to discuss the girl's preferences with some of the other staff members. She also went to visit the cats ready for adoption to determine which ones Emaleen might find interesting.

Grace was gone for about ten minutes. While the counselor was gone, Emaleen closed her eyes and her mind filled with many different cats and kittens of all different colors, such as gray, white, black, calico, and yellow/tan colors. Then she saw what looked like a baby tiger. Emaleen shook her head in surprise as she instantly thought that there couldn't possibly be a baby tiger at the shelter.

Aunt Zeraida quietly watched her niece with interest, observing her niece's expression change from serious contemplation to a look of surprise. It was interesting, thought Zeraida, with a mysterious smile.

When the pet adoption counselor came back, she said, "Emaleen, we have lots of different cats that I think you would just love to take home. I have some specific suggestions, but you are welcome to come into the kennel area and look at all of our cats. Do you have any preferences for the kind of cat you would like to see first?"

"Do you have any cats that look like tigers?" asked Emaleen. She didn't think there would be, but she thought that she should ask just in case. It may have meant something when she imagined a baby tiger. If they had such a cat, she should adopt it, she thought.

"I don't have any cats that look like baby tigers," Grace said, "but I have a very special kitten that we are very lucky to have that is close. He is a unique animal that requires very special care and a responsible owner. Would you like to see him before the other animals?"

Emaleen nodded with excitement. She couldn't wait to see this kitten. Somehow she knew this kitten would be right for her.

"Then come with me," said Grace, motioning for Emaleen and her aunt to follow her.

The counselor led them out of the room down a hall and through two different doors and then past a long row of stacked empty cat cages. She then led them into a large room, which contained an area enclosed by a three-foot high wall with a hip-high door for them to pass through. She led them through the door and closed it behind them.

"This first cat is a little kitten about five months old," said Grace. "He was brought to us just last night. He is a mix between a Bengal and a Savannah. We expect that he might grow to be quite large as a result."

"How did you get him?" asked Aunt Zeraida. "Aren't both breeds very expensive?"

"The owner who brought this kitten to us was very upset to have to give him up," replied Grace. "His cat had just had a litter, and he was able to sell all of them except for this one. He was smaller than the others and, like you said, these are very expensive cats. People are looking for perfection when they spend that amount of money. So, this is a very lucky time for you to come here."

Aunt Zeraida looked a little concerned as she asked, "Do you know any of the breeding history of this cat? How close to a serval is he? I've heard about these animals, and I don't want my niece to have a pet who could be inappropriate and potentially dangerous."

Emaleen didn't hear any of her aunt's concerns. She was too busy thinking about how this could be the tiger she had imagined. She was already falling in love with the idea of having this kitten, sight unseen.

The pet adoption counselor responded, "The owner informed us that the Savannah in this kitten's family tree is very far removed from a serval, probably an F7 or higher. The Bengal in his tree is also separated by several degrees from a wild cat. If you treat this kitten well and train him, he should be a very nice cat for you — a big one, though. You can also take these cats for a walk on a leash like you can for dogs. You can't do that with most other kinds of cat."

"I'd love to see him!" exclaimed Emaleen. "I read all about Savannahs and Bengals in my book last night. They are both very full of energy. So this kitten might be a lot of fun."

Grace nodded and then she left, returning shortly with a small kitten that looked more like a baby tiger than a cat. This kitten had a yellow-tan colored coat, black stripes all over his body, black spots between the stripes, and golden colored eyes.

Emaleen sat in the middle of the floor looking at the kitten with great interest and instantaneous love. The counselor put the kitten down on the floor, and it immediately walked over to Emaleen and sniffed her shoes. Then the kitten looked up at the girl, put a paw up onto her knee, and jumped onto her lap.

She then began to pet the kitten and scratch him gently on the top of his head between his ears. The kitten curled into a ball and purred, looking into Emaleen's eyes.

Grace smiled, knowing that a connection had been formed between the kitten and the child. She looked over to Zeraida, who nodded, indicating that she granted her permission.

"Is this the kitten you want?" Aunt Zeraida asked her niece. Then she observed, "He seems to have chosen you."

"Yes, he's perfect," declared Emaleen as she looked lovingly at the kitten.

"You will need to play with your kitten every day so that he releases all of that wonderful energy that he has in a good way," instructed Grace. "This breed of cat needs a lot of involvement from their guardians and a lot of exercise on a daily basis. If you don't do this, you will find him to be a difficult pet to own. He may use his energy in ways that you will not appreciate."

Emaleen nodded enthusiastically and said, "I will have no problem playing with my cat every day. I have lots of energy too!" Emaleen smiled a wide grin and looked hopefully at her aunt for an indication that her aunt would let her take this kitten home. Her aunt smiled.

Grace handed Aunt Zeraida another form to fill out. Aunt Zeraida filled out the form and paid the adoption fee.

The counselor then motioned for Emaleen to hand her the kitten. The girl complied, and Grace put the kitten in a temporary cat carrier specially designed for a trip home from the shelter. The kitten walked into the carrier without complaint.

Aunt Zeraida and Emaleen thanked Grace and left the shelter with the carrier. The kitten meowed loudly as they walked to the car.

"What are you going to name him?" asked Aunt Zeraida after they were seated in the car.

"I don't know yet," replied Emaleen from the back seat of the car. The kitten was in the carrier on the seat next to her.

"Emaleen, you will be in charge of taking care of this kitten," instructed Aunt Zeraida. "You must make sure he is fed every day and that you play with him. You will also need to clean the litter boxes."

Aunt Zeraida continued, "He will need to stay in the house for a while until he is used to his new home and he understands that you are his guardian. If he doesn't learn this, he might run away and get lost. So, please don't let him outside until I let you know that it's safe."

"I plan to be with him all the time," vowed Emaleen.

The two drove home in silence. Emaleen was busy thinking about playing with her new pet when she got home. She was also going through possible names in her mind.

Aunt Zeraida was thinking about what might happen now that her niece has a pet with whom she would be forming a bond. Emaleen's gifts with animals should start showing more clearly now. Aunt Zeraida would have to pay close attention without letting on too much to her niece just how much she was watching her for signs of her gifts. She would also need to be patient, but she hoped that the gifts that showed themselves would be substantial and that they would all appear soon. She had waited a long time for the first of Emaleen's gifts to reveal itself, and even now with a gift related to animals having done so, Zeraida wasn't sure what the extent of the gift was and how it would be useful to Emaleen in the future. Zeraida also knew that although she had to be patient, she was also unsure of how much time they really had to wait.

Aunt Zeraida had already decided that she needed to help the process along when she decided to start giving Emaleen the challenges. But before she even started with the challenges, one of Emaleen's talents had fortunately revealed itself on its own.

She would now need to create the right circumstances for Emaleen to develop whatever skills she had as quickly as possible without rushing them. Zeraida had yet one more animal surprise in store for

Emaleen that she thought might help her niece discover the full extent of her talents with animals.

When they arrived home, Emaleen walked quickly into the house, being careful not to shake the carrier with her kitten in it. As soon as she made it to the family room, she set the carrier down and opened the door for the kitten to escape the carrier. Once the carrier was open, the kitten poked his head out slowly and cautiously and then looked around. Then he pulled back into the carrier.

Emaleen called out, "Here kitty, kitty," in a sweet, high voice. Then she tapped her fingers on the floor outside the cat carrier to make the kitten curious.

The kitten once again poked his head out and then slowly left the cat carrier. He looked around the room at the furniture and then down at the shaggy carpet. As the kitten moved his paws, he discovered movement from the yarn in the carpet. The kitten started to play with the strands of yarn in the carpet, batting them between his paws.

Emaleen looked at the kitten, and he returned her glance. She softly said "no," and the kitten stopped his play and walked right over to her. She then sat down next to the kitten and motioned for him to crawl onto her lap. The kitten took a flying leap but landed softly in Emaleen's lap. He then curled up in her lap and started purring.

As she petted him, Emaleen thought about potential names for her new companion. She closed her eyes and thought to herself, "tell me your name." She opened her eyes and looked at her new kitten. Then a name suddenly came to her.

"Belenus," Emaleen blurted out, surprising herself. She didn't know where the name came from.

"Belenus," she said again. "That's your name. Do you like it?"

The kitten meowed and stared at the girl. Then he yawned, stretched, and went to sleep. It seemed to Emaleen as if the kitten liked his new name, or at least, had acknowledged it.

Aunt Zeraida then called out from the kitchen, "Did you choose a name? Did I hear the name Belenus? How did you think of that?"

"Yes, I did choose Belenus as his name," responded Emaleen. "It just popped into my head. But I have never heard the name before."

"That is a very unusual name," commented Aunt Zeraida, who was now with her niece. "That's the name of the Sun God believed in by the Druids, an ancient religious sect in Old England. It's interesting that you would pick that name on your own."

Aunt Zeraida added, "Some cats don't come when their names are called. You should use Belenus' name as often as possible so he gets used to it and learns it's his. Maybe he'll be one of those cats that answers to his name."

"Okay," said Emaleen, smiling. It would really be nice, she thought, if Belenus would come when his name was called.

"Also," instructed Zeraida, "you should set up Belenus' litter boxes, cat bed, and cat climber very soon." Then Aunt Zeraida suggested, "You should also get the cat toys out and play with him until he's tired out. Tomorrow, if all goes according to plan, I will have another surprise for you. But you'll have to wait to see what it is."

Aunt Zeraida turned as she finished speaking and headed back to the kitchen, leaving her niece with her new kitten. Emaleen then set up two litter boxes, one in a bathroom on the first floor and one in a bathroom on the second floor. She also set the cat bed and cat climber in her bedroom and brought out a cat toy made up of a long string with several colorful feathers attached to it. Emaleen traced the feathers on the ground for Belenus to chase. The kitten eagerly hunted the feathers, pouncing on them and grabbing them with his paws, and following them yet again when Emaleen pulled them away playfully. After twenty minutes of play, Belenus stopped and lay down on the ground on his side, breathing heavily. He was tired, and he had lost interest in the toy. So Emaleen put the toy in her closet.

Emaleen then carried the tired kitten up to her room. When she reached her bedroom, she put Belenus down on the cat bed. She then sat on her bed and started to read. The kitten left the cat bed, jumped up onto the bed next to Emaleen, curled up and went to sleep.

As Emaleen was reading, her phone rang. It was her friend, Skye, who had heard about the kitten and wanted to come over to see him. Emaleen agreed and invited Skye over for lunch.

When Skye arrived, she was astonished by the size of Belenus, who was a big kitten even though he was small for his breeding. She also loved his stripes and spots. Emaleen pulled out a ball of yarn from her aunt's knitting supplies, with her aunt's permission, and the girls took turns rolling the ball of yarn around for the kitten to chase.

As they were playing with Belenus, they couldn't help but notice that he would actually fetch the yarn and return it to them for them to roll it again. This was amazing to Skye, who had a cat once and had never seen her cat play fetch. Clearly, Skye thought, this kitten was not an ordinary cat, and it was not just because of his unique breeding mix.

After Skye left, the rest of the day was uneventful with Emaleen reading and playing on her computer, all the while accompanied by her new furry companion. After dinner, she fed Belenus some soft food made especially for kittens and reintroduced him to his fluffy and comfortable bed, which she had moved from the floor to a place up on a shelf in her room that she emptied so that she could allow Belenus to sleep there. She had been careful to secure his bed down with Velcro strips, one side of which she sewed to the bottom of the bed and the other side of which she stuck to the shelf with double stick adhesive. She was hoping to prevent the bed from sliding should Belenus decide to jump up into his bed. She also attached some steps to the wall that led up to his bed so that he could climb his way up.

At bedtime, Emaleen prepared for bed, said goodnight to Belenus, turned off the light and climbed into bed. Belenus jumped onto Emaleen's bed instead of his own. He then curled up and went to sleep instantly. It didn't take Emaleen long to fall asleep either, even though she was very excitedly thinking about what the next surprise her aunt had planned could be.

Chapter 8

The next morning, Emaleen awoke early as a result of Belenus pouncing on top of her and playing with her hair. When she opened her eyes, Belenus had a piece of her hair in his mouth. Emaleen gently brushed her hair away from Belenus's mouth. She crawled out of bed with Belenus hopping down behind her. She then got dressed and went down to the kitchen to feed the kitten and get some breakfast for herself. He followed behind her with his soft paws tapping on the hardwood floors.

Once in the kitchen, Emaleen put some soft kitten food out for Belenus. She then took a big red apple from a bowl on the kitchen table for herself. Aunt Zeraida was not in the kitchen this morning, which was unusual. Her aunt was usually in the kitchen waiting with breakfast for Emaleen, and they would usually discuss the events that could be expected for that day. Emaleen enjoyed her morning talks with her aunt. Now, she wondered where her aunt was.

Emaleen finished her apple, eating it in several large chunks. After throwing away the core, she walked out of the kitchen and to the front door. Maybe her aunt was outside, she thought. Emaleen walked out the front door carefully, trying to ensure that Belenus didn't escape into the outdoors. He was new to the house and couldn't go out yet. She successfully exited the house and entered the porch without allowing Belenus to escape. But as soon as she shut the door, she could hear the kitten meow. She looked through the screen and saw him sitting in front of the door looking up at her.

"I'll be back, Belenus," promised Emaleen softly. Belenus meowed in response.

Emaleen turned and walked down the steps from the porch to the lawn. She then walked around the house, looking for Aunt Zeraida and calling her name. As she turned the corner around to the side of the house, Emaleen saw her aunt talking with her uncle, Morvin Barsan, who must have just returned from his trip.

Uncle Morvin was forty-seven years old, and he had dark hair with some gray strands and green eyes. He was of average build, but was very tall, approaching six feet in height. He was wearing a button-down shirt with a tie, suspenders, and dress pants. Her uncle, more often than not, dressed up somewhat formally. She rarely, if ever, saw him in t-shirts or jeans. She often wondered about the stark contrast of dress between her aunt and uncle. But it didn't seem to bother them at all.

As she got closer to her uncle, Emaleen also noticed that there was a man with her aunt and uncle that she didn't recognize. The man looked to be about fifty, and his hair was completely gray. He was thin and short, about five-feet-six inches in height. He was dressed similarly to her uncle.

Emaleen also noticed that her aunt, her uncle, and the stranger were standing right next to a large structure that was new to the yard. The structure had wooden sides and a top, and a cage front. She wondered what it could be and stared at it, examining it carefully as she approached the three adults.

"It's called a mew," Aunt Zeraida called out as she saw Emaleen walking toward them with a curious look on her face. "It's a house for another animal that I want you to meet."

Emaleen looked over at the man with her uncle and saw that he had a large bird sitting on his arm, which was gloved. The feathers on the bird's back were black and gray, and its neck was covered with downy feathers that were light brown in color. On its underside, the bird had caramel colored feathers with short, horizontal black stripes of color. Its eyes were black. Its ankles were covered with what appeared to be leather bracelets. Attached to a metal ring on the bracelets was a leather strap, the other end of which was connected to the glove worn by the man. Also affixed to the bracelets on the bird's legs were small metal bells. The bells jingled as the bird readjusted its feet while it sat on the glove.

"This is Shaolin. She is a Peregrine falcon," stated Aunt Zeraida. "She's not for you to keep. She's just here to visit with you."

"Owning a falcon requires very special training between the animal and its falconer," added Uncle Morvin. "It takes many years to become a falconer and to learn how to take care of and work with a falcon."

"You also need a special license from the state to own a bird of prey, such as Shaolin," explained the man politely. "But you need to be at least fourteen years old in this state to apply for a license."

Emaleen looked at the man curiously and wondered who he was. Zeraida saw the quizzical look on her niece's face and realized that she had not yet made introductions. So, she introduced the man to her niece.

Aunt Zeraida said, "Emaleen, this is Mr. Earl. He is Shaolin's owner, and he is a master falconer. He is a long-time friend of our family. He will be staying in the guest house for a while."

"Hi, Emaleen," said Mr. Earl in a pleasant voice. "It is nice to meet you. I have heard so much about you. Your aunt and uncle speak very highly of you."

"Hi, Mr. Earl," said Emaleen. "It's nice to meet you, too. Your falcon, Shaolin, is very beautiful. Can I help with her sometime? Can I fly her sometime?"

"At some point, Mr. Earl may let you handle Shaolin with his supervision and instruction," said Aunt Zeraida. "You must be patient for a little while, though."

Mr. Earl nodded and said, "First, I have to be sure you are ready. You must listen to me carefully and follow all of my instructions before I can let you handle Shaolin. I have trained her to be friendly with humans because she was born in captivity, but she is still a wild bird by instinct and can be very unpredictable. It takes training and experience to safely handle a bird like Shaolin."

The falcon stared at Emaleen as she stared back at the bird. Emaleen tilted her head to the right slightly, and Shaolin tilted her head to the left slightly as if the girl and the falcon were mirror images of one another. Emaleen then waved her arms up and down and Shaolin, in turn, flapped her wings. Emaleen then hummed softly and in response Shaolin let out a couple of chirps and a screech. The others watched the interaction of the bird and girl with great interest.

Emaleen was fascinated and a little confused by this interaction with the bird. She looked over at her aunt and saw that she was smiling. It seemed to her that her aunt was actually proud of her, but she couldn't imagine why.

She then looked over at Uncle Morvin. She was glad to see him home. Her uncle was often away. But when he was home, he would spend time with her playing board games, playing ball games in the yard, such as soccer and catch, or having her assist him with home improvement projects. Uncle and niece were very close.

Uncle Morvin also sometimes sent Emaleen on scavenger hunts to find leaves from plants and trees shown in pictures that he provided to her. Sometimes, she would have to take a little shovel with her and dig roots out of the ground in the woods for her uncle. She didn't ask what the items were for because she had so much fun finding them. But as she grew older each year, her curiosity started to blossom, and she was getting close to asking her uncle about the items. She was still thinking fondly of the scavenger hunts when her uncle's voice broke through her thoughts.

"Mr. Earl is going to stay here with us for a few weeks," Uncle Morvin explained to his niece. "He'll be working with you so that you can work with Shaolin someday. While she isn't with Mr. Earl, Shaolin will be staying in this mew. She can only come out when Mr. Earl brings her out. Also, you will need to keep your new kitten, Belenus, inside at all times in case Shaolin is outside. You must keep him in anyway because he is so young and still unaccustomed to his new home. But keeping Belenus inside is also for the safety of both animals. I trust you will follow these instructions very carefully."

Emaleen nodded in agreement, knowing full well that when her uncle set down a rule there was a good reason for it. Her uncle was a man of few words who spoke only when he felt it necessary to do so. So Emaleen typically complied with her uncle's rules without question.

Suddenly, Shaolin started flapping her wings and making screeching noises. It looked to Emaleen as if the falcon was either very excited about something or nervous. Mr. Earl reached for a hood and placed it over Shaolin's head, and she instantly quieted down. They all stood there quietly for a few moments staring at the falcon.

Then Mr. Earl said, "Shaolin needs some time to herself for a little while. I'm going to put her in her mew."

Mr. Earl then opened the door to the mew and slowly pushed his arm and gloved hand on which the falcon was perched into the mew. With his other hand, he removed the bird's hood and the leash. He guided his arm toward a perch, which Shaolin set herself upon as it came near her. Mr. Earl then shut the door and walked away from the mew.

Aunt Zeraida then informed her niece, "Mr. Earl brought you a couple of books on falconry. They are on the table in the family room. You should start reading them as soon as possible. They will help you become prepared to work with Shaolin."

"She's really a cool bird!" exclaimed Emaleen enthusiastically. "I can't wait to have her sit on my arm!"

Mr. Earl looked at Emaleen and said, "I'm sure that you will soon be allowed to work with Shaolin if you follow instructions carefully. That is important for your safety and Shaolin's. Also, the bird and falconer relationship is a special one that requires work and nurturing. You will progress one step at a time. So, you must be patient."

"I understand," Emaleen assured Mr. Earl.

Mr. Earl smiled and declared, "Good. But for now, we're done for today. Tomorrow is another day."

"Thank you for letting me see Shaolin. She's beautiful," said Emaleen.

"You're welcome. It was my pleasure," replied Mr. Earl. "And, it seems that Shaolin was happy to meet you too."

Emaleen turned toward her uncle, whom she hadn't yet greeted because she was so curious about the falcon. She reached out to her uncle and gave him a big hug. She had really missed him. She hoped that he would not need to go away again for a long while to come.

"I missed you, Emaleen," said Uncle Morvin. "Soon, though, I will have a surprise for you that I brought back from my trip. But I'll have to give it to you when the time is right."

Emaleen smiled. She could wait for whatever it was that Uncle Morvin was promising to give her. A surprise was nice but having her uncle home was so much better than anything that he could have brought back for her.

Realizing that she was hungry, Emaleen excused herself and returned to the house to finish her breakfast. When she arrived in the kitchen, she fixed herself a bowl of cereal and sat down at the table to eat.

Chapter 9

Aunt Zeraida returned to the kitchen shortly after Emaleen finished her breakfast. She glanced at her niece for a few moments, carefully considering what she wanted to say to her niece.

"I will soon have a challenge ready for you," proclaimed Aunt Zeraida, "but before I can give you the first challenge, I have a special lesson to teach you. Follow me to the family room, and I will show you what you need to know."

Emaleen nodded and made her way to the family room. She sat on the couch and waited for her aunt, who was right behind her, to sit on the couch next to her. On the coffee table in front of the couch, there was some paper and colored pencils. She looked at the paper and pencils, wondering what her aunt had in mind. Her aunt sat down, faced her niece, and began to speak.

"I'm going to teach you some modern science based upon generally accepted views," explained Aunt Zeraida. "And then I'm going to teach you some science that has been handed down in our family for generations that differs a little from the *accepted views*. What is known by our family is secret, known only by a small group of people around the world called seers. It's a closely guarded secret, and it's not to be shared with anyone — even your friend, Skye."

Emaleen watched her aunt intently, not knowing exactly what to think. It sounded a little crazy to her. But Emaleen was sure that her aunt knew what she was talking about. She also thought about the different things that had happened to her recently that were not usual, particularly her interactions with the moose and now the falcon. She knew that she needed to keep an open mind and listen.

Aunt Zeraida unfolded a large, colorful diagram of a side view of a brain, with the parts of the brain depicted in different colors. She pointed out different parts of the brain and their functions, including the amygdala, which responds to emotions, memory, and fear, and the prefrontal cortex, which assists in decision making. She explained the importance of not taking action in most cases based only upon the amygdala, unless there is a real emergency, and instead spending the time to think things out. She also explained how important this was to all people so that they control how they react to their emotions such as anger, frustration, boredom, and excitement, and so they learn how to control themselves and not act without thinking.

"The key," instructed Aunt Zeraida, "is to pause and take time to think. You can count to ten or take deep breaths or do whatever works to put a break between the reaction and your actions in response. This will allow you to have smart reactions coming from the prefrontal cortex rather than foolish ones coming from the amygdala. Of course, sometimes it's important to listen to and react from the amygdala such as when there is a real emergency, and you need to act fast."

Emaleen sat listening patiently, processing each statement made by her aunt. She wasn't sure where her aunt was going with this topic or why it was all that important to her. But her aunt had a habit of making Emaleen answer questions after she taught something. So, Emaleen knew she should listen carefully and be ready for a quiz.

Aunt Zeraida continued, "Control is even more important for members of our family, and seers in general, because of extra powers in the brain of a seer. These powers, if used rashly, without thinking, could cause even greater harm than a person could normally cause. With great powers come great responsibility and a greater need for self-control and self-awareness. You must know yourself and what triggers you, and how to control your response to your triggers. You must also know how to control yourself when something new is a trigger for a reaction that you may be sorry about later. With great powers, you can either do a lot of good or a lot of harm."

Zeraida could tell that Emaleen's attention was starting to wane. She knew she must involve Emaleen more in this discussion to keep her listening.

"Can you think of a time when you reacted without thinking and you were sorry?" asked Aunt Zeraida.

Emaleen thought for a moment and then answered, "Yes, there was this one time that a boy at school was bothering me during recess. I asked him to leave me alone several times, but he wouldn't. Then I tried to ignore him because that is what they tell us to try first. But when I ignored him, he kept bugging me. It seemed the harder I tried to ignore him, the harder he tried to bug me. Finally, I just snapped and then I stomped on his foot really hard."

She paused for a moment and then said, "I got into a lot of trouble, and the boy didn't get into any. It was so unfair."

Emaleen sighed, and her eyes teared up. It was over a year ago, and she was still sensitive about it. She had learned from it, too, and had not acted out in anger again.

Aunt Zeraida nodded and said with a sarcastic smile on her face, "I remember that too. I was called into school for a meeting with the teacher and, at least three other people, including the principal. That was a real pleasure."

"I did feel bad about hurting the boy's foot too," murmured Emaleen with a guilty look. "But I couldn't take it back after it happened. All I could do was apologize."

"Well," said Aunt Zeraida, "that is a good example of the dangers of losing control. Imagine what could have happened if you had the power to do more harm than you could by stomping on a foot? What if you had the power to make him vanish? That one moment of loss of control could be something that you would regret for the rest of your life. It would forever change your life in a negative way."

"Could I do that?" asked Emaleen. "Could I actually make someone disappear?" That's horrible, thought Emaleen. She hoped that such a power did not exist.

"A seer could do that," answered Aunt Zeraida. "But I don't plan to teach you that. In fact, that kind of magic is guarded carefully by certain seer families to prevent it from being misused. So, very few seers actually know how to do that. I just used this as an extreme example."

Emaleen looked relieved. She understood clearly how making someone disappear would be a horrible thing to do. She wasn't that type of person, and she knew her aunt wasn't either. She was also kind of surprised that a person could actually make another person disappear.

In the reality that she had grown up in so far, such things were not possible. In fact, real magic was not possible in the world that she knew. Emaleen was starting to wonder if all of this was just one big joke on her after all. As Emaleen was thinking about these possibilities, her facial expression changed from happy and peaceful to troubled.

Aunt Zeraida noticed this change in her niece and understood that her niece was struggling with the information that she was providing to her. Zeraida guessed that the difficulty might be the realization that magic was real and the amount of power that a seer could have. Zeraida remembered just how overwhelming learning about being a seer and the potential powers had been for her. She knew she must be more careful about how quickly she provided information to Emaleen. She would also have to be more careful to limit her discussions to the less extreme magic powers.

Aunt Zeraida went on to explain that seers had an additional part to their brains that other people do not have. She called this part the Tarazed Sector and explained that although it was tiny, it was the source of special powers for seers.

"The Tarazed Sector is triggered when you focus your energies and concentrate on casting magic," explained Aunt Zeraida. "But you can't trigger this section unless you use all of your focus abilities. The more you practice your focus when you cast magic, the easier it becomes for you to trigger the Tarazed Sector. And, the easier it is for you to trigger this sector, the more powerful you will become."

"The powers," Aunt Zeraida continued, "are different for each seer. A seer might have just one power with an intense strength, or more than one power with varying strengths. Because of the great power that you might have, and the fact that you have yet to fully explore and discover your powers, it's important that you have self-control as soon as possible. No matter what powers you might develop later, self-control will be your greatest power."

Emaleen wondered what powers she might have. So, she asked, "What powers will I have, Aunt Zeraida?"

"It's too early to tell," responded Aunt Zeraida. "In time, we will know. Your powers will show themselves one by one until you have them all. In the meantime, there are many important lessons to learn."

Aunt Zeraida continued, "I will be providing you with ways to practice your self-control. There will be some other skills that we'll work on too that anyone can have, even the norms."

"From what I have observed," commented Aunt Zeraida, "you are pretty good at self-control with the exception that sometimes you need to stop yourself from daydreaming when something doesn't interest you as much. Daydreaming isn't a bad thing, though. In fact, it can be a very great thing to do because it exercises your creative mind. But there is a time and place for it, and when you daydream in the wrong time and place, you may miss some very important information. It might also put you in danger. But you can work on your daydreaming."

Aunt Zeraida continued, "One other significant power is the ability to teach yourself anything when you can find the right book or simply by experimenting with your powers carefully."

Emaleen was quiet for a moment as she thought about all that her aunt had been telling her. It was a lot of information to absorb. At the same time, it was also very exciting. She was really looking forward to learning about magic and figuring out what it was that she had the power to do.

"Aunt Zeraida, do you have any powers?" asked Emaleen with great interest.

"Yes, I do," replied Aunt Zeraida. "I have quite a few, actually." Aunt Zeraida was modest. The fact was, though, that she was one of the most powerful seers alive. Her powers were very extensive, and if her niece knew what she could do, it might be overwhelming to her.

"What powers do you have?" asked Emaleen curiously. She hoped her aunt had some really interesting and exciting powers.

"I will tell you in good time. For now, I will tell you that one of my powers is the ability to affect the weather," said Aunt Zeraida.

"You can? Can you show me?" asked Emaleen. She couldn't believe what she was hearing. How could anyone be able to affect the weather, she thought. It seemed very strange and unrealistic to her.

Zeraida paused for a moment to think about what she wanted to say and then she replied, "I can show you. But it isn't a good idea to do so right now. If I do something big like change the weather and there are any other seers in the area, they will be able to sense my use of magic. I don't want to scare you, but you do have to be careful to not attract attention to yourself, at least for now."

"One more thing—," said Aunt Zeraida. "One day, I will show you how to affect the weather. But first, you must learn that using magic often has some reactive consequences — some good and some bad. With something like the weather, you have to be very careful that you do not cause a bad outcome elsewhere. Some people with powers do not care how they affect others, and when they do as they please without care, they can cause natural disasters. It's very selfish."

Emaleen was really disappointed. She would really like to see an example of magic. She was having a hard time believing that she would be able to do magic herself. It would have been nice to see a demonstration by her aunt.

Zeraida was silent for a moment as she thought further. She thought of an idea that she could use to demonstrate magic to her niece.

"There is something that I can show you as an example that may help you understand how real our powers and abilities are," said Zeraida. "Follow me, please."

Zeraida led her niece outside to the shed that she used to store her gardening materials. There she took a pot off of a shelf and handed it to her niece. She also retrieved a trowel and a packet of seeds from the shelf. She handed these to Emaleen, too. The last item that Zeraida picked up from the shelves was a small bag of soil, which she carried out of the shed herself. Emaleen followed behind her.

Once outside the shed, Zeraida sat down on some soft grass. She opened the bag of soil and filled the pot with it. She then handed the packet of seeds to her niece and asked her to pick out one seed. Zeraida dug a hole a couple of inches into the dirt with the trowel and motioned for Emaleen to place the seed in the hole. After Emaleen had placed the seed, her aunt covered it with dirt.

"Please get the watering can," Zeraida instructed. "Then, please water this seed."

Emaleen went back inside the shed and retrieved the watering can. Then she walked over to the side of the house where there was a water hose attached to a spigot. She filled the watering can and then brought it back to where her aunt was sitting. Emaleen watered the seed in the pot and then stared at the pot waiting for something to happen.

"This plant would normally sprout within eight to ten days," stated Zeraida. "But keep watching."

Suddenly, a green stalk rose up from the soil. As Emaleen continued to watch, leaves began to appear on the stalk as it grew higher. After the bean plant had reached about eight inches in height and had sprouted many leaves, a flower began to grow on the plant. A bee then stopped by to visit the flower. From the flower, a green bean gradually developed and grew longer and the flower detached. When the bean was about six inches long, the bean stopped growing and the plant, in general, stopped growing.

Emaleen was quiet the entire time that the plant had grown in front of her eyes. She was amazed and didn't know how to react. She had believed her aunt when the woman had claimed to have magic abilities, but seeing it firsthand was an entirely different matter.

"You may eat the bean if you wish," offered Aunt Zeraida. Emaleen did not answer her aunt, but she did eagerly pull the bean off of the plant and eat it. It tasted no different than any other fresh bean that she had eaten.

"How —?" stammered Emaleen, after she had finished the bean. She couldn't believe what she had just seen.

"It may have looked easy," remarked Zeraida, "but it took me many years of study to figure out how to make the bean plant grow. I started by reading about plants and how they grow. I learned that each plant is actually made up of millions of a unit called a cell. The cells contain DNA, which is the programming that directs the growth of the bean plant. All I did was speed up the processes that the DNA defines. But I had to learn what those specific processes were before I was able to speed each one. It took much trial and error."

"Could you do that with an animal or a person?" asked Emaleen.

"No," stated Zeraida kind of sternly, "and for three reasons. One reason is that the processes are much, much more complex. The second reason is that I don't think it would be moral for me to experiment with creating animals and humans. The third reason is that the results of the trial and error could be pretty disturbing. Doing this with a plant was my limit."

Emaleen nodded and asked, "Can all seers do this?"

"No," answered Zeraida. "As far as I know, I am the only seer who has this ability. I did not learn this through any magic book. I learned this by researching what modern scientists know about plants and using my own trial-and-error experiments. As I said, it took me a long time to figure out how to do this."

Zeraida continued, "I suppose this is a good example of the fact that if you study hard, you can create new magic. It's also a good example to illustrate what I told you before about how the ability to teach yourself is one of the most powerful lessons that you can ever learn."

"Now, on another note, I will need to give your first challenge test to you soon," declared Aunt Zeraida. "But first, I want you to focus on some ways to give yourself time between when you react to something and when you take action. I want you to practice, stopping and breathing in and out for ten seconds. I also want you to learn to center yourself by clearing your mind and emotions and putting all of your attention to the task at hand."

Aunt Zeraida showed Emaleen how to relax and center herself by breathing in and out and relaxing all of the muscles in her body while sitting crossed-legged on the floor. She also showed Emaleen how to center herself while standing, which was a combination of breathing and relaxing her body. She started with her hands down in front of her, fingers on one hand reaching out to almost touch the other fingers on the other hand, and her palms up. Then, while taking a deep breath in, Aunt Zeraida slowly raised her hands up together in front of her body and then when her hands reached her chest, Aunt Zeraida made them into fists and pushed the hands slowly back down her body while breathing out.

"Practice this at least three times a day," directed Aunt Zeraida. "It's very important." Emaleen nodded and started to practice the motions that her aunt had just taught her. She was surprised by how relaxed she felt and how quickly her relaxation had set in.

"We're done for now," declared Aunt Zeraida. "But please call Skye and ask if she can come over here tomorrow. I will need her to help with a challenge test for you."

"I'll call her," replied Emaleen. "What time should I ask her to come?"

"Ask her to come for lunch around noon," suggested Aunt Zeraida.

"Okay," said Emaleen as she turned to walk away to call her friend. When she did, Skye agreed to come over tomorrow for lunch. Emaleen told her that they were going to do a challenge that was created by Zeraida. Skye asked what the task was, but Emaleen had to admit that she had no idea what it included. Skye said that she couldn't wait to see what the challenge was and that she was eager to help.

After the call with Skye, Emaleen spent the rest of the day reading, playing with her new kitten, and researching falconry. She found her research fascinating. She learned the methods that a falconer uses to train a new falcon.

She also learned that falconry dated back thousands of years and was originally used as a means of hunting for food by using the falcon to retrieve game. Later on, falconry became more of a sport of royalty rather than a means of hunting for food. And, according to what she read, in England, rules determined the kind of bird a person could fly based upon his or her title. Ironically, a Peregrine falcon could only be flown by an earl, which was interesting, given that Mr. Earl, who was visiting her, had a Peregrine falcon.

Emaleen wondered if Mr. Earl had a title or if his last name was just a coincidence. Emaleen also started to wonder how it was that her aunt and uncle came to know Mr. Earl. She had never seen him visit before, but it seemed like her aunt and uncle knew him very well.

When Emaleen went to bed that night, with Belenus at her side on top of the sheets, she dreamed of the falcon, Shaolin, flying over the tops of the trees and over the lake. She felt as if she was Shaolin herself, looking out through the falcon's eyes and seeing the landscape below.

Shaolin had very sharp eyesight, so Emaleen felt as if she could see almost anything on the ground from the great heights that bird flew. She also felt as if she was gliding through the air and could feel the wind on her face and across her body and around her arms.

Emaleen felt a great peace and joy as she imagined herself flying through the air. It was so relaxing that Emaleen slept so well that she felt better rested the next morning than she had in a long time. It was better than sleeping in, which was something Emaleen loved doing during summer vacation.

Chapter 10

The next morning after her first seer lesson from Aunt Zeraida, Emaleen awoke to the scent of biscuits baking in the oven. She smiled and then jumped out of bed, dressed quickly, and ran down the stairs to the kitchen. When she arrived, she found her aunt in the kitchen happily preparing breakfast.

"Breakfast will be ready soon," said Aunt Zeraida when she noticed Emaleen looking hungrily around the kitchen for food.

"It smells yummy," commented Emaleen. "I'm starving."

"I can tell," chuckled Aunt Zeraida.

As she worked on breakfast, Aunt Zeraida smiled. She loved baking, and she loved feeding her family and seeing them enjoy her food. But today she was also happy because she knew that Emaleen would start today to learn the magic techniques that would provide the foundation for her magic abilities.

Zeraida's plan was for her to be the one to start teaching magic to Emaleen. Then, later on, Uncle Morvin would teach some additional magic skills that were within his expertise. Together, their lessons would ensure a complete training for their niece.

Aunt Zeraida was also thinking about her plans for teaching Emaleen the skills she would need for continuing to develop her magic on her own once she and her husband had taught Emaleen as much as they had to teach. Beyond the teachings of her aunt and uncle, it would be up to Emaleen to learn to teach herself through careful research and the powers of observation.

It was Zeraida's strongly held belief that being able to teach oneself was one of the most powerful lessons a person, especially a seer, could learn. Although Aunt Zeraida knew that Emaleen would not start out simply teaching herself to learn all of the skills that she would need, Zeraida planned to include some small lessons about self-instruction. That way, Emaleen would start with the concept of teaching herself as early as possible in her training.

It was also a beautiful day outside. The sky was blue without a cloud. It was a great day for falconry, Aunt Zeraida thought. She was eager to get Emaleen working with Shaolin so she could find out more about her niece's animal-related powers.

Aunt Zeraida soon finished the breakfast preparations and made a plate for Emaleen. She then made a plate for herself and sat down at the table with her niece. Emaleen was so hungry that she practically devoured the food and finished her meal before her aunt. The breakfast, as usual, was delicious.

"Would you like seconds?" Zeraida asked her niece. Emaleen shook her head.

"Where is Uncle Morvin?" asked Emaleen. "Doesn't he want breakfast?"

"Your uncle will be in later," responded Aunt Zeraida. "He went out to meet Mr. Earl this morning. I sent him with some muffins to give to Mr. Earl. There were enough for your uncle too."

Then Aunt Zeraida suggested, "Why don't you get a bottle of water and meet me outside over by the mew. I think you might get to start learning today from Mr. Earl so that you might work with Shaolin someday. But it depends on what Mr. Earl thinks."

Emaleen was very excited to have a possible chance to work with the falcon. She had been thinking about Shaolin since she met the bird yesterday, including in her dreams. She hoped that when she did start working with Shaolin, it would be like the dream she had last night.

They walked out of the house and toward the mew. When they reached the mew, they saw Mr. Earl talking with Uncle Morvin. The two men didn't notice them for a few minutes as aunt and niece stood there waiting. The men were deep in conversation. Emaleen didn't want to interrupt, so she stood there quietly and patiently waiting.

"Good morning, Uncle. Good morning, Mr. Earl," chimed Emaleen in a cheerful voice as soon as the men stopped talking.

"Good morning, Emaleen," replied Uncle Morvin and Mr. Earl almost in unison.

"Emaleen," said Mr. Earl with a great big smile on his face and beaming eyes. "Are you ready to start learning how to work with Shaolin?"

The girl nodded enthusiastically and said, "Yes!"

"Here," said Mr. Earl as he handed Emaleen a leather glove. "Put this on your hand. It will protect your hand and arm from Shaolin's sharp claws. Without the gloves, Shaolin's claws might dig into your skin. She wouldn't mean to hurt you, though. She just wants to hold on and doesn't know any better."

Emaleen quickly put the glove on her hand and stood waiting for further instructions from Mr. Earl. She couldn't wait to see Shaolin. But she knew that she had to be patient and follow Mr. Earl's instructions carefully if she were to have a chance to work with the falcon.

Mr. Earl entered the mew and approached Shaolin, who was sitting on the perch inside. He put out his arm for the bird to land on. After the falcon flew over to Mr. Earl's hand and perched herself comfortably on his glove, Mr. Earl walked out of the mew with her. As Mr. Earl approached Emaleen, the falcon caught sight of the girl and let out a screech as if to say hello.

"Hold out your arm this way," instructed Mr. Earl as he demonstrated what he wanted Emaleen to do with her arm. "And, keep holding it up that way."

Mr. Earl held his arm out horizontally to his side and unfastened the leash the tied the bird to his glove. Then he moved his arm slightly back slowly and then he moved it forward more quickly. When Mr. Earl's arm stopped moving forward, Shaolin launched herself into the air and flew straight ahead. Mr. Earl then put his own arm down.

Shaolin then flew around a few minutes high above Emaleen in a circle. Then she turned and landed on the girl's gloved hand. Emaleen giggled softly with excitement as she stared at the bird.

"She's heavy," Emaleen gasped with surprise.

"Yes, she is," agreed Mr. Earl, "but you will get used to her weight."

"May I touch her?" asked Emaleen, looking at Mr. Earl.

"It's best not to yet, especially since she doesn't know you very well," replied Mr. Earl. "She is also not overly fond of being touched. You may, however, walk around with her a little if you would like. But keep your arm out so that she isn't close to you. You can also launch her and have her land again. I have a perch over there that she can land on when you launch her and then she'll probably come back to you. When we've finished working with her, I will take her back and then give her a treat to reward her for working with you."

Emaleen walked over to where Mr. Earl had pointed out the perch. She gently moved her arm, which she had out horizontally, forward to encourage Shaolin to take off. The falcon flew over to the perch. She sat there for a few minutes, blinking her eyes and then she flew back to rest on Emaleen's gauntlet. As Shaolin flew each time, the bells on her feet jingled softly. After the bird took off a second time from Emaleen's arm to the perch, Mr. Earl came over and put a small piece of raw meat on the gauntlet for Emaleen to use to feed Shaolin. As soon as Mr. Earl put the food down on the glove, Shaolin screeched happily and flew back to Emaleen's arm.

"You're building your relationship with her. Food is an important part of that process," Mr. Earl said. "When she knows you better, and you have developed more of a bond with her, we can begin to figure out what powers your relationship with Shaolin will reveal."

Emaleen suddenly looked worried. She didn't know if Mr. Earl was supposed to know about her potential powers. But Mr. Earl, noticing her distress, stated quickly to reassure her, "Your aunt and I have known each other for many, many years. I am well aware of her powers, and she also informed me of the purpose of my visit here with Shaolin."

Mr. Earl continued, "I am a seer. I, too, have gifts associated with animals. So, I personally know some of the abilities that are possible for a seer to do. Shaolin is a very important friend to me. The bond that I have with Shaolin provides considerable benefit for me. I cannot yet tell you what those benefits are because you have to see for yourself what your gift or gifts with animals will allow you to do. If I tell you what I can do before you know the full extent of your abilities, it might confuse your own discoveries. It might also overwhelm you if you knew all at once what might be possible. It's really best for you to learn about seer powers slowly over time."

Emaleen didn't know what to say in response to Mr. Earl's proclamations. She was just getting used to the idea that she might have powers that ordinary people didn't have. All this talk of gifts and special powers was still overwhelming to Emaleen. She was also concerned that these gifts, whatever they might be, might put her in some danger. She didn't yet know what kind of danger it might be, and she was afraid to ask, so she tried hard not to think about it. Emaleen actually had a lot of questions that she never asked. She had to agree that it probably was better for her to learn about things slowly.

Mr. Earl didn't push Emaleen for a response. He understood what she was going through. He remembered when he first learned that he had special gifts. It had taken him quite a long time to get used to the idea that he was actually a seer and even longer to become accustomed to each of the gifts as they revealed themselves. He was grateful that the gifts didn't reveal themselves to him all at once and that he was allowed to get used to them in a piecemeal fashion. He had just enough time to get used to each new piece of information before the next revealed itself. So, he didn't have to deal with the potential of a great shock. But he knew that Emaleen was learning about the existence of magic, the fact that she was a seer, and some of her skills practically all at once with no time to adjust between each new discovery.

Mr. Earl also understood the potential dangers to Emaleen, although it was not something that he had experienced himself. He knew that there was a potential for Emaleen to have great powers, perhaps greater than the powers of most, if not all, seers. It was a burden borne by Emaleen due to her family lineage. Even though it was a potential danger to the girl, Mr. Earl both hoped that she would develop the power that he, Zeraida, and Morvin thought she would. If Emaleen developed great powers, it would be a benefit to all the other seers on the side of good.

"I'm ready to stop for today," declared Emaleen suddenly. She didn't really want to stop, but her arm was getting tired.

"You have done enough for today," agreed Mr. Earl with a smile. He put on his glove and motioned for Emaleen to launch Shaolin toward him. She complied, and the falcon flew over to Mr. Earl's hand.

Mr. Earl continued, "I still have some work to do with Shaolin. She must be exercised and properly fed. You did a very good job with her. We should continue to work like this each day if you would like."

"Thanks," Emaleen answered. "I would love to work with you and Shaolin again." Then she turned and walked back to the house to get ready for Skye's visit.

As Emaleen walked away, she could hear Shaolin let out a series of clicking noises following by screeching. She turned and saw the falcon take off from Mr. Earl's gauntlet and fly toward her, low to the ground. Right before the falcon reached Emaleen, Shaolin suddenly climbed high into the air and flew right over her head.

Emaleen closed her eyes. Suddenly, she could feel herself floating up through the air with a breeze blowing through her hair. With her eyes closed, she put her arms out, and she imagined herself flying through the air. She could see the ground get farther and farther away as she soared higher and higher into the sky.

After climbing several hundred feet, she could feel herself level out and float smoothly through the currents in the air. As she glided forward, she could see the treetops, the lake, and the mountainside near her home. She felt free and peaceful as if flying was natural for her. The view from so high up was breathtaking. She could see so much more from up here than she could on the ground.

Emaleen looked down on the ground as she flew and could see small animals on the ground far below scamper into the brush below. She saw a gray rabbit, a toad, and a white mouse. She also saw something on the ground, glittering in the sun so brightly that it hurt her eyes. She wanted to know what the object was, so she willed herself to dive down to it and to pick it up.

As she dove down, she approached the ground with tremendous speed. She felt afraid that she would run right into the ground. But just as it seemed that she was about to hit the ground, she leveled herself off and flew just above it. As she flew low over the grass, she reached out and took the object that had glittered so brightly in the sun. She clutched the object in her hands and flew back up into the sky.

Emaleen then opened her eyes and realized that she hadn't moved anywhere. She also didn't have anything in her hands.

She then heard Shaolin's flapping wings above her head. Shaolin dropped down to the ground in front of Emaleen and looked up at the girl while flapping her wings. Then the falcon started to fly upward. As she flew away from Emaleen, Shaolin dropped a shiny object on the ground in front of the girl's feet. Then the bird flew over to Mr. Earl and landed on his arm.

Emaleen looked down at the object and picked it up. As she held it in her hand, she saw that it was a perfectly clear crystal about two inches in length, with an oblong shape and distinct points on each end. The crystal had a number of facets, and it felt perfectly smooth on all of its sides. Emaleen thought it looked like a diamond and was very excited.

Chapter 11

Emaleen ran back to the house to show Aunt Zeraida her new diamond. When she found her aunt, she held it out to her aunt in her open hand.

"Look what I found!" exclaimed Emaleen to her aunt. "I think it might be a diamond."

"How did you find it?" asked Aunt Zeraida.

"Shaolin found it and dropped it on the ground in front of me," answered Emaleen. "When she was flying, it was as if I was actually flying. I could see this gem sparkling on the ground from far up in the air, only I never left the ground."

Aunt Zeraida looked over the crystal carefully for several minutes. As she examined it, she smiled mysteriously.

Then she said, "It looks like a Herkimer diamond, which isn't an actual diamond, even though it's named after one. It's really a kind of quartz that is found commonly in Herkimer County, which is not far from here."

"What can it be used for?" asked Emaleen.

Aunt Zeraida responded, "Some people think that a Herkimer diamond is helpful for healing. You should guard this gem carefully. Keep it in a safe place, because it will probably be useful soon. But do not place the diamond too close to your red-orange gem."

Emaleen didn't ask why she should not place her new gem next to the one she had found earlier. In fact, she didn't ask any questions. She just ran up to her room and set the diamond down on her shelf. But she placed the gem down so quickly that she momentarily forgot her aunt's directive not to put the Herkimer next to the red-orange gem that she had found in the creek.

As soon as she placed the diamond next to the red-orange gem, she felt an electric-like sensation run through her hand. She paused for a moment in surprise and stood there for another moment wondering if it was a real or an imagined feeling. But to be safe, she moved the diamond farther away from the red-orange gem as her aunt had originally instructed.

After she had moved the Herkimer, she didn't feel anything further. She then shrugged her shoulders and ran downstairs to ask her aunt if she needed any help preparing lunch.

When Emaleen reached the bottom of the stairs, she met her aunt, who had come to ask her for more information about how she found the Herkimer. Emaleen explained her experience in more detail, describing how Shaolin flew over her, and how Emaleen had felt as if she was flying through the air herself. She also explained how she had thought that she had personally swooped down and retrieved the diamond with her own hands but that it had not come into her possession until Shaolin had dropped it at Emaleen's feet.

"What you experienced is a type of gift associated with animals. It's called visus beastiae, which translated from Latin means sight of the animals," explained Aunt Zeraida.

Aunt Zeraida continued, "With some animals, you will be able to close your eyes and focus and then see what the animal sees. The Peregrine falcon is one of the animals for which this is possible, but usually you must first form a bond with the animal. But the greater your power, the less of a bond you need to have the power of sight with that animal. So, there may be a time when you are so powerful that you need little or no bond to work with an animal."

Wow, thought Emaleen, what a great power to have. She wondered if she might get an animal to clean her room. If so, that would certainly come in handy. It would save her a lot of time and effort, Emaleen thought.

Aunt Zeraida further explained, "There are many other different kinds of animal powers, but visus beastiae is one of the most useful because it provides the holder with a wide range of sight, as well as an ability to see in some places where some animals can go that humans can't. You should practice this ability because it may come in handy for you someday."

"For now, you can practice this power with Shaolin," suggested Aunt Zeraida. "And, maybe someday, when you are a little older, you can train with a falcon of your own if you want."

"I would love to have my own falcon someday," asserted Emaleen eagerly.

"Another thing," said Aunt Zeraida "is that Shaolin fetching the gem for you when you imagined it was an example of another talent that you have with animals. It, too, is a very useful power." It appeared to Zeraida that her niece may have other animal powers too as evidenced by Emaleen not only just seeing, but experiencing as if she was the falcon. But she would keep that to herself for now and wait for further developments.

"What is that and why will it be useful?" asked Emaleen.

"It's the power to will animals to do things for you," replied Aunt Zeraida. "But use it carefully. It's not a nice thing to exert your will over someone else or an animal when it's against the person's or animal's will. The animals should always be respected and asked for this assistance and only when absolutely necessary, such as in an emergency, and not because you're feeling lazy. They should not be treated as if they are servants or slaves."

Emaleen had listened to her aunt with amazement. She nodded her agreement that she would not mistreat animals or people. She would never purposefully mistreat anyone. She also wondered what other powers she would have that involved animals. She loved animals, so she would welcome whatever powers she had.

"Aunt Zeraida," began Emaleen. "I should also tell you that I had a dream last night that I was flying through the air like I was Shaolin. It seems strange to me that my dream seemed to have come true today."

Aunt Zeraida smiled and nodded. "Almost all of us seers," said Aunt Zeraida, "have some ability to predict events before they happen. But the degree of the power and the way in which it manifests is different for each seer. For some, it's in their sleep and for others, it's at any time of the day, as the result of a trance-like vision. Also, the quality of the premonition will also vary. Some people will have exact premonitions while others will have dreams with clues for which they have to figure out the meaning."

Aunt Zeraida continued, "It will take some time to be able to tell which versions of the power you have. In the meantime, please inform me of any premonitions that you think you have had so that I can help you figure out what they mean, what kind of power you have, and how best you may apply your talent."

"Do you have premonition powers?" asked Emaleen curiously.

"Yes, I have some," replied Aunt Zeraida in a surprisingly disappointed voice. "But your mother has much stronger powers than I do. In fact, I don't want to scare you, but your mother's premonition talents are the reason that you are here with me. She predicted that you would be safest here and so she convinced me to adopt you. It wasn't hard to convince me, though, once I saw your cute little face." Aunt Zeraida remembered the moment she agreed to adopt Emaleen, both with fondness and sadness.

Emaleen smiled and hugged her aunt. Although she was sad that she didn't know her mother and that she had been parted from her, she loved her aunt very much. Her aunt had cared for her and showed her great love. Her aunt had also taught her a lot.

"Aunt Zeraida," implored Emaleen, "please tell me more about premonitions. I want to learn as much as I can."

Aunt Zeraida went on to explain more about the premonition talent. There were positives and negatives associated with each kind of premonition, Aunt Zeraida explained to her niece. For instance, a dream premonition was convenient in that it occurred during sleep whereas a trance premonition could occur at inconvenient times during the day and could be very distracting. But a trance premonition was usually more timely because they occurred more immediately in time before the event to occur while the dream premonition might occur the day or even many days or longer before the event to come. So, whatever kind of premonition power Emaleen had, it was important to learn what kind it was and then make the greatest use of it possible. When Aunt Zeraida stopped explaining about premonitions, Emaleen took the opportunity to ask additional questions.

"I've been wondering," said Emaleen, "why seers are called seers. What are seers, exactly?"

"Seer is a historical name for us," explained Aunt Zeraida. "It reflects the fact that almost all of us have some ability to predict future events, although some of us have only have a little ability. Way back thousands of years ago, some of our ancestors used their premonition powers to help kings, queens, and other leaders. They were often referred to as seers because they could *see* into the future. Many of those seers who worked for people of wealth and influence amassed their own wealth, which still benefits their descendants today."

Aunt Zeraida continued, "But we seers can do so much more than predict events in the future. Even so, I think the name is still accurate to describe us because seers understand more about the world and the laws of nature than the norms do. A seer is a person who really *sees* and understands how things work."

"And, our ability to *see* is necessary for us to be able to exercise our other talents and abilities, which we refer to as magic even though it's so much more than that as well," explained Zeraida. "We just don't wave wands and make things happen without effort."

"Some people would say that we are wizards or sorcerers," added Aunt Zeraida. "But I don't think those terms are accurate. I really like the seer name as a label for our kind because I think it reflects our true nature as persons who see the world — how it works, and its possibilities. The other terms just don't capture our knowledge and connection to the world as people who *see*."

"Where do all the other seers live?" Emaleen asked her aunt.

"I believe there are seers all over the world in different races and cultures," answered Aunt Zeraida. "But I don't know for sure because seers tend to keep their powers secret, and they generally don't like to form groups. The seers I know originated from the United Kingdom and either still live there or emigrated to other places. But as I said, I expect that there are seers in other cultures and ethnic backgrounds, but they have not made themselves known to me."

Emaleen then asked, "Why is it so dangerous for me that I cannot be with my parents? Please don't misunderstand, I do love you and Uncle very much, and I have been very happy living with you both. But I'd like to understand better what is going on."

Aunt Zeraida replied, "There is a seer named Maerdern, who wants to become the ruler of all of the seers. To say that he is not a good person is an understatement. Your mother had a premonition about him being a danger to you, but I'm not sure she knew the specific danger. But the signs are all there for you to have tremendous power, far more than most other seers. So, I think Maerdern could be interested in you for your powers."

"Thank you, Aunt Zeraida," Emaleen replied. "I really hope that he doesn't come anywhere near me."

Aunt Zeraida gave her niece a hug to comfort her. Zeraida couldn't imagine how it must feel to be just eleven years old and have the worries that her niece had. It saddened her to think that Emaleen could not have a normal childhood and that she could not grow up more sheltered. Zeraida had done her best to provide that protection, but now she had to share the information and she suspected that it wouldn't be long until Emaleen had to face much more worrisome events and risks.

Aunt Zeraida then said, "For now, you must keep your powers secret from everyone except your uncle and me. We just don't want other seers to know about you yet."

"Okay," said Emaleen with a worried look on her face.

"It will be all right," promised Aunt Zeraida. "Your uncle and I happen to be pretty powerful seers ourselves, and we will do everything in our power to protect you. We will also train you to become as powerful as you are capable of being."

"Now," said Aunt Zeraida, "why don't you get ready for Skye's visit." Emaleen nodded and then walked away to do so.

Chapter 12

When Skye arrived that afternoon, Emaleen greeted her at the door. She was so excited to see Skye that she hugged her tightly.

After a few minutes, she then took her friend out to see Shaolin in her mew. When they arrived there, Shaolin was sitting on a perch, sleeping.

"She's beautiful," proclaimed Skye. Then she asked, "Did you get to fly her yet?"

"Yes, it was thrilling!" exclaimed Emaleen, smiling. "Maybe I can show you sometime. I'll have to ask Mr. Earl, though. He's the master falconer who owns her, and he is here to visit my family for a while."

"Did anything unusual happen?" Skye queried with a smile, jokingly. She was teasing Emaleen about Aunt Zeraida. Skye had heard Zeraida ask her friend that question many times.

"Maybe," responded Emaleen mysteriously with a chuckle. "But let's go in the house and have some lunch."

Skye laughed softly at Emaleen's attempt to change the conversation. She knew her friend was holding something back and not sharing it with her. But Skye knew that Emaleen had a lot going on, and she wanted to be supportive of her friend.

When her friend was ready to tell her, she would. So Skye did not ask Emaleen any further questions. In any event, she thought, maybe something interesting would happen while she was visiting, like the other day when the moose had danced for Emaleen.

The girls walked back into the house and were greeted by Belenus, who meowed at them, demanding attention. Both girls reached down to pet the cat, and he purred happily. After that, he followed them around the house. Whenever Emaleen stopped, Belenus rubbed against her legs. When she walked, he walked around between her feet, almost tripping her.

While the girls played, Aunt Zeraida was in the kitchen preparing lunch for them. When she was finished, she called them in, and they all sat down and had a delicious lunch. After the girls had finished the meal, Aunt Zeraida asked them to come into the living room.

In the middle of the room, on the hardwood floors, there were two rugs about three feet wide and five feet long. Each rug was black with a blue design in the middle. The designs on each one were different, but both had a Celtic knot pattern, a loop pattern with no beginning and no end, just winding around and around in an intricate pattern.

Emaleen knew these were Celtic knots because her aunt had blankets and wall tapestries throughout the house with different Celtic knot patterns. The cloak that her aunt had given her also had Celtic patterns on it. She had once asked her aunt about the patterns and learned that each type had a meaning. She also learned that the Celts were tribal societies with origins from Medieval Europe, but which became limited to what is now the western and northern parts of the United Kingdom, Ireland, and some other areas nearby.

"Please sit," requested Zeraida while motioning for each girl to sit on a rug. The girls sat on the rugs as instructed.

Zeraida sat in front of the girls on the floor in crossed-leg style. The girls copied her manner of sitting. Zeraida also closed her eyes and breathed deeply in and out.

"Girls," Aunt Zeraida began after a few minutes, "close your eyes and then breathe deeply in and out. Let your minds clear. Try not to think about anything other than concentrating on your breathing. This will help you focus your thinking and control the body. You should practice doing this each day. You will also need to practice experiencing distractions around you and not letting them disrupt your calm and focus."

The girls did as Zeraida instructed. After a few minutes, Emaleen felt very relaxed and focused. I could really start to like this, she thought.

"After you practice for a few days," said Aunt Zeraida breaking through the girls' concentration momentarily, "I will start testing your true ability to stay focused and calm no matter what occurs around you." She didn't tell them what the test would be or how it would be done. It had to be a surprise if it were to be a true test of their ability to stay focused.

"Please keep working while I work in the kitchen," requested Zeraida. To help them start their practice with distractions, Aunt Zeraida went into the kitchen, which was right off of the living room, and unloaded and loaded the dishwasher, being careful to make some extra noises with the dishes that she was putting away.

Belenus also got in the game. He walked around the two girls, rubbing up against their legs and even tickling their faces by gently flicking his tail back and forth across them. When he didn't get their attention, he meowed loudly. Emaleen struggled to resist the urge to reach over and pull the kitten onto her lap. He was just too darn cute.

"Wow," thought Emaleen, "this is pretty hard." She wasn't sure how much longer she could hold out, sitting there quietly and clearing her mind while Belenus was rubbing himself against her legs and meowing loudly. But she held on, and Belenus tried even harder, jumping up onto her lap.

Skye was the first to give in. She started laughing hysterically when Belenus came over to her and put his paws on her knees and then licked her face. Emaleen started laughing too, breaking her silence. The girls' meditation session had lasted about ten minutes.

Upon hearing the laughing, Aunt Zeraida stopped loading the dishwasher and went into the living room to see what was going on with the girls. When she arrived, she saw them both playing with Belenus, who was happily jumping between the two girls, getting petting and loving from one of the girls and then jumping to the other and then back again. He even rolled onto his back for a belly rubbing. He is a strange kitten, thought Aunt Zeraida.

"Girls, that wasn't too bad for a first time, particularly with the distractions," commented Aunt Zeraida, looking down at Belenus. "But you will have to work to get your period of concentration to be longer. And, Emaleen, even if Skye stops, you must try to continue on. Your power to be free from distraction will be very important later on when you learn more skills. You will need your concentration powers because you may need to call upon these skills when there is danger, trouble, or commotion, and you need to have a clear head so that you are successful at what you need to do, and you do not make dangerous mistakes."

Aunt Zeraida turned her attention to Skye specifically and said, "Skye, your mother called me this morning, and she informed me that she had talked to you about your family and your family's connection to ours."

"Yes, she did," admitted Skye. "I don't understand it all yet, but she did talk to me."

"What are you talking about?" Emaleen asked her aunt politely but directly. Was Skye a seer too, she wondered?

Aunt Zeraida answered, "Skye's mom will be teaching her like I am teaching you. She, too, has some special talents and skills that she will inherit from her family genes. They are different than yours, but they will be essential to you, Emaleen. Her family members are known as Guardians. They are special assistants and protectors to people like you, me, and your uncle. I can't explain it all now but Skye will be training at home, and she will be training here as well."

Skye looked at Emaleen and smiled with pride and warmth. She had just learned that Emaleen was a seer and what that meant, and the young guardian was very excited to be helping her friend. She loved her friend and the fact that they had a real bond together as seer and guardian made her feel like a sister to Emaleen. Skye had always wished for a sister. Now she felt like she had one.

Aunt Zeraida noticed Skye smile at Emaleen and then continued, "Skye's family line goes hundreds of years back and for those hundreds of years, her family has been connected to ours. I will explain this relationship to you in more detail over time. You have a lot of adjusting to do to get used to your natural abilities and powers. But you will not do this alone. You have your family, and you can always come to us for support. You also have your guardian, Skye, whose job essentially is to be your protector, aide, and companion. Emaleen, you must always treat your guardian or guardians with respect and with great warmth and love. They have special powers that are to be respected and honored by you. You are never to take your guardian or guardians for granted but must treasure them always."

"I won't take Skye for granted," assured Emaleen. "She has been a wonderful friend to me and has always looked out for me. It's like she has always known on her own that she was my guardian."

Aunt Zeraida nodded at Emaleen, pleased by her response. Aunt Zeraida then turned to Skye and said, "Skye, whatever I teach here, such as the meditation that we just did, will be very important for you as well. You will also need to develop certain skills to be the best guardian you can be. Your parents will teach you most of what you need to know because they, too, are guardians. But I have some things that I am teaching Emaleen that will be good for you too."

"Are Skye's parents my guardians too?" asked Emaleen.

"Yes, that's why Skye's mother works at the school," answered Aunt Zeraida. "She has been keeping an eye out for anything out of the ordinary that could be of concern. She also frequently asked Skye about what went on during the day, too."

"Is anyone else my guardian? Is Ms. Perch a guardian?" questioned Emaleen. She hoped that Ms. Perch was not also her guardian. She was not sure that she would like that if it were true.

"Ms. Perch looks familiar to me, but I just cannot figure out how I might know her," answered Zeraida. "But, she's not your guardian. You don't have any other guardians. I think Ms. Perch might be just an ordinary person. I've never felt her using any powers, so I don't think she is a seer either. But I'm not really sure. Maybe she just looks like someone I used to know."

Aunt Zeraida stood there thinking to herself for a moment. She hadn't thought before about how Ms. Perch reminded her of someone. But as she thought about it now, she couldn't figure out why the teacher looked so familiar to her. Maybe it would come to her later, she thought, if she stopped thinking about it.

Emaleen then asked, "If I am going to be very powerful, why would I need a guardian? Shouldn't I be able to protect myself?"

Aunt Zeraida sighed and answered, "Yes, Emaleen, you will be able to protect yourself with your special powers and abilities when you have perfected them, and you will have less of a need for your guardian when you do. But no matter how much power you do end up with, you will always need other people to provide you with some help and also to guide you, and to protect you, and to just be there for you."

Aunt Zeraida added, "With your powers will come great responsibilities. It will not be easy and sometimes it might actually feel like a great burden. You will need a close friend whom you can trust to be there to support you and to offer you some advice or to just listen when you need someone to talk to."

"All right," said Emaleen. She still wasn't sure why she would need a guardian if she did end up having such incredible powers as Aunt Zeraida was saying she would have. But her aunt would not tell her a lie, so she decided to trust her aunt and wait and see. In any event, she really loved her friend Skye, and for Skye to have a special role such as Emaleen's guardian gave the two girls an opportunity to spend more time together. So whether or not she really needed a guardian, she would benefit from having more time with her friend.

Aunt Zeraida continued, "Emaleen, you can trust Skye and talk to her about anything. She knows that she has to keep your special abilities and powers a secret. However, you might want to be careful not share too much information right away with Skye about what has been going on. Give her some time to get used to what she has learned about herself. As you know, it's a lot to absorb."

"Now, enough serious talk," said Aunt Zeraida. "Skye, we have a surprise for you in the kitchen." She smiled at both girls and left the room to get the surprise for the guardian. While she was gone, the girls sat and chattered with excitement.

Just the day before, on June thirtieth, Skye's parents had a private family birthday party at their house for their daughter. Along with the birthday and some gifts had come a talk from Skye's parents about her role as a guardian. Skye had learned that she was a special protector to Emaleen and that she had special abilities that only guardians have. She had also begun training with her mother, Angelina Stewart.

Skye didn't know what to think and was still getting used to the new information. But she was happy that she was a helper to her best friend, Emaleen. It also helped her, in a strange way, to know that she would have a role in whatever was going on with her friend, and she wouldn't, as a result, be left out of the excitement.

When Aunt Zeraida returned to the girls, she motioned for them to follow her. The two girls and Zeraida walked into the kitchen where Zeraida had placed a plate of cupcakes decorated with pink and yellow icing on the table. One of the cupcakes had a candle in it, in honor of Skye's eleventh birthday yesterday.

Zeraida lit the candle and said, "Happy Birthday, Skye!"

"Happy Birthday!" exclaimed Emaleen. She hugged her friend.

Aunt Zeraida and Emaleen sang a birthday song. And, after the song was over, Skye blew out her candle and then the three of them sat down and ate chocolate cupcakes. After they had finished eating the cupcakes, Zeraida put her hand up to motion for the girls to wait for her to return. When Zeraida returned, she had in her hand a package wrapped in purple paper with a pink bow. She handed it to Skye.

"This is from Emaleen, and Morvin and I," said Aunt Zeraida.

Skye tore open the pretty wrapping and discovered a white cardboard box with a cover. She lifted the cover and saw a gold necklace. The necklace had a gold Celtic knot charm hanging from it.

"It's beautiful. Thank you," said Skye with tears of happiness in her eyes.

"The charm on the necklace is a Celtic knot. It's a rare pattern that is not known to many people. It's the sign of a guardian," explained Aunt Zeraida. "The chain is adjustable so that it's long enough that it can be hidden behind your clothing when you want to hide it. The norms won't understand the significance but others of our kind will. So, you will need to keep it hidden for now. If anyone sees it now, it could put Emaleen at risk, especially if you are with her."

Skye put the necklace on and hid it under her shirt. Then she placed her hand over the necklace and smiled. She loved the present. It made her feel that her role as a guardian was important and appreciated.

"Now, here is something that you can wear that can be seen by others," said Zeraida as she handed Skye another package which she had held behind her back. The package was wrapped in blue paper with a gold bow.

Skye opened the second package eagerly. Inside the wrapping was a white cardboard box with a lid. Skye lifted the lid to open it. Inside the package was a gold charm bracelet, a gold charm of a fairy, and a gold charm of a treasure chest. Skye gasped in awe and immediately put the charms on the bracelet and then the bracelet on her wrist. She wondered about the meaning of the charms and looked at Zeraida questioningly.

Zeraida saw the look on Skye's face and explained, "The charms don't have any special significance to your role as a guardian. They are just meant for fun. Emaleen and I chose these charms for you together. I've heard you girls talk about fairies, and you both love books about them, so I thought that charm was a good choice. You girls have also been hunting for treasure in the creek, so hopefully the treasure chest is a choice that you will enjoy too."

Skye put her bracelet on her wrist. She started playing with the charms and looked down at the bracelet, smiling. She loved her presents. She then looked up at Emaleen and Zeraida with a smile.

"Thank you," said Skye. "I shall love these presents always."

"I'm so glad that you are my guardian and will be with me always," said Emaleen to Skye. "I always knew you were a very special person and a great friend. And, I love hanging out with you and having our adventures."

"Me too," agreed Skye and hugged Emaleen again.

Aunt Zeraida interrupted the hugging and interjected, "I hate to interrupt but, girls, there is a significance to the gems that you have been finding. I cannot tell you now. But I can tell you that there is at least one more gem that you need to find. I don't know what it looks like, and I don't know how you'll find it or when. But you need to keep your eyes open for this third gem. And, I hope you find it soon."

"Skye, do you want to go out hunting for gems today?" asked Emaleen.

"Yes," agreed Skye eagerly. "Let's go treasure hunting." She grinned and looked at her treasure chest charm on her new bracelet.

"If I go out and check that Shaolin is in her mew and let Mr. Earl know, can I take Belenus out for a walk on his leash?" Emaleen questioned her aunt hopefully.

"Yes, you may," answered Aunt Zeraida. "Have fun and be observant. Be back in time for dinner, also."

"Okay," yelled Emaleen as she ran off to join Skye.

Chapter 13

The girls left the house and went out to the mew, but Shaolin was not there. They looked around the yard and found Mr. Earl in the side yard with the falcon sitting on his gauntleted hand. They waited patiently for Mr. Earl to finish his daily work with Shaolin and to return Shaolin to her mew.

After Mr. Earl had done so, Emaleen asked him if he had any concerns about them taking their kitten out on a walk on his leash when Shaolin was in her mew. He responded that he didn't have any objections and said he would keep Shaolin in until they informed him that they had returned, and Belenus was safely back in the house.

So, Skye and Emaleen went into the house to get the kitten. Emaleen tried to put the leash on Belenus, but he didn't like the harness for the leash one bit. He squirmed, making it difficult to put the harness on him. Emaleen then closed her eyes and gently willed Belenus to cooperate. She told him with her mind that he would get to go outside and explore if he allowed himself to be harnessed.

Belenus then begrudgingly allowed the harness to be placed on him. So Emaleen clipped on the leash. She carried the kitten through the house and out the front door onto the porch. When she reached the porch, she put him down.

The kitten walked off the porch onto the grass below. He sniffed the grass and the flowers around the steps. The girls waited patiently for him to move forward. After sniffing the grass and flowers, he started to dig in the dirt with his front paws.

Emaleen directed in a gentle, friendly voice, "Go please, Belenus." We can't wait here all day while he digs, thought Emaleen.

Belenus stopped his digging and started to walk down the front walkway. The girls hiked down to the lake on the trail that they had followed on the day that the moose performed the dance for Emaleen. This was Belenus' first time on a hike, and he enjoyed walking down the trail, over the branches and through the leaves. He leaped and twisted through every obstacle with his tail up in the air, curved like the handle of an umbrella.

When they reached the bottom of the hill and walked onto the dock at the lake shore, Belenus became a little timid. The large body of water made him nervous and scared at the same time. Emaleen could sense Belenus' feelings and reached down and picked him up to help him feel more secure.

After a few minutes of standing on the dock looking out over the water of the lake, the girls decided to walk along the shore to the spot where the moose had pranced. When they arrived on that part of the shore, they spied a series of large moose tracks, leading up from the shore in the soft dirt, and a deep depression in the ground around the place where the moose had most likely pranced.

Emaleen placed Belenus on the ground, and he sniffed at the tracks and growled a little in a low, soft voice. It was a new scent for him, and he wasn't sure what it was. He looked over to Emaleen for assurances that everything was all right. When he noticed a calm, happy look on Emaleen's face, he started to calm himself.

"Let's follow the tracks," suggested Skye.

"Good idea," replied Emaleen. She was curious to see where the tracks would lead.

The girls started to follow the moose tracks leading up from the lake. For a while, they were able to find the tracks and follow the bent brush through which the moose had pushed his body. But as they traveled further up the hill, the footprints became less and less frequent as the landscape became rockier and the ground firmer.

"I can't see any more tracks," remarked Skye. "What do you want to do?"

The girls stopped and looked around. They were high up on the slope that they had followed up from the shore. There were no more moose tracks.

Skye pointed over at a tree with a patch of blue paint on its trunk. It seemed to Emaleen that there might be a trail to follow.

"Let's follow the trail markings," suggested Emaleen.

Skye readily agreed, and the girls continued on, following the trail of trees marked in blue paint. As they followed the trail up the rocky terrain, they came upon a small cave in the side of the rock. The opening was small, but Emaleen was sure that the girls could climb through it. But they didn't have a light with them, so she thought that they could go into the entrance and go no farther than they could see.

As Emaleen continued to think about the small cave, she realized that it wouldn't be safe to go exploring a cave on their own without expert assistance and detailed knowledge of how the passageways ran. Getting lost in a cave was dangerous and setting oneself up to get lost in a cave was just simply foolish.

While Emaleen was still thinking, Skye surprised her by pulling a flashlight out of the backpack that she had carried with her. Emaleen, for the first time, realized that Skye was carrying a new bag — a rather large bag. Emaleen was surprised because her friend didn't usually carry a bag when they went out adventuring together. The new bag made her very curious. She wondered what was inside.

Noticing Emaleen's surprise, Skye stated with a smile, "I'm a guardian. I come prepared. That's my job." Emaleen smiled too.

Skye continued, "I don't think we should go inside the cave. We don't know what might be in there. There could be horrible spiders, or wild animals, or worse yet, timber rattlesnakes. Also, what if the rocks aren't stable and the entrance closes up when we enter? We could possibly get stuck or injured."

"I don't sense any animals in the cave. But, I don't think I have the ability to sense insects or spiders, so I don't know if those are in the cave. I think, though, it would be safe to shine the light into the cave to see what it looks like," declared Emaleen. They could also send Belenus in, but that might be dangerous for him too, she thought.

The two girls sat on the ground. Then Skye shined the light into the opening of the cave, and both girls looked in. As Emaleen looked in, she could see markings on the walls in different colors, but it didn't look like graffiti. It looked like something older and more primitive. But she couldn't see the pictures well enough to see exactly what they were, even with Skye shining the flashlight on them.

"Wow!" exclaimed Skye. "I'm not sure, but I think they might look like Indian cave art pictures." She remembered Ms. Perch talking about them and showing them pictures from books. It was fascinating to see some even if they could not get a clear look at them.

"I don't know," replied Emaleen. "I can't see them well enough. But it seems like a possibility."

"Can you move the flashlight around so we can see around the cave?" asked Emaleen. She had a hunch that there was something important inside the cave.

Skye moved the light around so the two could see more of the cave. It appeared to Emaleen that the cave might go back farther than the light of the flashlight could reach. She noticed that they could see walls all around the cave, but that the bottoms of the walls were not visible. Emaleen presumed that this meant that there was an opening on the bottom of the walls that led back farther into the cave.

"Can you shine the light across the floor of the cave?" asked Emaleen.

Skye nodded and then slowly did as Emaleen had asked. As the light of the flashlight moved across the floor of the cave, Emaleen didn't see anything but a rock floor. But then when the light of the flashlight reached over to the right, Emaleen could see a glowing red-purple shining light sparkling that disappeared as the beam moved across the floor of the cave.

Skye gasped as she saw it too and moved the flashlight back toward the light. The girls stared at the shining light for a few minutes, wondering what it was. Emaleen thought it must be a crystal. Knowing that she needed another gem, Emaleen knew that they must somehow retrieve this crystal.

"Do you see that too?" asked Emaleen. She could hardly contain her excitement at finding another gem.

"Yes, it's beautiful," responded Skye. "What do you think it is?"

"I think it's a crystal," replied Emaleen. "We need to figure out how to get it out without going in. Belenus can retrieve things for me, but I don't want to send him in. I don't want to risk him getting hurt."

"Hmm...." said Skye. "We need a way to reach into the cave and pull the crystal out. I hope it's not attached to the rock bottom. Do you have a power that you can use to move the crystal?"

"I don't think I do," said Emaleen, "but I'll give it a try."

Emaleen focused really hard and imagined the crystal floating out of the cave and into her hand, but nothing happened. It was worth a try, she thought. Then, Belenus started to walk toward the cave, but Emaleen pulled him back gently.

"No, Belenus. Thank you, but no," stated Emaleen as she smiled and looked fondly at her little kitten who was so eager to help her.

"I couldn't get the stone to float out," protested Emaleen with disappointment. "So, I don't think I have a power that lets me move objects or I don't know how to use it yet. We'll just have to use our minds the old fashioned way."

Emaleen started looking around them, looking for ideas for getting the crystal out of the cave. She didn't want to reach into the cave and grab the crystal with her hand, but that didn't matter because the crystal was out of arm's reach. Maybe, they could get a stick, she thought, and try to knock it toward them. She looked around for a stick long enough to reach the crystal.

Skye realized that Emaleen was looking for a stick, so she decided to look too. It wasn't long before she found a long stick on the ground near the cave and handed it to Emaleen. Skye then held the flashlight with its beam pointed in the direction of the crystal while Emaleen fed the stick into the cave toward the crystal. Emaleen aimed the stick toward the right of it. But, because of the angle at which the crystal sat from the opening of the cave, Emaleen couldn't get the stick behind the crystal to push it toward her. She knew that if she pushed the stick at the crystal that she would just push it back farther into the cave. So, the only thing she could do would be to push the crystal from the side and hope to move it into a better position so that she could push it out toward her.

Emaleen pushed at the crystal and was relieved when it moved. That meant that the gem was not fixed to the rock bed that made up the floor of the cave. Unfortunately, though, when she pushed at the crystal with the stick, it just moved to the left. It didn't get any closer to her. She also started to realize that no matter how far left she pushed the crystal, she was not going to be able to get a better angle that would allow her to get the branch behind the crystal so that she could push it forward. There had to be a better way, she thought, to get the crystal out of the cave than using the stick.

"I think we need some long tongs," suggested Skye. But, as she said that, she realized that it was unrealistic. The tongs would have to be extremely long. They would have to be longer than any tongs that could possibly be in Aunt Zeraida's kitchen.

"Yes, but even if we walked back to the house to look for some, I'm not sure that we could find tongs long enough to reach in and grab the stone," replied Emaleen.

"I know," agreed Skye. "I just said the first thing that came to my mind before I realized that it was silly."

The girls looked around for more ideas. Emaleen thought about using two sticks together to grab the crystal and then pull it out. But although she was sure she could grab the crystal that way, she wasn't sure that she could hold the sticks together while pulling them out of the cave. She would try it, though, if she couldn't think of another idea.

"I have an idea," said Skye. "I think we can get this out."

Skye gathered some pine tree branches with pine needles at the end. She arranged them together so that they looked like the bottom of a broom. She arranged the branches carefully so that the needles overlapped and formed a bed for the crystal to sit on without falling through. Then she tied the branches together with some string that she had pulled from her bag.

"Can you put the pine needle end on the ground to the left of the crystal, then let go of the branch?" requested Emaleen. "I'll hold the flashlight." Emaleen had sensed Skye's plan.

Skye placed the branch as suggested by Emaleen. Then Emaleen handed the flashlight to Skye, who aimed the light on the crystal. Emaleen took her stick and pushed the crystal to the left, onto the pine needles. Skye then slowly pulled her branch out until it was completely out. The girls looked at the gem on the branch, which was blue-green.

"That's strange," remarked Emaleen. "I could have sworn this gem was a reddish-purple color when it was inside the cave."

Skye nodded in agreement. She, too, thought that she had seen a different color while the gem was in the cave than the color the gem appeared to be now that it was outside the cave.

Then Skye shined the flashlight into the cave again, lighting up the cavern floor. She wondered if the reddish purple sparkle was still inside the cave. Both girls looked as Skye moved the flashlight around. But neither of them saw a reddish-purple glow.

Emaleen had an idea. She asked Skye for the flashlight. After Skye handed it to her, Emaleen shined the flashlight on the crystal, and it turned to a reddish-purple color. Emaleen moved the flashlight away from the crystal, and it turned to a blue-green color. She couldn't wait to get home to look this gemstone up on her computer to see what it was and why it changed colors.

"We should get back," suggested Emaleen. "We can show this to Aunt Zeraida. I think she'll be pleased." She placed the crystal in a pocket of her pants.

Skye nodded, and the two made their way, with Belenus, back down the hill, following the trail markers and then the moose tracks until they got to the lakeshore. Then they made their way around the lake to their dock and back up the hill.

When they were back at the house, the two girls and Belenus were tired and very hungry. Once inside the house, Emaleen unhooked him from his leash and took off the harness. Belenus meowed happily. He was happy to be back in the house and free from the harness. Emaleen then sent a text to Mr. Earl to let him know they were back in the house.

"Are you hungry, Skye?" asked Emaleen.

"Yes, I'm starving," replied Skye.

"I'll be right back with some food," said Emaleen. She ran into the kitchen and fixed a small snack of cheese and crackers. She brought the plate with her into the family room.

When they finished eating, Emaleen suggested they go upstairs to her room, and Skye agreed. Once in her room, she put Belenus onto his bed. He immediately went to sleep. He was tired from the walk.

Then she removed the crystal from her pocket and placed it on her shelf. But she was careful to keep it far away from the other two gems in case putting it too close to them would cause a problem. She remembered the reaction she felt when she had placed the first two gems next to one another.

The girls then sat on Emaleen's bed and talked about their adventure that had resulted in the finding of the gem. After a while, she went over to her computer to research her new crystal. Skye joined her and looked over her friend's shoulder as Emaleen researched.

Based on what Emaleen read, she thought her new gem might be an Alexandrite. But like her first gem, her research showed that an Alexandrite needs to be polished to look like the gem that they had found in the cave. She wondered how the polished gem came to be located in the cave and how it was that she was lucky enough to find it. It seemed unlikely that someone would lose a polished Alexandrite in a cave near her home.

Emaleen also researched the magical properties of Alexandrite. She found references to the gem balancing the mind and emotions, and to the gem being used during meditation to increase focus. She knew she would have to ask her aunt for information about this stone as well as the others. She trusted her aunt's knowledge more than the information that she found on the Internet. But her aunt also seemed to know more than she was sharing, Emaleen thought.

Chapter 14

After the girls had played in Emaleen's room for a while, it occurred to Emaleen that she should talk to her aunt about the Alexandrite. So she suggested to Skye that they find Aunt Zeraida. Skye nodded her head. Emaleen then retrieved the Alexandrite from her shelf and placed it in her pocket. The two girls proceeded down the stairs with the expectation of finding her in the kitchen.

When they reached the first floor, they couldn't find Aunt Zeraida, so they went outside to look for her. But they did not find her outside. They went over to the mew and saw Shaolin. Next, they went over to the guest house and knocked on the door, but no one answered.

There was no sign of Emaleen's uncle either, but the young seer knew that sometimes her uncle went off on long walks so that wasn't unusual. However, Aunt Zeraida was usually easy to find. She was usually in the house, often the kitchen, or in the yard working in her flower garden. But now she was in none of those places.

"Maybe she's upstairs, and we didn't see her," speculated Skye encouragingly. She could see that Emaleen was getting more and more nervous the longer it was that she could not find her aunt.

So the girls stomped their way back upstairs to look for Aunt Zeraida. There they found that the bathroom door was open with no one inside. Next, they knocked on Aunt Zeraida's door. No one answered but Emaleen did hear a strange swishing and whirling sound that she had never heard before and wasn't sure what it was. She looked at Skye, unsure what to do. Skye shrugged.

Emaleen paused for a moment listening to the strange sounds and then not knowing what else to do she knocked on the door softly, almost timidly. As soon as she knocked, the sound stopped. Emaleen heard a creak as if a door was being opened, which was strange because she had been in Aunt Zeraida's room many times and she had never seen a door on hinges. The closet in the room was a walk-in closet, but it didn't have a door.

From the other side of the bedroom door, Emaleen heard footsteps. But they were not heavy steps. They were light and made only a little sound. Aunt Zeraida then opened the door and came out of the room.

Emaleen tried to look into the room, hoping to figure out the source of the noises that she heard. But everything looked normal to her. Nothing seemed to be out of place at all. There was also nothing unusual in her aunt's room that could explain the sound. Aunt Zeraida seemed normal, as well, as if nothing strange had been going on just a few minutes before. It appeared that her aunt didn't want to explain, so Emaleen decided not to ask her aunt what had been going on.

"What can I do for you girls?" asked Aunt Zeraida.

Emaleen opened her hand and held out the Alexandrite. She informed her aunt that they thought it was an Alexandrite because of its color changing when the light hit the gem. Emaleen also explained to her aunt how the girls had found the gem and how it was that they were able to retrieve it from the cave.

Her aunt was pleased that the girls had made the wise decision not to crawl into the cave. She was even more pleased with the creative problem solving that they had used together to retrieve the gem without going into the cave. To Aunt Zeraida, this was evidence that they were going to make a great team.

Aunt Zeraida was further pleased that although her niece was experimenting with possible powers, she was still ready to use her mind for solutions when she didn't have a power that she could use. Hopefully, Emaleen would realize just how important an asset her mind would be to her and that she could not always rely on her supranormal gifts and abilities. But better still, Zeraida was pleased that Emaleen had found the third gem, and she smiled with pride and hugged her niece snugly.

"I think that you are right that this is an Alexandrite," agreed Aunt Zeraida. "And, I'm so pleased that you have found it. An Alexandrite is good for focusing one's attention and its ability to calm the person holding the gem. It will be a very useful gem for you, Emaleen, and you too, Skye, when you are with Emaleen, particularly during a very stressful moment."

Aunt Zeraida added, "You should use this when you two next meditate."

"I don't understand how it is that I'm finding these gems," said Emaleen. "Some of these aren't usually found around here and even if they were, I don't think they would be in a polished form, but instead they would be in a rough rock form. Also, I have found these in such odd places."

Emaleen then asked her aunt, "Are you putting these out for me to find?"

"No, I'm not," Aunt Zeraida assured her niece.

"Then how am I finding them?" queried Emaleen.

Aunt Zeraida took a breath in slowly and then started with her rather long explanation. "It's kind of hard to explain and it will probably take a very long time for you to fully understand. There are even things that I don't understand fully, and no other seer understands fully either. It's just that complicated."

Then Aunt Zeraida added, "Each person, whether gifted with supranormal abilities or not, has a spirit. For us seers, the spirit has an extra feature that allows us to control our environment to some extent. Sometimes we are aware of this control because it's in our conscious mind, which is the part that we are aware of. When we use our conscious mind, we can use our will to effect a change."

"But sometimes," continued Zeraida, "the control is subconscious, in the part of our mind of which we are not aware. The subconscious mind is what controls how our body works without our direct knowledge or control over it happening. The subconscious part of our spirit determines the right combination of crystals and gems for you and helps bring them to you as your powers develop. But they must be found by you as you are ready to find them. So, you don't really find them by accident. Instead, the subconscious spirit guides you to the crystals and gems. Later, when you become more experienced with your abilities, you will learn to know when the subconscious spirit is attempting to lead you."

Aunt Zeraida looked over at Emaleen and Skye and noticed that they were in a stunned silence. A worried look crossed Zeraida's face. Maybe she had shared too much all at one time. She sighed. It was so hard to explain all of what she needed to explain in a gradual way so that Emaleen and Skye only had to process a small amount at a time. Emaleen was so obviously curious and had been trying very hard to be patient and not ask her aunt a lot of questions. But she did need to start learning.

Emaleen broke the silence and stated, "That was a lot, but I think I understand it — at least some of it. Thank you for explaining. I understand that there is a part of me that helps gather the crystals that I will need and helps me to find them even though I don't realize that this is what is going on. But I don't understand how the gems get there in the first place."

"How they get there is complicated," responded Zeraida. "I don't fully understand it myself. But I believe your subconscious mind uses some powers that you cannot use consciously to get those gems into the places in which you find them. Some of these gems might have been placed where you found them long before you even started to realize that you had powers. There is really no way to know."

"Will I ever be able to control this subconscious part of me?" asked Emaleen. "Will I ever be able to use these subconscious powers consciously?"

"No, you won't be able to control the subconscious part of your mind, but you will learn over time when it's telling you something," promised Aunt Zeraida. "And, this subconscious part also becomes less dominant once you start to develop your conscious powers. In fact, it can and often does become a very minor part of you. But it will always be there. You must develop self-awareness so you can figure out how to interpret the messages from your subconscious mind. But you cannot make decisions based solely on your subconscious mind.

You must think about what it is telling you and then make a decision with your conscious mind."

"What do I do with these gems?" asked Emaleen.

"For now, you keep them apart, very far apart," instructed Zeraida. "If they are close together they will start generating some magical energy. Others of our kind can feel this magical energy and will become aware of you if they are near enough. We don't want that to happen yet. You are not ready. So, it is very, very important to keep these gems away from one another. Soon enough, we will put them together, and you will see what they are for," answered Aunt Zeraida.

"Do I have all of the gems that I will find?" asked Emaleen. She hoped that there would be more gems to find. It had been exciting for Emaleen to find each gem.

"I don't know," admitted Aunt Zeraida uncertainly. "You need at least three gems to be able to generate extra powers. Some of us have only three gems. But some have many more. We will never know if you have all of your gems. You might never find another one, or you could keep finding them for a while. You could even think you have all your gems because you stop finding them only to find one many years later."

"Do you have gems, Aunt Zeraida?" asked Emaleen.

"I do have gems. I have five in all," Aunt Zeraida replied in a matter of fact tone of voice.

"Can we see them?" asked Emaleen.

"I will show you some time," promised Aunt Zeraida. "I have them in a special place. You'll be surprised when I show it to you."

"You mentioned before that some people call our powers magic, but you said it's more than that. Can you explain?" asked Emaleen.

"Yes, I'm glad you asked. Our powers are a kind of magic but not like what you might think," declared Aunt Zeraida. "If we think of our powers as just magic, then we might take them for granted."

"What do you mean? Isn't magic just magic? What could it be otherwise?" asked Emaleen.

Zeraida replied, "I don't feel that the way people think of magic as something that happens when you cast a spell is an accurate description of the powers that we have. We don't cast spells and then something just happens. We have certain talents and abilities that let us tap into events that occur naturally, and we use our will to cause something to happen, to stop something from happening, or to lessen, strengthen, speed or slow something that is already happening or about to happen. This is why you need to learn about science and nature. You need to understand how things work so that you can influence them in some way."

Emaleen asked, "Can we call our talents and abilities magic?"

"Yes," replied Aunt Zeraida. "In fact, most other seers do call our powers magic. It's just easier to refer to them that way. I just want you to understand there is a lot of work that goes into effecting a change of some sort. It's not like in the fairy tales where someone says a magic phrase and something happens."

"I understand," said Emaleen. Then she asked, "Why do you gather herbs and plants? Is it for making magic potions?"

Aunt Zeraida sighed and then smiled as she replied, "No, I don't make potions with magical powers. As far as I know, there is no such thing as magic potions."

Emaleen looked slightly disappointed at this response. She had read a lot of books about people with magical powers. And, when she first started learning that she would have magic powers, it was these books that she thought of and used to form her impression of magic. The way her aunt described it, seer magic seemed less interesting than the magic in the books.

Aunt Zeraida continued, "I make natural medicines, soaps and other solutions for every day, ordinary uses. There is no magic in what I make. It's just the use of knowledge. Anyone can do what I do with herbs, plants, and other materials. It just takes some time and patience to study all the properties of the materials so that you know what they do and how they react to one another when you mix them together.

The medicines and other items are very useful, and it's good to be able to make medicines and other items when you are not near any stores."

Emaleen asked, "Aunt Zeraida, if we use our minds to change things, then why is it that the gems give me extra powers? Are the gems magical?"

"The gems don't make magic," explained Aunt Zeraida in a serious tone. "However, they can provide you with some extra abilities but only because they build upon abilities that you already have and then help focus and enhance those. It really is difficult to explain. But someday you will understand, and you may even learn more about all of this than I can teach you. Maybe you'll teach me something someday."

"By the way, your uncle has a special gift that he has been keeping for you so that he can give it to you when you have your third gem," Aunt Zeraida informed Emaleen. "He went out for a walk earlier. Let's see if he's back in his workshop."

"His workshop?" asked Emaleen. She didn't know that her uncle had a workshop.

"Oh, sorry, I forgot," said Aunt Zeraida with an embarrassed look on her face. "Your uncle has a workshop in the woods around our house where he creates things out of wood. I never mentioned it to you before because it is hidden by magic — like a cloaking. It's a special technique that I will teach you someday. In the meantime, I'll have to help you get there. Follow me, and I'll show you."

Chapter 15

Aunt Zeraida led the girls down the stairs and out the front door to the porch. She then led them down the porch and toward the creek. But just before she reached the creek, she turned right and walked through some brush. Skye and Emaleen followed Aunt Zeraida down an unmarked trail for at least ten minutes before they reached a spot where it appeared they could go no farther through the woods because the trees and brush became so thick that it seemed impassable. Aunt Zeraida stopped in front of a large tree that was wider than any of the other trees; at least two or three times wider. It was even wider than any tree that Emaleen had ever seen.

Aunt Zeraida raised both hands into the air with her palms outward toward the tree but not touching the tree. Aunt Zeraida closed her eyes and then lowered her hands so that they touched the trunk of the tree. She held her hands on the tree for several minutes and then she knocked on the tree three times, pausing increasingly longer periods between each knock. Aunt Zeraida then stepped back from the tree and stood still. Aunt Zeraida quietly turned to the girls and put her finger up to her lips, motioning for them to be silent.

They all stood there for several minutes waiting silently, but nothing happened. Emaleen was starting to wonder whether her aunt knew what she was doing or if she might be playing a joke on them. Then, suddenly, a wooden door appeared to the right of the tree in midair. The door had a frame, but it didn't seem to be attached to a building. It just sat there on the floor of the forest. Green light shone through the gaps between the door frame and the door. Aunt Zeraida turned the handle to the door and opened it inward.

Emaleen peered over her aunt's shoulder, but there didn't seem to be anything on the other side of the door other than the forest that was already there as if you could walk through the door and go nowhere but to the forest sitting on the other side. There was also no green light shining through the door, which was curious given the light that shone through the cracks of the door before Aunt Zeraida opened it. But then her aunt stepped through the door and then disappeared. Emaleen shuddered for a second; her aunt's unexplained disappearance disturbed her and made her nervous.

Aunt Zeraida called out for the two girls to follow her. But they both just stood there, stunned, and didn't move. Aunt Zeraida reached a hand out and motioned them forward. Her hand looked like it had appeared out of thin air.

Emaleen was the first of the two girls to go through the door, although she did so reluctantly. Skye followed behind her. As Emaleen passed through the door, the trees disappeared from view and instead of stepping into a forest as she had expected, she found herself in a room with wooden walls and a set of wooden stairs leading up. From inside that room, Emaleen looked out into the forest that she had just left behind.

Then Emaleen turned and faced the steps leading upward. Just then Skye arrived. The two girls followed the steps up, as they spiraled upward, and led into a room with wooden walls and a stone floor. After they had stepped into the room, a door that hadn't been there before closed behind the girls.

Still stunned by her inexplicable passage through the door that had appeared in the woods, Emaleen stopped and took a moment to look around the room. In one section of the room to her right were various tools hanging on the walls and some large machines on the floor. All around the machines were piles of sawdust. One of the machines held a long, circular piece of wood that was shaped in such a way that it looked like a bedpost or a banister for a stairway.

Straight ahead was a small fireplace, but inside there was no fire burning. Even so, there was light mysteriously glowing from the fireplace. Over the fireplace was a mantel upon which were some wooden cups with fancy handles. There were also a few wooden plates displayed on the mantel, some of which appeared to have words written on them in dark staining.

There were no windows in the little house. But the house was full of light as a result of the light in the fireplace and candles on the walls.

As Emaleen looked around over to the left, she noticed her uncle in a corner. He was sitting, facing them, in a rocking chair with a knife and a long staff, cutting into the staff with his knife. He looked up and smiled at his niece and then looked back down and continued his carving, softly whistling a tune that Emaleen recognized but couldn't identify by name.

Next to her uncle was a bookshelf that covered part of one wall from the floor to the ceiling and was as wide as Emaleen was tall. The bookshelf was full of books, so full that some books were stacked upon the books that stood up on each shelf. Emaleen squinted and tried to read one of the titles. She could just see some lettering, but she couldn't make out any titles. The words she could make out were unfamiliar and appeared to be words from some foreign language.

"Girls," said Aunt Zeraida breaking through the silence, "as you can probably guess, this workshop is a secret location. Please don't tell anyone about it. Skye, you may, of course, tell your parents. But no one outside our two families can know about this."

Aunt Zeraida continued, "This workshop is Morvin's. It's hidden by magic from the view of normal people and others of our kind. Your uncle makes special items in this workshop. Most are wood. Some are metal. He has been working on a special item for you, Emaleen."

Uncle Morvin stopped his carving and stood up from his chair. With the wooden staff in his hands, he walked toward Emaleen. When he reached her, he twirled the staff so that he was holding it horizontally. He held it out for Emaleen and nodded for her to take it.

Emaleen reached out and took the staff. She held it horizontally and examined it. It was reddish-brown in color and had many different carvings on wooden rings that wrapped around it. She saw a carving of a falcon, a kitten that looked like Belenus and a moose. At one end of the staff, she noticed that the wood split off into three pieces that looked kind of like prongs on a ring. But the prongs were empty.

She then turned the wooden staff vertically, setting the end without the prongs down on the ground in front of her. As she set it down on the ground, she could feel it thud as if she had placed it down with force, but she had set it down gently. She also felt a strange buzz of power flow through her as she held it. At the same time, Emaleen felt calm and a sense of well-being and power. She felt strong, as if she could face any obstacle that might come her way. All these feelings were powerful for her, and she started to feel a little light-headed. She swayed just slightly but then steadied herself with the staff.

Uncle Morvin smiled and stated, "Emaleen, this is your staff of power. We also sometimes call it a wand. But as your aunt will teach you over time, it's so much more than just a wand. It has several uses, actually. The staff is also not the source of magic power, but it's a means of focusing and enhancing your powers."

"It feels like wood, but it's an unusual color. What's it made of?" asked Emaleen.

Uncle Morvin answered, "It's made of a type of wood that comes from a magical forest in southeastern England that is long lost and known only to a very few people — only those of our kind who have powers. I brought it back many years ago and have been waiting for the right time to start working on it for you. Just a few weeks ago, I started working on it and have been slowly carving, shaping, sanding it, and staining it so that it's just right for you. I have personalized it for you with the carvings and I can add more as you wish."

"It's beautiful," gasped Emaleen as she admired the staff in awe. She couldn't believe that her uncle had made something so beautiful. It was so well suited to her tastes, thought Emaleen.

"I'm glad you like it and think it's beautiful," responded Uncle Morvin humbly, "but it's also a very significant tool of magic, which should be with you always from now on. You must take very good care of it. You will have this all of your life."

Uncle Morvin went on, "The three prongs are for the three gems that you have found. When you are ready, you can add them to the staff. But we'll have to wait to add the gems for a while yet. When we do add them, you can decide which prong will hold which gem. Once you've placed them, though, they will remain permanently on the staff. If you find additional gems, the staff will grow a new prong on its own when you present the new gem to it."

"How can I carry a staff with me all the time?" asked Emaleen. "What do I do when I go to school or when I go anywhere in public? People don't carry staffs around with them, unless they are hikers."

"You are absolutely right, Emaleen. In ancient times, our people carried our staffs proudly, and we were revered by the normal people for our skills. But today it's different. The norms are not aware of us, and we actually like it better this way because, believe it or not, it's less complicated. But our secret existence has required us to find creative ways to disguise our staffs," explained Uncle Morvin.

"So, how do I disguise my staff?" asked Emaleen.

"The answer to your question is one of my most favorite features of the staff that I've made for you. Hold your right arm out, and lean the staff against it while you support the staff in your left hand," instructed Uncle Morvin.

Emaleen gave her uncle a confused look for a moment. His instructions didn't immediately make sense to her. But then as if it had suddenly become clear to her, Emaleen held her right arm out and then touched the staff to her held-out arm. She supported the weight of the staff with her left hand, balancing it as best as she could.

As she supported the staff, she noticed that it started to feel lighter, and the longer she held it against her arm, the lighter it felt. Looking down at the staff, she noticed that it was becoming thinner and thinner. Then slowly it started to twist and wind around her right arm, into a bracelet. The bracelet looped horizontally around her wrist once at the base of Emaleen's wrist and then wrapped up and over the top of Emaleen's arm diagonally and then it wrapped horizontally around her arm, about four inches from the loop around Emaleen's wrist. The result was a bracelet wrapped around her wrist and arm.

The carvings that were on the staff appeared across the top of the loop on Emaleen's arm. On the loop around Emaleen's wrist were three raised flowers with holes in their centers that looked like they could hold three small jewels. These flowers, thought Emaleen, must be the prongs that hold the gems. She wondered if the gems would shrink when they were installed in the staff and the staff turned into a bracelet.

"You should leave this bracelet on always unless you have the staff itself activated. The wood is specially treated so that you don't have to worry about it getting wet or dirty," Uncle Morvin explained to his niece.

"How do you activate the staff so that it changes from a bracelet to a staff again?" asked Emaleen.

"I will show you some other time," answered her uncle. "For now, it's important that you don't have the staff activated because it might generate some magic that could be detected by others of our kind. None of us, you included, is ready for you to be detectable yet. Your staff is now only slightly detectable, and it's only a little risky. To activate the staff even by itself would be dangerous. But, I promise that I will show you when the time is right."

"Do you and Aunt Zeraida have staffs?" Emaleen asked her uncle.

"Yes. Ours too are hidden," answered Uncle Morvin and he nodded at Aunt Zeraida.

Aunt Zeraida stepped forward to show her hidden staff. It was a bronze-colored, thick, stiff rope necklace wrapped around her neck. It was coiled loosely three times around her neck. Each coil was separate from the others and differed in the length each traveled her neck. On each of the coils was a small gem. One gem was red and triangle shaped. Another was green and was an oval shape. The third was a dark blue diamond shape. And, on the smallest coil, there were another two gems, both of which were clear, one of which was a circle shape and the other which was a crescent moon shape.

Uncle Morvin pointed to one of his suspenders, which appeared to be made of leather and which had five tiny gems affixed to it. The suspender seemed to have a wood-grain-like finish on it as if it had been painted to look that way.

"Uncle Morvin," asked Emaleen, "do you have two staffs? You have two suspenders."

"No, I just have one. But suspenders don't come in singles; they come in pairs. So the other is just a copy," answered Uncle Morvin.

"Pretty clever, Uncle," laughed Emaleen.

"I can also turn my staff of power into a cane or a walking stick if it's not convenient to carry my wand as a suspender," added Uncle Morvin. "Sometimes, as you can imagine, it can be awkward to reach for a suspender and turn it back into a wand."

Emaleen nodded. "I can imagine," she remarked with a laugh. She momentarily pictured her uncle trying to pull off his suspender strap and turning it into a wand.

Uncle Morvin's five gems were separate colors. They were yellow, orange, black, white pearl, and dark purple. Unlike Aunt Zeraida's gems, which were differently shaped, all of Uncle Morvin's gems were oval shaped. Emaleen wondered if there was any significance to the shape of the stones. But she decided not to ask just yet because she felt that she had already received far more information than she wanted for one day.

"I also have a ring that I wear that has certain powers," said Aunt Zeraida, holding out her hand. "This is actually my wedding ring that your uncle gave me on our wedding day." Aunt Zeraida smiled as she looked down at her ring as if she was recalling a past happy memory.

"What does it do?" asked Emaleen.

"Someday I will explain what this ring can do. Or I may show you," answered Zeraida, mysteriously.

"I have one, too, that I received on my wedding day to your aunt," stated Uncle Morvin with a bright smile. "It, too, has special powers."

Emaleen noticed that the two rings both had clear gems with a hint of yellow to their color. They looked to her like they were diamonds, and both were trilliant cut. As she stared at her aunt's ring, she noticed that the numerous facets of the gem picked up the colors around the room and reflected them back. She also thought for a moment that she saw a ray of light sparkle from the gem. Emaleen continued to stare at the jewel as if she were under a spell.

As if she sensed that Emaleen had learned enough for the day, Aunt Zeraida suggested, "Why don't we all go back to the house and have a snack? I have freshly baked oatmeal raisin cookies."

Aunt Zeraida had baked the cookies that morning and put them away in airtight plastic containers for later and for several days to come. But cookies did disappear quickly in Aunt Zeraida's kitchen, and she suspected that it was not the result of magic.

The girls eagerly agreed. Emaleen hoped that it would be chocolate milk because that was her favorite kind of milk to drink with cookies.

"I have some more work to do here," said Uncle Morvin. "I will be by later for some cookies."

They waved goodbye and went down the stairs. Aunt Zeraida opened the secret exit from the little house, and the girls and Aunt Zeraida left, leaving Emaleen's uncle to his work. They walked back through the forest and back to the house to enjoy the cookies and milk.

After their snack, both girls felt refreshed. Then Aunt Zeraida shooed them off to play. She knew that they needed some free time to absorb what they had learned and also to just be kids.

She had promised herself, as she had promised Emaleen's mother so many years ago, that she would allow them to be kids for as long as possible and would protect them from having to shoulder the serious responsibility that came with their powers and abilities for as long as she possibly could. But she still had to teach them so that they would be ready when the time came. She wouldn't let them be caught unprepared by danger. Aunt Zeraida smiled as she watched the girls run out of the house to play, giggling as they chased each other.

Chapter 16

The next couple of weeks were uneventful and peaceful for the girls. They played in the creek and explored the trails in the woods. They played with Belenus frequently and watched him grow bigger. They baked and cooked with Aunt Zeraida. They played in the house together and read books. They also walked over to Skye's house and played there too.

Between their play sessions, the girls worked on the lessons and challenges that Aunt Zeraida planned for them. They routinely practiced their meditating and became very good at not being distracted by anything while they were on their meditation rugs, including Belenus jumping on their laps and licking their faces. They could hold their concentration for a half hour straight without being distracted by even a loud, startling noise. Aunt Zeraida was very pleased with their progress and praised them frequently, which made them beam with excitement and joy.

Aunt Zeraida also gave the girls various challenges to test how closely they observed things. She had them go on scavenger hunts for hard-to-find items. Some of the items were very rare to find in the woods, but they could be found if a person looked hard enough. There were also other items that she had planted so well hidden that only the smallest piece of the object was visible.

The girls became so good at observing things that Aunt Zeraida wondered what other things they might observe and figure out. She was very pleased and thought that she would have to make the challenges more difficult.

Emaleen also frequently worked with Shaolin and had become very good at seeing through the falcon's eyes. She also had developed some skill at gently willing Shaolin to fly in certain directions and to search for certain things. She could have probably used the bird to give her an advantage on the scavenger hunts that Aunt Zeraida had given her and saved a lot of time. But she knew to do so would not honor her aunt's wishes and expectations, nor would it help Emaleen develop the skills that her aunt was trying to teach her.

Emaleen, however, had Shaolin fly over her former teacher's house just for fun to see what her former teacher was doing. She saw through Shaolin's eyes that Ms. Perch did a lot of gardening outdoors and that she was a perfectionist about pulling up all the weeds in her garden. Ms. Perch also liked to drink iced tea as she lay in a hammock hanging between two trees next to her garden as the hammock swung gently in the summer breeze.

She had really only thought of Ms. Perch as a teacher and had not thought of her as a real person who had interests and a life outside of school. Emaleen realized then that the teacher was just a person like everyone else. As she began to realize that Ms. Perch was a real person, Emaleen stopped thinking of her as someone out to get her and she realized that the woman was probably just doing her best to try to help her.

She soon lost her fascination with her former teacher and what she might be doing. Not long after that, she stopped willing Shaolin to fly over the teacher's house and yard.

Ms. Perch had wondered about the bird that kept flying over her property, which she mistakenly thought was a hawk. The hawk seemed to be watching her while it circled above her. It would also occasionally land on the power lines nearby her house and sit there for long periods of time. She dismissed these thoughts as a crazy fantasy, but she also smiled a strange, seemingly knowing smile, as if someone had shared a secret with her. She also did notice when the hawk stopped flying around her house.

After she stopped flying Shaolin over Ms. Perch's house, Emaleen really started to explore with the falcon. Shaolin could fly to places that would not be accessible to Emaleen otherwise. She saw through the bird's eyes all sorts of things that she never expected to see. Some of what she saw from the sky, she would have probably never seen even if she were in the places herself.

One such sighting that shocked and surprised Emaleen was when she saw a large manlike creature covered in fur walking alongside a creek in an area that looked to her as if it would be difficult for a person to access. She thought that the creature must be a figment of her imagination, or that Shaolin must have been seeing a bear and that the angle of view was simply off enough to appear differently from the sky than it would appear from the ground. So, she had the falcon fly back over the area to get another look.

Although she didn't want Shaolin to get too low because that might be too close to the creature, the falcon was able to get close enough that Emaleen was able to determine that it was an ape-type creature walking on its hind legs. She decided to keep her discovery a secret to protect the creature. No one would believe her anyway, she thought, except of course her family and Skye.

Emaleen also worked a lot with Belenus, taking him on walks and working with him to listen to her will so that she could make requests of him using her mind to communicate with him. However, as Aunt Zeraida had instructed, Emaleen was careful to respect her kitten and not to treat him like he didn't have his own will and, as a result, mistreat him. Belenus, in Emaleen's opinion, was a loved companion and not a servant or a slave.

As she did with Shaolin, she also learned how to see through Belenus' eyes. But the kitten's view was different than the one she had with the falcon. Belenus' view was at ground level, which allowed Emaleen to see things more closely on the ground than she could through the falcon's eyes from high up in the sky. Through the kitten's eyes, she could also see in places that she couldn't personally go because Belenus was so small and could move into areas in which Emaleen could not fit.

Except for one advantage, Emaleen really didn't think the ability to see through Belenus' eyes was that useful since there usually wasn't much to see on the ground. But through practicing with Belenus, Emaleen had learned how to turn her view through an animal's eyes on and off so that she could use it when she wished and that she would not constantly see the images.

As she continued to work with the animals, Emaleen reported to her aunt her findings about seeing through animals' eyes. Her aunt was very pleased by how her niece had progressed.

One day, in a conversation about the animal sight ability, Aunt Zeraida explained to Emaleen, "Since the power you have comes in different forms and different strengths, you should continue to experiment to see what you are able to do with the powers. It's most common for the power to be limited to animals with whom the person has formed a special relationship and bond. However, a very small group of seers can use the animal sight power with almost any animal within a certain distance of the person. For such people, the greater the power the person has, the greater the distance at which the person can detect an animal and then connect to it so that the person can see through the animal's eyes. I know of only one person with that most extreme form of the power. But even that person did not have the power with all types of animals."

In addition to direct training and explanation, Aunt Zeraida also gave Emaleen books to read with instructions to read certain pages. The books were about science and nature, including biology, physics, chemistry, and the properties of herbs and the healing arts. After she had finished each book, she would report it to her aunt, who would quiz her on the reading and then send her back to read some more if she did not do well enough.

Aunt Zeraida wanted Emaleen to have as much knowledge about any related science and nature as possible before she started to explain the proper way to work magic. In Aunt Zeraida's opinion, this was the foundation of all properly performed magic. She also thought that Emaleen should fully appreciate the effect of her actions and ensure they were carefully measured to avoid unintended consequences.

Emaleen enjoyed the reading and loved learning about new topics. She couldn't wait to learn more about magic. She constantly wondered about what her wand would be able to help her do once the three gems were added to it. But she knew she had to be patient and that Aunt Zeraida would teach her when the time was right.

It was now the last week in July. Several weeks had gone by since the end of the school year. Now, the summer was half over, with August on the verge of starting. Emaleen wasn't quite ready for the start of the next school year. She hoped the month of August would provide her with plenty of time to play and explore, swim in the lake, and to learn more from her aunt before the summer ended.

She wondered what school would be like for her now. Emaleen was different after all that she had learned and practiced in just a few weeks.

Emaleen had a greater self-awareness, very refined powers of observation and attention, and an increased ability to think of creative solutions to problems. She also had more self-control and was able to react more logically, rather than emotionally, because she could stop and think about a situation and not react immediately based upon her emotions. She also had a lot more focus and attention and was putting more of mind and effort into her tasks. Her personal growth this summer so far had been quite remarkable, particularly given the short time frame. But Emaleen knew that she still had a lot more to learn.

After all her hard work, Emaleen felt very powerful. She loved the feeling of control that she had over how she reacted to things that happened. She also loved how aware she was and how she noticed details that she hadn't noticed before. It made her feel even more alive and connected to the world than she had felt before.

Even with all her newly-learned powers and abilities, Emaleen was not all powerful as a seer. She also had weaknesses. For example, she did not have full control over herself, but she was working on that.

However, Emaleen was starting to understand what her aunt meant by being able to *see*. She also loved that she could *see* even so much more with her animals than she could normally see. Her aunt had told her, though, that this was just the beginning of being able to *see* and that she would learn so much more as they went along. Her aunt would continue to instruct her and guide her in developing her full ability to *see*. But her aunt also informed her that even after Emaleen had gained what would seem to be all of her powers, she would always be learning more. The better she paid attention and focused on what was happening and she was doing, and the harder she worked, the more she would learn. But it would also require many lessons over a long time.

Aunt Zeraida had sensed Emaleen's new feelings of power one day and cautioned, "You need to be careful that however powerful you become, you don't to let the power go to your head and take control of you. It's always important to make sure that you are in control of yourself. If you aren't careful, you could lose control and let a thirst for power start directing your actions. The result could be very bad."

Aunt Zeraida also explained to her niece that she should also maintain respect. Not only should she respect the power that she had by not misusing it, but she should respect all living things. She should respect all people, and she should not let their differences, including their differences in career choices, cultures or backgrounds affect how she treated anyone. All people were special in their own ways, and all were to be respected and treated with dignity and kindness.

Further, Aunt Zeraida instructed that Emaleen should be careful not to disrespect the norms, who did not have the powers that Emaleen and her kind were lucky enough to have inherited through birth. She taught her how there were some seers long ago who had abused their powers and how some of them had treated the norms oppressively. She also instructed Emaleen that she was not excused from following the rules of society, including all laws and all rules of the places in which she found herself, such as school. She was also not to use her powers to give her advantages over norms, unless the purpose was to protect her personal physical safety and only after she had exhausted all other means of escaping the situation.

Aunt Zeraida continued, "I hope you don't feel that I am lecturing you. I just want to help you cope with your powers and be happy in life. Letting your power control you instead of you controlling your power can lead to great unhappiness and distress."

Aunt Zeraida also had a sense of fairness, justice, and ethics and wanted to make sure that her niece understood the same values and would only act with these in mind. She respected their powers and felt that having them imposed a duty to be careful with those powers and to use them only when it was appropriate. To do otherwise would be disrespectful to the awesome powers that they were fortunate to have.

What she didn't tell her niece was that at some point, Emaleen would probably have to draw upon her powers to actually confront Maerdern, who had let the powers go to his head and now was abusing them. Zeraida had told Emaleen that Maerdern was a danger to her niece, but had not yet shared the possibility that Emaleen may have to fight him. She didn't yet know how to explain that to Emaleen or how to prepare her for that knowledge. She was concerned that the information would be very distressing to Emaleen and might interfere with her niece's training. She would have to address it later when Emaleen was more mature and more fully trained and prepared to think clearly and logically instead of reacting with her emotions. Emaleen had made great progress in these areas, but she was not yet ready.

Chapter 17

Early one morning in the first week of August, Emaleen woke up suddenly and bolted straight up to a sitting position. At the same time, she cried out in a panic and gasped for a breath. She wasn't yet quite awake but was still partially asleep. A second later she was fully awake, and she then knew that something horrid had happened in her dreams. But she had no specific memory of what her dreams were about. Shaking still from fear, Emaleen slowly climbed out of her bed and put her slippers on. She went downstairs to find her aunt.

When she arrived downstairs, Emaleen found Aunt Zeraida in the kitchen making tea and some breakfast muffins. She sat down next to her aunt in a chair at the breakfast bar that separated the kitchen from the dining area. She glanced over at her aunt with a look of fear on her face.

Aunt Zeraida reached over and hugged her niece. She knew from the look on Emaleen's face that something was very wrong, but she could also tell that her niece wasn't yet ready to talk about it. So, she just waited and smiled pleasantly at her, hoping to comfort her.

When the breakfast muffins were finished, Aunt Zeraida set them out on a cooling rack. She then prepared some fresh-squeezed orange juice and took some jams out of the refrigerator. She set some muffins out on a plate in front of Emaleen and motioned for her niece to take one. Emaleen took a muffin and spread some strawberry jam on it and ate in silence. She then grasped the glass of orange juice with both hands, holding the glass tightly as if she was afraid that she would drop it. She was still shaking slightly as a result of her dream, but she still couldn't remember what it was about.

"What's wrong?" Aunt Zeraida finally asked her niece.

Emaleen paused for a moment, gathering her thoughts together and trying to calm her emotions before she answered, "I don't know. When I woke up this morning, I felt upset and afraid. I don't know why, though."

"Did you have a bad dream?" asked Aunt Zeraida.

"I think so, but I can't remember what I dreamed," answered Emaleen.

"It might have been a premonition dream," suggested Aunt Zeraida. "But since you don't remember what you dreamed, it's hard to tell for sure."

"You mentioned that before," said Emaleen. "What is it exactly? I didn't understand what you meant when you mentioned premonition dreams before."

"Premonition dreams are dreams about things that may happen in the future," answered Aunt Zeraida. "But usually, you would remember the dream. Since you do not remember, it's more than likely that you had an ordinary, everyday bad dream that means nothing at all. Sometimes, dreams like these happen to the norms as well as seers. So, if I were you, I wouldn't worry. I would just try to shake it off."

"I'll try," said Emaleen uncertainly.

"Why don't you have some tea?" suggested Aunt Zeraida. "It has some herbs in it to help you feel less stressed." She handed her niece a caffeine-free herbal tea, which Emaleen immediately accepted.

Emaleen took a few sips of the tea and started to feel calmer. Then she noticed that there was a small bird sitting on the outside kitchen window sill looking in at her. It looked to her as if the bird might be a red robin. But she couldn't see its wings, so she wasn't sure if it was the bird that she had seen before. She decided not to tell her aunt because it sounded crazy to her that a bird would be watching her.

A few minutes later, the doorbell rang. Aunt Zeraida went to answer the door and discovered Skye on the doorstep. Zeraida was surprised to see her niece's friend there so early, but soon discovered the girl's purpose. Skye had a note from her mother, Angelina.

The note was sealed in an envelope, upon which Zeraida's name was written, that she handed to Zeraida unopened. Although Skye had been curious about the contents of the note, she respected her mother's wishes and had not opened it.

"Skye," asked Aunt Zeraida, "would you like to come in for some breakfast?"

"Yes, I would love to," replied Skye, who was pleased to accept the offer because she had not yet had breakfast. Her mother had woken her up early and had given her the note to deliver to Zeraida, and had directed Skye to deliver it immediately. Skye hadn't stopped to eat but had brought the note to Zeraida without any delay.

Skye was also pleased to see Emaleen. But she became concerned when she saw the look on her friend's face. So, Skye suggested that they finish breakfast and then play with Belenus. Skye knew that playing with the kitten would cheer her friend up and help ease whatever was troubling her.

"Thanks, that's a great idea," commented Emaleen. "I'm so glad that you're here." Emaleen gave her friend a big hug.

"You girls can take your breakfast into the family room to eat, if you promise to be careful not to spill," suggested Aunt Zeraida. "You can play with Belenus while you eat. But don't feed him any of your food because it may not be healthy for him to eat it."

After the girls had left the room, Zeraida took the note out of the envelope and along with it came a yellow piece of paper, which fell to the floor. Aunt Zeraida read the note while drinking her tea. The note simply stated, "Please stop by this morning. Bring Emaleen with you."

Although it was so short that it hadn't taken Zeraida long to read it, Zeraida held it in her hands for several minutes while she sat thinking and drinking her tea. Zeraida could tell by the direct tone of the note and the yellow color of the piece of paper that had come with it that it was a message indicating that there was no immediate danger but that there was some reason for caution.

If the paper had been orange or red, it would have been a signal that matters were much more serious. But with yellow, Aunt Zeraida knew that she didn't need to hurry, but could take her time to get ready to go over to the house. After finishing her tea, Aunt Zeraida stood up from her chair and went into the family room.

"Girls," Zeraida said calmly when she entered the family room, "when Skye is finished eating breakfast, we all need to go over to her house. I am going upstairs to get dressed to go out and wake Uncle Morvin so that he can come with us."

Emaleen thought it strange that Skye would come so early in the morning with a note and that Aunt Zeraida would then state that they needed to go to Skye's house as soon as possible. And, although her aunt had acted so calmly as if nothing was wrong, Emaleen was still worried. She thought about how she scared she had been this morning about her dreams and wondered if there was a connection.

Zeraida noticed the worried look on Emaleen's face and stated reassuringly, "Girls, everything is probably fine. You don't need to worry right now. I just need to talk to Skye's mother."

But Emaleen was still worried. She wondered why they would need to have an early morning meeting. It seemed urgent to Emaleen, and it worried her. They had never had a morning meeting before. She also couldn't shake her feelings caused by her dreams last night even though she couldn't remember what had happened in the dreams.

Skye looked at Emaleen with compassion and asked, "Are you okay, Emaleen?"

"I am fine. I just woke up this morning with feelings of fear, I think from my dreams, but I can't remember what I had dreamed last night. And now I am concerned about there being a need to meet at your house with your mother. It sounds to me like something is wrong. Aunt Zeraida is so calm, but I sense trouble."

"I sense something too," agreed Skye. "But I think it will be okay. We have my parents and your aunt and uncle to look after us and keep us safe." Skye gave Emaleen a big hug.

The girls then played with Belenus to distract themselves. Belenus, as usual, loved playing with the girls and brought out his energy full force. Belenus jumped and spun through the air, chasing the toy that the girls wiggled in front of him until he was exhausted and panting for breath. Belenus then lay down on the floor and let the girls pet him while he purred happily. The girls then turned to their food, which they had not yet touched, and started to eat.

A few minutes later, Aunt Zeraida came down the stairs and into the family room with Uncle Morvin. Aunt Zeraida motioned to the girls that it was time to go. Then they all went outside and got in the car and drove over to Skye's house. Although Skye's house was just down the road from Emaleen's and within walking distance, Aunt Zeraida was eager to get to the house and hear whatever news Skye's mother had to share. She didn't want to take the time to walk, although normally that would have been her first choice.

When they reached the house and the car stopped, the girls jumped out and ran up onto the porch of the Stewart house. Skye's mother, Angelina Stewart, and Skye's father, Jay Stewart, who had been waiting for them, met them at the door.

Angelina had blonde hair just like her daughter, and she was taller, about five-feet-ten inches. Her husband, Jay, had brown hair, and although he was of a slight build, he had fairly developed muscles from working out.

The Stewarts, who were in their thirties, were younger than the Barsans. Neither of them had a particular style of dress that they favored. Instead, they preferred wearing the correct clothes for the particular event at hand. Today, they were dressed for tea with friends. But they were not dressed too fancy, so as to make their guests uncomfortable, particularly Zeraida, who they expected would be in an informal long skirt with a comfortable cotton top. Rather, they were dressed in somewhat casual clothes that were stylish and semi-dressy.

"Girls, why don't you go up to Skye's room to play," suggested Skye's mom, Angelina. "We adults just need some time to talk."

"Mom," asked Skye, "is everything okay?"

"Yes," answered Angelina. "There is nothing right now to worry about. At the moment, everything is all right."

"Thanks, Mom," said Skye as she motioned for Emaleen to follow her, and she started to run toward the stairs that led up to her room.

"Girls," called out Angelina, "I have left some ice cold lemonade and vanilla scones in Skye's room in case you get hungry."

The girls ran up the stairs to Skye's room, leaving the adults behind. Emaleen forgot that they were there for some serious business and was grateful to go upstairs to play.

Chapter 18

As soon as the girls left, Angelina Stewart turned her attention to Zeraida and Morvin, who had entered the house behind the girls and had been standing in the doorway. They had been waiting for the girls to leave the room before they started to speak.

"Zeraida and Morvin, it's good to see you," said Angelina. "Please come into the living room. I have some herbal tea and biscuits ready for us."

After they all sat down, Angelina poured tea for each of them and then served the biscuits. Then after a few more minutes, Angelina started to inform Zeraida and Morvin about the reason why she had invited them over this morning.

"I have received a message from the spy who is watching Maerdern Baleros for Emaleen's parents," explained Angelina. "We need to discuss what to do."

Angelina handed the message to Zeraida. The message was short and to the point. It simply stated, "He's on the move. Lots of activity and buzz in his household. Don't know why. No evidence that he knows. But be careful and watchful. He has bird sight now, but it is so far limited in range and only with his own bird. He is traveling with his bird."

Zeraida read the note and then handed it Morvin, who also read it. Both Zeraida and Morvin sat there thinking about it for a few minutes. It was unsettling for Zeraida to hear that something was going on with Maerdern but not knowing exactly what. Hopefully, she thought, he still had no knowledge of Emaleen's existence. They would have to keep vigilant. Without more information, though, it would be difficult to know what to watch for.

"It's tough to know what to do," said Uncle Morvin. "There isn't enough information in this message to indicate what's going on."

"I agree," said Zeraida. "But I am very concerned about Maerdern having bird sight. That power could be particularly dangerous since

Emaleen has that power too, and especially since she has been working with Shaolin. If Maerdern develops the power further and is able to see through Shaolin's eyes, he may be able to see Emaleen."

"We need to find a way to protect Emaleen then," asserted Morvin, "so that Maerdern can't access Shaolin's sight."

"At least, he is now far enough away that the risk of Maerdern using Shaolin's bird sight is low, isn't it?" asked Angelina.

"That's true," agreed Morvin. "But should Maerdern come near and we aren't aware of that, it might be a significant risk. It just depends on how Maerdern develops the power."

"Even if Maerdern were close, and could use bird sight with Shaolin, wouldn't he need to know about Emaleen and what she looks like for his bird sight to be a risk to Emaleen?" asked Jay.

"That might be true," answered Zeraida. "But if Maerdern were to use bird sight and he saw Emaleen, he might be able to see the signs that she has power. If he were able to do that, he could figure out about Emaleen through just the bird sight."

Maybe, thought Zeraida, she could find a way to cover up those signs so that they could not be noticed so easily. But, she and her husband would need to research that possibility before she shared that idea with others.

Morvin turned to Zeraida and said, "I don't have any magic that can be used to prevent Maerdern from using Shaolin for bird sight. Do you know any magic that would protect against that, Zeraida?"

"No, I don't know of anything," answered Zeraida with a sad sigh. "But I will definitely go through my books when we get home and see if I can find something. You should go through your books too, Morvin, just in case there might be something in your books that you aren't thinking of right now. And we should probably also consult with Mr. Earl. He may have some ideas too, particularly since he works with Shaolin."

"We might also have to rethink our use of pigeons to carry messages," suggested Morvin.

"Yes, we will. But I am nervous about using telephones or email," countered Zeraida. "I am afraid that Maerdern might have a way of spying on those communications."

"Well, he might not actually suspect our use of pigeons," said Morvin. "It is so old fashioned that it might be safe."

"You might be right," agreed Zeraida. "At least, I hope so."

Zeraida decided that as soon as they got back home, she would look through the books in her library and see if she could find a way to make Shaolin undetectable to other seers, or to find some other way to keep another seer from being able to use Shaolin's eyes. She would also have to research to discover whether there was a way to keep another seer from tapping into their pigeons too.

"Should we contact the Andarsans?" asked Jay Stewart. "Do you think they might have some ideas?"

"Hmm," said Morvin slowly. "I think we should limit our contact with the Andarsans at this time. We don't know what Maerdern is up to, and we don't want to blow Emaleen's cover just yet. She's got quite a lot of training to do before she is even remotely able to defend herself against Maerdern."

"There is not enough information for us to know what is going on with Maerdern," claimed Angelina. "The buzz in the household could be about anything. The same thing is true for whatever trip Maerdern is starting. His opinion of himself is quite large. He could be creating his own drama just to feel important. There is just no way to know yet."

"We also do not know for sure that he has no knowledge of Emaleen," remarked Morvin. "Since we have no idea why he is traveling, we should assume the worst until we know." They all agreed, nodding their heads.

"So what should we do now?" asked Jay. "Should we organize the other seer families against Maerdern?"

"I don't think we can make an alliance with the other seer families right now," volunteered Zeraida. "Many of the seer families don't even see Maerdern as a threat. They feel that he isn't powerful enough to be a concern to them. I believe they dangerously underestimate him, though. But hopefully, someday, we will be able to bring the families together because I believe that is the only way that we will be able to defeat him."

The adults were all silent for a moment. Each was thinking over Zeraida's words and the difficulty of their situation. They all realized that it would be difficult to form an alliance with the families for any reason. And, if they didn't take Maerdern seriously, it would be even harder to get their attention to the issue.

"Well, I don't think we should overly panic," suggested Morvin interrupting the uncomfortable silence. "We should stay where we are, but keep an extra eye out for anything out of the ordinary. If we discover information that gives us actual cause to worry then we should leave here and move to somewhere more remote and safe. But in the meantime, we should remain calm and stay put."

"I agree," said Zeraida. "I think, too, that we should ask Mr. Earl to use Shaolin to keep watch for Maerdern and his people. I'll figure out a way to protect from Shaolin's sight being accessed by other seers. I'm sure there is a way."

"We also have to be ready to move to the emergency relocation point that we have planned, though," contributed Angelina. All of the adults nodded.

Having talked out their plans, they turned their conversation to other topics while the girls continued to play upstairs. It had been a long time since the adults had gathered together, so they had much to discuss. The remainder of the conversation was light and fun.

Upstairs, the girls were playing happily in Skye's room. They had no awareness of what was being discussed by the adults downstairs. The girls were also too busy playing to be interested.

"I have done some more work on my dollhouse since you were last here," said Skye proudly. "Would you like to see?" Emaleen nodded with enthusiasm.

Skye showed Emaleen her large, two-story dollhouse that she had been decorating over the last couple of years. The house had rooms with carpeting, hardwood floors, and tiles. It also had rooms with wallpaper and some rooms with hand-painted murals on the walls. The rooms were all furnished with the appropriate furniture, including lamps on tables, and in a couple of the rooms there were chandeliers.

Skye explained that her father had made the wooden furniture for her, but she had designed it. She was proud of all her hard work on her dollhouse and was very pleased to be able to show her friend the work that she had done since the last time Emaleen had come to visit. Skye was a tomboy, but she liked how the dollhouse allowed her to be creative.

"Would you like to help me decorate one of these rooms that I haven't finished yet?" asked Skye.

"Sure, how about this one," suggested Emaleen pointing to a room on the first floor. "I think we should paint the walls light blue."

Skye agreed and brought out the light blue paint and two paint brushes. It was fun work, and Emaleen found herself in a more relaxed state only a few minutes after she started painting. The girls also painted some purple flowers on the walls, at Emaleen's suggestion.

Skye was pleased to see her friend having so much fun and becoming so relaxed and much more like herself. Emaleen's previous tense state had made Skye uncomfortable. Skye thought it must be her role as a guardian as well as best friend that had made her feel unhappy and uneasy when Emaleen was so obviously stressed and unhappy.

Emaleen was thrilled to be on a visit to Skye at her house. It had been quite a long time since she had visited Skye here. Usually, Skye went over to Emaleen's house. Emaleen had not realized that before. Skye also had never thought about it before either; it had always seemed more natural for her to go over to Emaleen's house.

The young seer looked around the room and noticed that Skye's bed and bedspread matched the bedding in one of the bedrooms in the dollhouse. She also noticed that Skye had a wooden chest at the end of her bed that was also matched in the dollhouse. The wooden chest was a dark walnut color and had pictures of roses carved into its top. The wooden chest caught Emaleen's eye, and she could not take her eyes off of it. She was very curious about the contents of the chest.

Skye noticed her friend was staring at the wooden chest, and so she asked, "Would you like to see what's in the chest?"

"Yes, I would love to," replied Emaleen.

The two girls walked over to the chest. When Skye opened it, Emaleen saw burgundy-colored lace fabric at the top. Skye took the lace out and showed Emaleen that it was part of a dress that included lace with a rose design as an overlay.

Under the dress, were several different colored woven belts, including white, yellow, blue, red, brown and black. Skye took each of these belts out and placed them on her bed. Next inside the trunk were two outfits with a top and pants. They were both white.

Skye explained that she had earned the belts in martial arts classes, and the outfits were the uniforms that she wore in her classes. Emaleen knew that Skye had taken martial arts classes, but never before had Skye told her that she had a black belt.

The young guardian's parents had started her in Tae Kwon Do classes when she was just three. They had explained to her that they had her learn Tae Kwon Do so that she would be able to defend herself if the need should arise and also to help her build her confidence, focus, and ability to set and achieve goals.

As they were going through Skye's Tae Kwon Do items, Skye stated, "You know, I've been thinking since I found out that I am your guardian, that my parents might have put me into Tae Kwon Do as part of getting me ready to become a guardian. I'm really glad that I worked so hard and became a black belt. There were times that I wanted to quit because it was so hard, but I knew that I had to keep working and earn the black belt."

Skye still continued to study Tae Kwon Do so she would not only maintain her skills but so that she could continue to grow and develop them. She had also learned how to use weapons, such as a bo staff and a pair of nunchucks. She hoped that she would never have to use her skills in martial arts, but she was willing to use them to protect Emaleen, if needed.

Under the martial arts items were pillows and blankets that were of no special interest. Emaleen helped Skye put the items back into the wooden chest. Skye was careful to arrange her martial arts uniform and belts in a certain way as she returned them to the chest.

The girls had just finished putting the items back into the chest when they heard Aunt Zeraida call from downstairs for the girls to come back down.

"Emaleen, we are finished talking," called out Aunt Zeraida from downstairs. "It is time for us to go home."

Skye hugged Emaleen and told her, "It was wonderful to have you come over for a visit. I hope you come again soon."

When the girls arrived downstairs, Aunt Zeraida informed Emaleen, "When we get home, we will have lunch and then get started on some new lessons that you should work on as soon as possible."

Aunt Zeraida then turned to the Stewarts and said, "Thank you for having us over. I hope you both have a good day." Aunt Zeraida also asked, "Can Skye come over tomorrow? I'd like to show Skye and Emaleen some more skills."

"Yes, of course," said Angelina. "I'll send her over right after breakfast."

Zeraida then waved goodbye and turned to exit the house. Morvin and Emaleen waved, too, and then followed behind her to return home.

Chapter 19

When they arrived home, Aunt Zeraida made a quick lunch. While they ate, they were quiet. Each was thinking about the day's events so far. Emaleen was thinking of her play date with Skye. Zeraida and Morvin were both thinking about Maerdern and how they should protect Emaleen.

After Emaleen, her aunt, and her uncle had eaten lunch, Emaleen helped her aunt clean up. Then, although Zeraida had plans to research in her magic books to address the issues they had discussed earlier at the Stewarts' house, she knew she had other more important work to accomplish first. Zeraida knew that she needed to work more quickly to get Emaleen ready just in case she needed to face Maerdern in the near future.

"Emaleen, we need to work on something," said Aunt Zeraida. "Please get one of your gems, and meet me in the upstairs hallway."

Emaleen ran up the stairs and into her room. She took the Herkimer diamond off of her shelf. Then she left her room with the Herkimer in her hand. She stood in the hallway, waiting patiently for her aunt to join her. Aunt Zeraida stepped out of her own room and joined Emaleen in the hallway.

"Have you noticed anything strange about the length of this hallway and the width of my bedroom?" asked Aunt Zeraida.

"No," replied Emaleen slowly and uncertainly. She wondered if it was a trick question.

"Well, this hallway is longer than my bedroom, and the two should be equal in size. Do you wonder why that is so?" asked Zeraida.

"Yes," agreed Emaleen smiling. "I would love to know." Emaleen looked up and down the hall quickly, but she still wasn't sure what the answer to her aunt's question was.

"Well, the reason is that there is a secret room in which I practice seer skills and abilities, which you would call magic. This room has a secret entrance and is generally hidden from everyone but your uncle and me. Now, you'll be able to access this room too, but only with me at first. Eventually, you'll have your own," explained Aunt Zeraida.

Aunt Zeraida continued, "The room is also protected so that the magic that I do inside can't be detected outside the room. That way, other seers who could be near us won't sense my use of powers and will not know that we are seers. I call this room my closaid."

"Why did you want me to bring one of my gems into the hallway, Aunt Zeraida?" Emaleen asked.

Aunt Zeraida responded, "We are going to construct your wand. But we can't do it out here. When we first bring the three gems together with the wand, it'll cause a gigantic ripple of magic that will be felt far and wide, and the seers will all know that a new seer is gaining power. So we need to do it in the protection of the closaid, so that the magic is concealed. We must keep your existence a secret from the other seers for as long as we possibly can. You will need to be fully trained before we can risk the others knowing about you."

"Why did I need just one gem then?" asked Emaleen.

"We need to keep the gems separate until they are put together into your wand," answered Aunt Zeraida. "Do you remember how I asked you to keep the gems separate from one another?"

"Yes, and I have done that," affirmed Emaleen. Except for that one short moment, she thought, which she hoped was not a problem.

"Good," said Aunt Zeraida. "I'm pleased that you followed my instructions." But she had once felt a brief, small ripple, she thought.

"How do you get into the room?" asked Emaleen. "I've never seen any doors in your room. Even your closet in your room doesn't have a door to it."

"There isn't a fixed door to the room," explained Aunt Zeraida. "The door floats around on the outside of the room. It appears on any of the two interior walls whenever you need it. But it is magically concealed, and it only becomes visible when I will it to. I will make it appear for you now. But whenever you want to go into this room, you will need me to reveal the door for you."

"How do you open it?" asked Emaleen.

"Making the door reveal itself is a skill that I'm not ready to teach you yet. But someday I will, and you can reveal this door yourself. In the meantime, I'll explain it generally," answered Aunt Zeraida. "As I said just a few minutes ago, the door isn't attached to the room. It floats around the outside of the room. The door appears when I call it."

Aunt Zeraida knocked on the wall softly three times, then paused a short time, and then knocked one time loudly, and then three times more softly. She closed her eyes, took a deep breath in and a deep breath out, and said, "Appear."

Slowly the outlines of a door appeared on the wall where Aunt Zeraida had just knocked. The door was green, and it glowed softly in the light of the hallway. There was no knob on the door to use to open it. But Zeraida pushed on the door, and it opened inward.

From the hall, Emaleen could see yellow light shining out from the door. Aunt Zeraida stepped into the room and was no longer visible. Emaleen stepped into the room behind Aunt Zeraida, and the door shut behind her with a soft click. Emaleen turned and looked behind her, but the door was already gone.

Emaleen looked around the strange room, and she was struck by its unusual characteristics. It was unlike anything she had ever seen, and it seemed to Emaleen as if it might even be a place not located in this world. She wasn't sure if the room was actually attached to and a part of the house or if it was some magical domain, or even out in space. It was both ugly and beautiful at the same time, which made the room appear even stranger to Emaleen.

As Emaleen continued to look around the room, she noticed that the walls were a bright, light yellow color except for one wall on the back side of the room that was completely covered by a floor-to-ceiling bookshelf. The ceiling was black with numerous small lights twinkling against the dark, like the stars in the night sky. The floor was a dark blue color and because of the way the floor surface shone and seemed to absorb the light, it appeared to be made of glass. The floor also had a slick, but not slippery, surface, and it felt solid as if the glass was very thick. The blue color was dark enough that the floor was not transparent but was translucent. The strange combination of colors of the room seemed somehow to work together. Emaleen also felt warmed by the yellow glow of the walls. She felt safe and protected in the room.

Then Emaleen looked around some more and began to focus on the objects in the room instead of the colorful borders of the room itself. In addition to the bookcase that she had already noticed, there was a small wooden desk along the wall to the left, and next to that desk was a long workbench. The workbench was filled with bottles and lab equipment, including a Bunsen burner, test tubes, and a mortar and pestle. The workbench also contained several different scales. Above the workbench was a peg board with various dried herbs and other plants hanging from pegs.

Over near the right wall, but not immediately against the wall, was an area with a rug. The rug had a Celtic knot pattern woven into it, and on top of it there were some cushions for sitting. In the middle of the rug was a small table with short legs. It must be a table was for people sitting on the carpet, thought Emaleen. There was also a fireplace along that wall, not far from the carpeted area.

Aunt Zeraida watched Emaleen look around the room and said nothing. She allowed her niece to take her time exploring the room with her eyes. She knew that much of what was in the room would come as a big surprise to her niece, especially the lab area and the colors of the room. She was prepared to answer some of Emaleen's questions, but as with many other matters, she would have to leave some items for a later discussion since they might overwhelm her niece.

After several minutes, Aunt Zeraida finally spoke and said, "Emaleen, it's important that we start more serious training so that you can learn more about your powers and abilities. It is important that all your attempts to access your powers and use what you would call magic are done only in this room. As I mentioned before, this room has special properties that prevent magic that you work in here from being detected outside so that we can train in here without the other seers discovering us."

"What is the floor made of? Is it glass? Will it break?" asked Emaleen curiously.

"It's actually a special type of crystal that reflects light and other waves," answered Aunt Zeraida. "It won't break."

"Why is the floor made of crystal?" asked Emaleen.

Aunt Zeraida answered, "The reason that other seers can detect the magic is that it creates a series of waves similar to a light wave. The seers can feel these waves. The more powerful the waves, the farther the distance they will go, and as a result, the greater the number of seers who will feel the waves. The floor here reflects any of those waves that would otherwise escape through the floor into the outdoors. Instead of passing through the floor, the waves reflect back into the walls and ceiling. The walls are painted yellow and made of special materials so that they absorb the waves. And, the ceiling is actually the night sky, way out into space. Any waves that are not absorbed by the walls are reflected straight up out into space."

"That's amazing!" exclaimed Emaleen. "How is the ceiling reaching out to space? It doesn't seem that high."

"The ceiling is actually much farther away from us than it looks," explained Zeraida. "The ceiling is also not flat. It's a dome that starts at the tops of the walls and reaches up far into the sky. But although the walls and the ceiling do meet, their junction bridges a gap between where the walls actually end, and the start of the sky in space. The gap is the sky between the walls and the start of space. The junction is basically what seers know as a fold. The sky that is missing is basically folded out so that the tops of the walls and space meet."

"Huh?" exclaimed Emaleen. What her aunt had just said sounded unbelievable. It made no sense to her. How could the walls reach up into the sky, and the sky look like it was so close to her, she wondered?

Aunt Zeraida smiled and said, "Imagine a piece of paper. At the bottom of the paper is a junction with the top of the ceiling, and at the top of the paper is a junction with a point in space. If you were to fold that paper in half with the top end and the bottom end touching, that is like what this room is. With your piece of paper, you have made a gap between the junction with the ceiling and the junction with the point in space go away because you folded out the paper in between so that the ceiling junction and the space junction touch."

"So, if I were to make a fold between here and school, I could make it so that I could walk right out my front door and into the school yard?" asked Emaleen.

"No, this fold is only a fold of the image. You cannot make a fold for you to use to travel to another location. But the waves will go straight up through the image because the fold only creates a shortcut for the straight line that the waves would travel anyway and traveling through the fold cannot affect the waves at all. But we humans can't travel through the fold of the image. It would be dangerous for us to try," replied Aunt Zeraida.

"Now, we need to start getting some work done. We need to put your wand together with your three gems," continued Aunt Zeraida. "Did you bring your first gem?"

Emaleen held out her hand, palm up, and opened her hand to reveal one of the gems, the Herkimer diamond. The diamond, which was a clear, glass-like gem, appeared to turn yellow when Emaleen opened her hand.

Aunt Zeraida then instructed her, "Now, place your gem on the workbench right there, please." She then provided her niece with instructions for activating the wand that was currently wrapped around her wrist as a bracelet.

As instructed by her aunt, Emaleen closed her eyes and turned her right hand palm up. She then raised her palm up to her shoulder, almost touching her shoulder, and then briskly flung her hand straight down, with the palm remaining up. She repeated this process two more times.

Each time, the wand started to straighten from its position wrapped around her wrist and began to let go of its hold on her wrist. On the third time, the wand slipped entirely from her wrist and ended up in her hand, changed from a bracelet into a straight, wooden wand. Emaleen caught it without even thinking as if to do so was natural for her when it was actually her first time converting the bracelet into a wand, and it was unlike anything she had ever done before.

She hadn't held the wand as an actual wand since that day in her uncle's workshop in the forest. At that time, the wand felt very heavy to her. Now, it felt incredibly light.

"Aunt Zeraida," asked Emaleen. "Why is this wand light? The last time I held it, it was heavy."

"I can't explain exactly why this happens, but as you gain more powers your wand will become less heavy," replied Aunt Zeraida.

"Hmm — very interesting," said Emaleen.

Emaleen waved the wand around a little bit more, being careful not to knock over any items in Aunt Zeraida's closaid. The wand was easy to wave around and holding it did not tire her hand as might be expected given its size.

"Please bring your wand over to the workbench, Emaleen," requested Aunt Zeraida while motioning to her niece to move toward the workbench. When Emaleen did so, Aunt Zeraida handed her the Herkimer diamond.

"Now, pick one of the prongs on the wand that you want to put your Herkimer diamond into," instructed Aunt Zeraida.

The young seer looked carefully at the prong sets on the wand. They had originally appeared to all be the same. But upon closer inspection, she found that the prongs were indeed different. They were different in many ways, but one big difference was the number of prongs on each prong set. Emaleen wondered what the reason for the difference was. She hoped that she made a good choice when selecting each prong set. She hoped that her selections would not in any way impact the amount of power that the wand or the gem would yield.

Another difference in the prongs that Emaleen noticed was that a symbol was carved into the wand underneath each prong set. She hoped that these symbols did not have an important impact on the power of her wand that would be affected by her choice of where to place the gems.

Emaleen looked at her aunt for help, but her aunt simply nodded as if to encourage her niece to go ahead and make her choice. Clearly, she thought, her aunt wasn't going to tell her where to put the gems.

"You can't get this wrong, dear. Your subconscious mind will guide you in this task and tell you where to put each gem if you stop and listen to it," assured Aunt Zeraida.

Emaleen picked the set with five prongs on it and slid the Herkimer diamond between the prongs. As she placed the diamond, the prongs began to close around the diamond, and when she let go of it, they shut tightly around the gem.

"Now, please get the next gem. Just get one gem. If you get more than one at a time, they will let off some energy and power that can be detected by other seers. I'll hold the door for you, but please be quick," Aunt Zeraida requested.

Emaleen ran out of the room when her aunt opened the door and then into her room to pick up the next gem, which was the Alexandrite. When she returned, the door closed behind her.

"Now please place this next gem in an empty prong set, following the same process you followed for the Herkimer diamond," instructed Aunt Zeraida.

Emaleen picked a prong set with a star design carved into the wood under it. She proceeded to set the gem in that prong set. When the gem was locked into place, it lit up momentarily, glowing brightly.

"Now, get the last gem," requested Aunt Zeraida. "Again, I will hold the door open for you. Please be quick."

Emaleen ran out of the room and retrieved the last gem from her room, which was the red-orange sapphire. When she returned, Aunt Zeraida closed the door.

"Please wait for a moment," directed Aunt Zeraida, "before you install your last gem."

"The insertion of the last gem will activate your wand for the first time," instructed Aunt Zeraida. "You should hold on tightly to your wand when the wand is activated. Do not let it go until it is clear to you that the wand is fully activated. If you are not sure, please ask me before you let go of the wand. This is very important. The wand activation could be a non-eventful process or it could be very powerful and dramatic. So, you need to be ready for anything. And, if you let go of the wand too soon, you may lose it forever. So, please be very careful."

Before she set the last gem, the red-orange sapphire, into the last prong set, Emaleen took a deep breath. As she placed the gem between the set, the prongs closed around the gem. Emaleen felt a strong current of power flow through the wand. The three gems on the wand started to glow, and the staff of the wand started to vibrate, making a buzzing sound. Emaleen could feel the power building up inside the wand, and the vibration steadily grew stronger, and the buzzing sound grew louder. Suddenly, the gems on the wand shot out thousands of beams of light all over the room, and the buzzing sound stopped. The light reflected off blue crystal floor and the yellow walls. The room lit up as if there had been a sudden explosion.

Emaleen then felt as if an electrical charge was running throughout her whole body as she held onto the wand. The charge made Emaleen feel powerful. After a few minutes, Emaleen herself started to glow. She could see it in her hands and arms, which she held out in front of her in amazement as she continued her tight grip on the wand. After several minutes, the electrical charge stopped, and Emaleen no longer glowed. Emaleen was a little tired, physically, but she also felt very energized and empowered mentally.

Aunt Zeraida stood there stunned. She had expected a big reaction when her niece activated her wand for the first time. And, in her many years, Zeraida had seen many first-time wand activations. All of these had been unique, not one the same as another. But Zeraida was stunned by the amount of power generated by Emaleen's wand. She had expected that Emaleen's wand activation would be extraordinary, but the activation had actually exceeded Zeraida's expectations.

After the gems stopped glowing and it seemed like the wand activation was complete, Aunt Zeraida asked Emaleen, "How do you feel? Do you feel anything else going on or does it seem to you as if the process is over?"

Emaleen responded stating, "I don't feel anything right now other than an increased power generally. The wand feels quiet and still."

"I'm glad we did the activation here. It created so many powerful waves that it would have been picked up by seers thousands of miles away," commented Aunt Zeraida. "Do you feel any different?"

"I don't know," replied Emaleen. "Right afterward, I felt this incredible amount of energy. Now it seems to have calmed down."

"Well," said Aunt Zeraida, "now that the wand has been activated, you might start discovering more new abilities and powers. A seer's wand usually transforms special properties in your gems into a surge of power that will make changes in the part of your brain where your seer skills and powers reside. Usually, this will mean a combination of an enhancement of the powers and abilities that you already have and the development of brand new powers and abilities. We will have to be watchful to see what new powers you develop."

"In the meantime," continued Aunt Zeraida, "I suggest that you put your wand back into bracelet form and you get some rest. You might have felt a surge of power and energy from the activation, but your physical being will have been stressed from the process and may be drained. You should take a nap or at least lie down for a while, even if you don't feel like you need it. I will make you a snack and bring it to your room."

Emaleen converted the wand back into a bracelet. Then, Aunt Zeraida opened the door. Emaleen immediately followed her aunt's suggestion and went through the door, down the hall, and into her room. When she got to her room, she saw Belenus waiting for her. He looked up at her and meowed and rubbed against her legs and then jumped upon onto her bed, leaving room for Emaleen to lie down beside him. She crawled into bed next to Belenus. He started purring, which was comforting to Emaleen.

When Aunt Zeraida arrived with the snack, Emaleen was already asleep, curled up next to Belenus. So, Aunt Zeraida placed the snack on the little table next to Emaleen's bed and walked quietly out of the room and shut the door. Emaleen slept deeply and peacefully for several hours.

When she awoke, she went downstairs and had dinner. Aunt Zeraida offered to play some board games with Emaleen and kept the mood light and stress-relieving for her niece. She knew that Emaleen needed a little time to relax before she would feel like herself again. Although there was nothing wrong with Emaleen and she should be happy about her wand activation, it still was a significant event that had great effects on Emaleen's physical state. The wand activation had started a growing process that would lead to the growth of additional brain matter from which she would develop new powers. After some rest and relaxation, she would be ready to start training again, and once she did start training again she would start exploring new powers that the wand activation had started to make possible.

Chapter 20

Aunt Zeraida was correct to be increasing the speed of her niece's training and the activation of her wand. Although she did not know what Maerdern was currently up to, she did have some knowledge about him and what he was capable of doing. She knew his character, and she knew that he was ambitious. Zeraida also knew that he had plans to use magic in an unethical and evil way. It was her hope to prevent him from doing so.

Maerdern was thirty-six years old and was of average height and weight for a man of his age. Although he was far from being elderly, his hair was completely white, and his eyes were gray. Despite the white hair, he was otherwise physically young. He frequently went on long hikes and exercised. He usually dressed in jeans and t-shirts. He rarely, if ever, dressed up and, in fact, he despised ties and dress shoes. He found them uncomfortable.

He had been an only child of two fairly powerful seer parents who were kind and who had high hopes for their child, whom they had named Halwyn Gruem. They had provided Halwyn with a beginning education in magic, but they had been waiting for a full education until he was an adult. They wished their child to have as normal a childhood as possible. Halwyn loved his parents very much, and he had been a well-behaved, respectful child as he was growing up.

Unfortunately for Halwyn, both of his parents had died in a car accident when he was just sixteen years old. Despite the tragedy, he was not left without family. He had aunts and uncles who loved him and would have been happy to take him in and raise him as their own. They would have also provided him with seer training.

But even though Halwyn could have moved in with family and had a good life, he foolishly chose to take care of himself and live on his own, and he changed his name to Maerdern Baleros. He also decided to drop out of school and, as a result, he did not graduate from high school. Because of these choices that he made for himself, his prospects in life were limited, and he could not expect to be employed in positions that would afford him a comfortable living.

Maerdern supported himself with low-paying, part-time jobs and committing various crimes, such as stealing money from people on the streets late at night. Maerdern essentially became a thug who didn't care about anyone but himself. He would do just about anything that he felt suited him, whether or not it hurt other persons.

He was not the young man that his parents had raised and had they been alive, they would have been extremely shocked and hurt by the man he had become. Not only had he not lived up to his potential, but he had chosen a path of evil.

If Maerdern had chosen to live with other family members, he would not have had to resort to such acts. He could have finished school and been fully trained in magic by his family.

He could have also changed his mind at any time and lived with his other family instead of continuing on his path of malevolence. But Maerdern was stubborn, and he could not admit to anyone else or himself that he was ever wrong. He also had a habit of blaming others for his problems even when they were problems that he created himself. As he grew up in such undesirable circumstances of his own making, he grew bitter and felt cheated by the world. His bitterness turned his heart to evil.

Although Maerdern was intellectually smart and had also developed street smarts, he lacked ordinary common sense and emotional maturity. He had made bad choices that set him on the wrong path in life, and it was no one's fault but his own.

A little more than a dozen years ago, Maerdern had formed a desire to gain control over all the other seers. His plan was to eventually rule over all of the norms after he had gained his power over the seers. He worked quietly to recruit other seers to work for him and to follow him.

His plan was to recruit as many seers as possible to his following before the other seers caught on to his evil intentions. The more seers he recruited, the more powerful he became, and the more of a threat he became to the rest of the seers and also to the world of norms.

Except for a few seers, such as the Andarsans and the Barsans, the seers who did not join Maerdern's following largely ignored Maerdern and his efforts. Seers, as a group, did not typically band together under one leader. They were free spirits with strong wills who lived independently and followed their own self-perceived destinies. They also typically didn't interfere with what other seers were doing.

But Maerdern was different. He thirsted for power and wanted very much to be worshiped and followed. And, he had allowed his powers to influence his view of himself, and he lost his self-control. The evil seer no longer used his logic and intellect to make his decisions. What controlled him was his ego, and his never-satisfied need to feel important and be powerful over others.

A significant part of Maerdern's plans and the part that created the greatest threat to Emaleen was the evil seer's wish to have an apprentice with extraordinary powers so that he could make up for his own insufficient magic powers. His magic abilities were not as fully developed as they would normally be for a seer of his age. But that was his own fault since he had given up his opportunity to be raised by a seer family. Thus, he did not receive the training he would have had from his family.

Maerdern had been watching, waiting, and searching for a young seer to become his apprentice for a long time without success. He had gathered information on the various families of seers and the powers of each individual and was keeping a close watch on new births in the families. Although the potential powers of a new seer are difficult to predict, there were some characteristics that if observed could help to predict how powerful a baby might later become. Maerdern had carefully studied these clues and had sent spies to bring back information about each new baby and young child.

Emaleen's parents, Seanna and Mannix Andarsan, who were now thirty–two and thirty-five respectively, had believed, at the time

Emaleen was born, that Maerdern could be a credible threat for Emaleen. They had predicted that Maerdern would look for a young apprentice. When Emaleen was born, they saw in her signs that she might become a highly powerful seer, perhaps more powerful than her parents. She might even become a peerless seer — a very rare kind of seer with powers that surpass those of all the other seers.

As much as they loved Emaleen and it pained the Andarsans to part with her, they knew that to protect her, they needed to hide her. They also needed to make sure that Emaleen had a great upbringing and full training in the powers that she would someday grow into. They decided to entrust their daughter to Mrs. Andarsan's only sister, Zeraida, who was a recluse with respect to the seers in general. As a result, Zeraida's whereabouts and even existence were not known to many seers. The same was true for Zeraida's husband, Morvin. So Emaleen's parents thought Zeraida and Morvin would be good substitute parents to care for Emaleen and to train her to be a powerful seer.

The Andarsans selected the Stewarts to become Emaleen's guardians. They were the Andarsans' closest friends, and they trusted them to keep their daughter safe. That created a slight risk since there was a direct connection between the Stewarts and the Andarsans. But there were more guardians than seers, and they thought that Maerdern would be unlikely to track down all of the guardians.

Because of their premonition regarding Maerdern's plans to find an apprentice, the Andarsans were able to hide Emaleen before Maerdern started to gather information on the families and their composition. They could only hope, however, that Maerdern would have relied only upon his check of who was in the family when his spies came around and that his spies would not figure out and report back that Mrs. Andarsan had been pregnant, or worse still, that she had given birth to a daughter. The Andarsans believed they had taken enough precautions to prevent Maerdern from learning about Emaleen even if his spies were thorough. But they could not be sure.

Fortunately for the Andarsans, the spy that Maerdern sent out to check out the Andarsan family was tired after a long journey of visiting many different seer families and gathering information. The Andarsan family was the spy's last family to visit after many, many weeks on the road away from his own family. So when he arrived at the Andarsan house, in a small town in East Sussex, England, he simply sat for a day and watched who came in and out. He didn't spend any time inquiring of neighbors or checking public records to find out if there had been any children in the family who might be away. And, all he saw was Mr. and Mrs. Andarsan coming and going, so that's all he recorded in his report about the family.

If Maerdern had learned how little effort the spy had put into gaining information about the composition of the Andarsan family, he would have been angry. Of all the seer families, the Andarsans had some of the greatest potential of having a child with extraordinary powers. Emaleen's parents were some of the most powerful seers on the Earth.

Maerdern would have also been angry because of the influence of Emaleen's family and their interest in forming an alliance against him. Although the seers as a group did not have a leader to follow, there were certain families that the seers tended to respect more than others. The Andarsans were particularly held in high regard. If the need arose for the seers to unite on the side of good, the Andarsans were one of the families who might be able to unite them, if that were possible. Having an Andarsan family member as his apprentice could potentially advantage Maerdern.

Chapter 21

Maerdern Baleros was on a trip, just as the spy's note to the Stewarts had stated. In fact, he had left his home in a remote mountain town in the Pacific Northwest. He and his many followers who were traveling with him had just arrived at the first location on their trip, a small town outside Memphis, Tennessee, after a three-day journey by chartered bus. After several days of traveling, he was happy to arrive finally at their destination, which was in the outskirts of the city.

Maerdern was traveling with about a dozen followers. He was never alone. He always had several followers with him. His ego and need to feel important required that he have lackeys on hand at all times to compliment him and tell him that he was right about anything and everything that he formed an opinion on, even if he was wrong. He also needed to be known as the source of all ideas, and no one could make any suggestions to him or disagree with him.

Although he liked being surrounded by his followers as a show of his power, the days on the bus journey convinced Maerdern that in the future, he should leave the bus to his followers and he should ride along in his own private car. He wanted his followers to respect him and to compliment him frequently, but some of them had become very annoying during the trip.

He needed some time to think without being bothered. He needed to think about what he was going to do when he arrived at his destination and made contact with the first seer family from whom he planned to steal magic books. But there were a couple of followers, Lanus Aimsley and Bruce Letneir, who seemed to be competing with one another over which follower could earn better favor with him. Their constant boasting and other banter, and attempts to get his attention, kept him from having any time to sit and think without being bothered.

When they arrived and checked into the hotel that had been booked for them, Maerdern gave instructions that no one was to bother him until the morning, unless they were specifically called for. He also instructed two of his followers, not the ones who had bothered him on the bus, to sit outside his door for the night.

The two followers were brothers, named Baldolf and Rycroft Bisbane. They were very large, muscular individuals in their twenties who didn't talk very much or ask many questions. They were not seers or guardians but were norms. Maerdern used them as personal security guards because they appeared intimidating to him and because they did not otherwise have any special talents or skills. They also were sent out to run errands for Maerdern.

After settling into his room, Maerdern instructed Baldolf, one of the two followers stationed outside his door, to summon one of his spies that had come with the group. When the spy arrived, Maerdern sent him out with instructions to watch the Jaimeson family and to report back to him anything unusual that he saw. He also asked the spy to prepare a general report on the family's circumstances, such as information about their house, so that he could form a plan to wage an attack on the family. He instructed the spy to stake out the house with another one of the spies. Once he had finished arranging for the spying on the family, Maerdern went to sleep.

The next morning, the spies came back early with a little information for Maerdern about the family. They hadn't discovered as much as Maerdern had hoped they would. But it was a short period of time in which they had to work so it was to be expected. In any event, Maerdern had awakened with other ideas on how he would get additional information.

Maerdern opened the door to his room and motioned to Baldolf to enter his room. Baldolf had been sleeping outside Maerdern's door on the floor and had only just awakened. His brother was still asleep.

Once Baldolf entered the room, Maerdern said to him, "Baldolf, I want you to go down to the front desk and ask for a meeting room. Then I want you to gather all of our followers for a meeting. Let them know that I expect everyone to attend and to be on time."

Baldolf nodded and left the room to accomplish his task. He returned in less than an hour and informed Maerdern that the meeting was to be at 10 a.m. and that he had arranged the room and notified the followers.

"Good," said Maerdern. "Now, leave me and go out to continue to guard my door." Baldolf nodded and left the room.

A short while later, Maerdern met his followers in the room arranged by Baldolf. He stood in front of the room for a few minutes surveying the group. He took a mental attendance, and he looked each person in the eyes for an uncomfortable moment. He wanted to generate some fear and unease among the followers before he started the meeting.

Despite the appearance that he had created among his followers that he was a dangerous seer to cross, Maerdern's own powers were only fairly average for a seer. But he had somehow managed to convince his followers that he had great powers through coincidental happenings or magic performed by other seers that Maerdern took credit for. He would often secretly direct his followers to carry out magic for him, of the type that Maerdern was unable to do himself, and then claim to other seers that he had performed the magic himself. He had some of his followers convinced that with all of his amazing powers, the performing of certain magic was beneath him. That made it easy for him to get his followers to perform magic on his behalf.

Maerdern also used the willingness of his followers to please him and to win his favor, often competing with one another, to his benefit to get seers to do tasks for him. So, Maerdern was able to accomplish what he wanted through the powers of his followers without exposing just how meager his powers and abilities really were.

Maerdern also had Baldolf and Rycroft stand on either side of him at this meeting to add some physical intimidation as well. Maerdern had prearranged signals with the two security guards for them to act should any of the followers overstep his or her bounds and act in any way that Maerdern determined to be disrespectful.

After Maerdern was satisfied that he had set the right tone for his meeting — fear — he began to speak to his followers. "I will be sending one of my followers out to the house of the Jaimeson family," shared Maerdern in a quiet voice. "This follower will earn great favor from me for a very important task — if he should succeed, that is. This follower will befriend the family, gain their trust, and then seek to find out information about the magic books that they hold so that he can steal the books with information about the most powerful skills and abilities for me."

Maerdern paused for a few moments for dramatic effect. He looked around the room as if he was deciding right then who he would choose to send on the mission. Several of the followers avoided Maerdern's gaze, and he noted these individuals. Some of the followers eagerly looked at Maerdern, hoping to be chosen. Some of them, however, were too enthusiastic, which Maerdern interpreted as a threat to himself.

"The follower that I have chosen is named Tristan Gollach," Maerdern announced. Maerdern chose Tristan, a twenty-one-year-old man with blond hair and soft, blue eyes, because he was a very friendly person, who was also a little foolish and naive. With Tristan's personality, he wouldn't raise any suspicions on the part of the family, and he had a very good chance of gaining their trust. He also had avoided Maerdern's gaze, which Maerdern had interpreted to mean that Tristan was afraid of him. This was satisfying to Maerdern because he believed Tristan would do his duty for fear of disappointing his leader. He also was not any threat to Maerdern's authority.

There was a hushed silence from the group of followers after Maerdern announced Tristan for the special mission. They all turned and stared at Tristan. Some of them viewed Tristan with envy and jealousy and others glared at him with hatred.

Tristan just stood there, stunned. He was not excited about being chosen for the mission. He was a Maerdern follower as a result of a mistake in judgment, and he had remained a follower only out of fear that Maerdern would punish him if he tried to leave. Tristan knew that if anyone were ever foolish enough to refuse to do Maerdern's bidding or worse still, disagree, Maerdern would punish the person severely. Tristan knew that Maerdern had thrown one such person in a dungeon that he had constructed in the basement of his home. Maerdern had also imprisoned another person in a small glass flask that he wore around his neck and used as a warning to his other supporters should they think about questioning or defying him.

The other followers, including those who had wanted to be chosen for the mission, were quiet. Some were glad they were not selected and were relieved. They had been afraid to be chosen. It was a chance to fail Maerdern, and none of them wanted that.

There were also some of Maerdern's followers who were angry not to be chosen but didn't dare to speak. In addition to fear as a means to control his followers and keep them under this rule, Maerdern also promised his followers great riches when he and his followers succeeded in their goal of achieving domination over all of the other seers. Maerdern had convinced them that he would succeed and that when he did, those followers who had helped him in his efforts would be rewarded and those who did not would suffer a more difficult life. So, some followers were angry at the lost chance to please Maerdern and gain position in his organization. They wanted to increase their chances of being rewarded should Maerdern's efforts succeed.

Maerdern continued, "The rest of you will wait here in this hotel and await further instructions from me. You may now leave this meeting and return to your rooms. Tristan, you will come with me now." Maerdern wanted to converse privately with Tristan to provide him with instructions and to let him know just how important his mission was and that Maerdern would expect success. But he waited to speak to Tristan until all of the followers, but for his two guards, had left the room.

"Tristan, this mission is critical to our work," declared Maerdern. "I expect success from you. Failure is not an option." Just for emphasis,

Maerdern pulled out the glass vial that was hanging around his neck, and he showed it to Tristan. When Tristan caught a glimpse of the man trapped in the vial, his eyes widened, his heart started to race, and he thought he was going to pass out. Maerdern smiled when he saw the effect that his vial was having on Tristan. It made him more confident that Tristan would take any and all steps that he needed to take to encourage the family to trust him so that he could steal from them.

Maerdern continued, "All of us, except for you, will be leaving this location in the morning to move on to another seer family. You will stay and fool the family into trusting you so that you can gain access to their magic books. If that fails, you will use whatever methods possible to obtain those books for me. As soon as you have information about the books that the family has in their possession and the magic contained in them, you will contact me. I expect that you will use all possible means to obtain their books."

"Do you have any questions?" asked Maerdern sternly with a look that communicated that he really did not want any questions.

"No," replied Tristan in a quiet voice as he stared down at the floor. Tristan was trying desperately to conceal from Maerdern just how terrified he was.

Maerdern then dismissed Tristan, saying, "Go now! And, whatever you do, do not disappoint me. It may be the last thing you do." He glared at Tristan with narrowed eyes to ensure that Tristan knew and felt just how important Tristan's success on this mission was.

Since he had not yet found the apprentice that he felt he needed to augment his powers, Maerdern had recently decided to obtain as much information about magic as possible from the other families, including the most powerful families. He knew that it was customary for seers to keep books that provided instruction on different magic techniques.

Maerdern was convinced that the families with the greatest powers were simply more powerful because of the books that they had and the information that they passed down from generation to generation. Maerdern thought that if he could gather up these books, he might be able to increase his own powers beyond his current abilities and training. Maerdern was also convinced that these powerful families had books explaining how to perform magic that was long rumored to exist but not generally known to most seers.

One such power that Maerdern suspected these families had knowledge of was the power to give a person immortality so that the person would live forever and never die. Maerdern did not know of any seer who had such a power, but he believed that the most powerful families held the secret of achieving immortality and kept it from the other seers to prevent it from being misused. In fact, it was rumored among the seers that in the past seers all had the power of immortality until a particularly misbehaved seer had misused the power so badly that the most powerful families banned the use of immortality and locked away the secret books that provided instruction on how to invoke the power. Maerdern wanted to seize the information on how to achieve immortality for himself and to keep it from all the other seers, to give himself an advantage against them so that he could have ultimate power over them.

There were other powers that Maerdern wanted to seize for himself, too. He wasn't sure what they all were, but he was sure that these families guarded the books that were the key to extremely powerful magic.

As Tristan was leaving, Maerdern called out, "I expect to hear from you within a week."

Maerdern would give Tristan Gollach a week to win over the family and steal the books. If Tristan failed, Maerdern would punish him severely.

Chapter 22

Immediately after the private meeting with Maerdern was over, Tristan traveled out to the Jaimeson family house. Tristan decided to spend his first day on the task by watching the household to figure out how he might approach the family. He needed a plan for gaining the family's trust.

Tristan was not thrilled to have this assignment. In fact, he was not happy to be a follower of Maerdern. He wasn't even sure how he had become a follower, but he was now so involved that there was no way out. He was simply a nice, naive person who was not very assertive for himself. He wanted very much to be accepted and to fit in.

His need to fit in was so great that it made him an easy target for Maerdern, who sized Tristan up quickly and figured out how to compliment him and provide him the acceptance he wanted. It wasn't long before Tristan was looking up to Maerdern and was willing to follow him.

Maerdern was careful to hide his true nature from Tristan as long as possible. Maerdern reeled Tristan in slowly, bit by bit, before showing his evil side to him, which he only showed a little at a time so as not to scare Tristan away before he had power over him.

As Maerdern's true nature became more and more apparent to Tristan, he began to realize that Maerdern was not the person he originally appeared to be. Maerdern was actually evil. It started with small bad acts, which he overlooked because they were minor. Then when the acts became just a little worse, he still overlooked them. When the acts became even worse, he then made excuses for his friend and focused on the sense of belonging that he felt by being accepted by Maerdern. Eventually, the acts were just too bad for Tristan to ignore and justify with excuses.

Around the time that Tristan was figuring out that Maerdern was evil and stopped looking up to him, Maerdern started to realize that his influence on Tristan was waning. So, he changed his tactics from providing Tristan with acceptance to ruling him by fear. Although Tristan recognized the need to get out from under Maerdern's power, he felt that it was too late to leave because of fear of what Maerdern might do to him. In sum, Tristan feared for his personal safety should he leave Maerdern.

Tristan also regretfully realized too late that the signs had been there all along that Maerdern was evil and that he should have stayed far away from him. Tristan thought that, if and when he ever got out from under Maerdern's influence, he would be sure to be much more selective about the friends he chose for himself.

This was the first time that Maerdern had asked Tristan to do something awful for him. Previously, it had been Tristan observing Maerdern committing bad acts.

It made Tristan feel ill that he would have to earn the trust of a family of seers only for the purpose of stealing from them. He was a nice guy, and this wasn't the kind of thing he would have ever thought of doing or wished to do. He was also somewhat shy and was nervous about whether he would be able to befriend the family. So, he was not sure how to go about accomplishing his mission. But he was very afraid of Maerdern and did not dare try to escape him now, nor did he dare fail his mission. So, as much as he didn't like his mission, he felt that he had no choice but to undertake it and do his best to succeed so as not to disappoint Maerdern. But he needed time to make a plan.

Later that afternoon, Tristan arrived at the Jaimeson house after a short walk from the hotel. It was a two-story, white colonial with a white fence around the front and back yards of the house. Tristan tried to take a close look at the house while walking down the sidewalk that ran parallel to the street and across the front of the house. There was no one in the yard, and the curtains were closed in the house. So, about all that he could determine was the general shape and size of the house.

After Tristan had passed the house, he walked around the neighborhood to get a good look at the surrounding area. Then he turned, crossed the street and walked down the sidewalk on the opposite side. A few houses down from the Jaimeson house, Tristan sat down on a curb and opened a can of soda that he had brought with him. As he sat, he watched the Jaimeson house.

If either of the Jaimesons was looking out from the house, he hoped he was far enough up the road that he would not be seen. If he was, he hoped that he would not alarm the family. His lack of experience as a spy showed as he sat there out in the open.

As he drank the soda, Tristan looked around the neighborhood out of the corners of his eyes without moving his head. He did not want the Jaimesons to realize that he was casing the neighborhood. His survey of the neighborhood revealed to Tristan that there was no vantage point from which he could station himself to spy on the family. He was going to need to come up with a plan for learning about the family to figure out how to become trusted enough to be in their house.

Inside the house, Mr. Jaimeson had been looking out the window. His wife had told him earlier in the day that she had a feeling that they would be visited by Maerdern and his followers. So, he had remained vigilant and had watched quietly for some sign that Maerdern was nearby. As he looked out the window after a few hours of watching and waiting, Mr. Jaimeson noticed a man sitting on a curb a little way down the street from their house.

The Jaimesons were one of three seer families that were commonly considered by other seers to be the most powerful. The three families had become aware of Maerdern's intentions of gaining power over the seers. Unbeknownst to Maerdern and Tristan, the Jaimesons together with many other families, including lesser powerful ones, which did not have any family members who were followers of Maerdern, had started to communicate with one another about Maerdern and his activities. However, they were unable to form a plan together to do anything other than watch Maerdern and his followers. The families who would like to see an alliance formed, including the Jaimesons, could not seem to overcome the general objection of other seers against the formation of seer alliances.

If necessary, the three most powerful families had agreed that they might organize together to fight Maerdern if a larger alliance of seer families could not be established in the near future. But they had not yet agreed on who would lead the families or how decisions would be made.

The disagreement over who would lead the families should the need arise to fight Maerdern was a significant hurdle to the families actually uniting, and it created frustrations for the Jaimesons. They knew that it was possible that the seers would not ever be able to unite.

Another barrier to forming an alliance was that even where a majority of a family's members agreed that the right course of action was to form an alliance, some of the members of these families still did not take seriously the potential threat that Maerdern posed. These other family members thought Maerdern was inept and lacking in enough power to accomplish an effort of dominating all of the seers.

Unfortunately, as the Jaimesons knew, the difficulties in forming an alliance among the good seer families were creating a significant advantage for Maerdern in pursuing his plans of conquering all of the seers because there was no effort made to stop him. Further, each family was on its own if Maerdern were to attack a family, and it was in this predicament that the Jaimesons currently found themselves.

Mr. Jaimeson said to his wife, "They are here. A follower is now spying on our house. He is sitting on the curb down the street drinking soda, hoping that we won't notice him."

"I wonder what they want and why that follower is here?" commented Mrs. Jaimeson. "My vision didn't show me what would happen. I only saw that someone would be coming."

"We could send out our spy cat, Annabel, to watch and follow him," suggested Mr. Jaimeson. Then after a short pause, he said, "But it might also be too dangerous for her. What if she doesn't return?"

Mr. Jaimeson was worried that Annabel might either be discovered by the follower or face other perils, including the potential danger of being run over by a car. He didn't like sending Annabel out, even though he knew that they had trained the cat well to avoid dangers and to follow a person without being seen. But he and Mrs. Jaimeson had grown to love the cat, and he would not willingly place Annabel in a dangerous situation.

"Maybe we should wait and see what happens with this follower," suggested Mrs. Jaimeson hopefully. "Maybe he will leave and not come back." She knew, though, that this was an unrealistic hope.

"We should put some cameras up around the house to keep an eye on the outside. We should also put up some motion sensors in the yard too," suggested Mr. Jaimeson.

"But we have magic to protect us," countered Mrs. Jaimeson. "There is no need to get a security system."

"We should use all available means of protection," answered Mr. Jaimeson. "Modern technology is something that we should never overlook as a tool. We can deploy it without causing a stir like we would with powerful magic. We can add magic later if we need to."

Mrs. Jaimeson reluctantly agreed. She would rather take some direct action and send out a magic attack to take care of the spy currently threatening them. But she knew that her husband's plan of avoidance of direct conflict would probably be safer for them than a magic battle.

About fifteen minutes later, when Tristan stood up as if he planned to leave, Mrs. Jaimeson suggested that they send their robin out to follow Tristan as he left. Mrs. Jaimeson had the power of animal sight. She could watch Tristan through the robin's eyes. The robin might also face less risk than the cat since it would be less noticeable and could fly over the cars. Mr. Jaimeson agreed, and so they sent the robin out.

After Tristan had left, Mr. Jaimeson called a security company and arranged for the cameras and motion sensors to be installed later that day. They had to pay extra for the rush job, but it was worth it, he thought. No one would be able to enter their property without setting off an alarm and alerting the family.

Mrs. Jaimeson also saw through the robin's eyes that Tristan had gone to a hotel not far from their home. Later they sent out a spy to find out who, if anyone, was staying at the hotel with Tristan. They learned from their spy that Maerdern and the rest of his followers had left the hotel and that Tristan was staying at the hotel by himself.

After Tristan had returned to the hotel, he spent several hours in his room. He hadn't yet figured out what to do. He didn't know the Jaimeson family or anyone in the town. And, he was naturally a shy individual who did not know how to make new friends easily in ordinary circumstances, let alone under circumstances that required him to be deceitful. But he did not want to let Maerdern down.

As he sat there wondering what to do, there was a knock on the hotel room door. When Tristan answered the door, he found a man standing there with an envelope. The man handed Tristan the envelope without saying a word and then turned around and walked away. Tristan closed the door and walked to the nearest chair and sat down.

Tristan opened the envelope and found a note from Maerdern and some additional papers. The note stated that the envelope contained information about the Jaimeson family that Maerdern's spies had gathered. In the note, Maerdern also reminded Tristan that it was important that he not fail his mission and that there would be severe penalties if he failed, but great rewards if he was successful. The additional papers with the note contained information about the Jaimeson family, such as the background, history, and known magic abilities of Mr. and Mrs. Jaimeson, and the names of their extended family members, friends, and neighbors, and their backgrounds and known abilities.

Chapter 23

After reading the information that Maerdern had sent, Tristan decided to gather up his courage and take a direct approach. He decided to go to the family and tell them that he was a fellow seer and that he had heard that the Jaimeson family had great powers and that he hoped that they would take him in and educate him. He would tell him that he had lost his parents when he was young and that he had not received a full training. It was not the truth, but Tristan had no idea how to approach the family and he only had a short time to gain their trust. So he borrowed Maerdern's unfortunate story as his own. He hoped that it would be enough to get the family to work with him and begin to trust him.

So, Tristan ate a quick meal and headed off to the Jaimeson house. As he walked, he rehearsed in his head what he would say to the family. The wrong approach with the wrong words would threaten his mission immediately and might make it unsalvageable. The pressure of the importance of this first conversation weighed heavily on Tristan.

He felt his stomach churn as he walked up the walkway to the porch and rang the doorbell. He heard footsteps inside the house, and whispering, but no one came to the door. Tristan, however, stood there patiently waiting.

After several minutes, he heard a male voice on a speaker state, "Hello. Please state your name and your business."

Tristan sighed. They had an intercom system and hadn't bothered to open the door so that he could talk to them. That would definitely make it harder for him to explain his situation and obtain the family's confidence in him. He also wasn't sure who was speaking to him. It could be a member of the family or someone else.

Tristan decided to change the story he had planned and pressed a button next to a speaker and, "I'm Tristan Gollach. I was adopted when I was a young boy, and I am seeking my birth parents. I was hoping you might have some information that might help me."

He hadn't planned to say this before the words came out of his mouth, but after he had spoken them, he thought that maybe this might encourage the person talking through the intercom to come to the door and discuss the matter with him face to face. But he was wrong. The male voice responded back instead.

"No one in this house has ever given a child up for adoption. Nor do we know anyone who has. So, I don't think we would have any information for you. Goodbye, and have a good day," said the voice on the intercom.

Tristan paused for a moment. He wasn't sure what to say next. What he had said was not part of what he had planned on the way over, and it wasn't going very well. He didn't want to give up on his mission so easily.

He pressed the button again and said, "I think it is very possible that someone in the family or one of your friends might have been keeping an adoption a secret. So, please don't dismiss me so easily. Please come talk to me. I'd really like to find my birth parents."

Tristan heard more whispering. Inside the house, Mr. and Mrs. Jaimeson were quietly discussing their next move. They knew Tristan was lying to them. But they were trying to figure out how best to handle him. They did not want to come to the door to talk to him, but they suspected that if they didn't handle him well enough he would just find another way to come at them. At least now, he was doing so visibly. They also weren't sure how powerful his magic was, so they didn't want to underestimate him.

The Jaimesons also believed that Tristan could be a source of information on what Maerdern was up to, but they weren't sure how to find that out without using magic. If they started using magic when Tristan had not, that might inspire Tristan to use it also, and that could spiral into a war of magic. They also knew that Maerdern was not at the hotel that Tristan was staying at, but they had no idea where Maerdern had gone. If they started a magic war with Tristan, they couldn't be sure whether Maerdern or another follower could be around to join. A big magic fight would create a significant danger that they would like to avoid. So they had to be very careful.

Since the voice on the intercom had not responded for some time, Tristan pressed the button on the speaker and spoke, "I don't understand why you don't come to the door so that we can talk. I can explain better if we can speak in person instead of through this intercom."

The voice on the intercom responded, "You came to our house unannounced, and we don't know you. We know of no adoptions, and we have no reason to come to the door. It's time that you leave. This conversation is over. Good day."

Tristan sighed. He had done his best to get someone to come to the door to speak with him. But it wasn't working. If he pressed further, he would certainly ruin any chance that he might have to make a connection with the family later. So, Tristan turned around and walked back down the walkway of the house and back to his hotel room. He would have to give some more thought to figure out another way to approach the family. But he was feeling very defeated. This was going to be even harder than he first had thought it might be.

The Jaimesons watched with relief as Tristan left their front door and walked away. But they knew that they had only dodged the danger temporarily. They would need to come up with a longer-term plan because they were certain that either Tristan would keep coming back or that Maerdern would send more followers when he realized that Tristan had failed.

Later that day, the Jaimesons came up with a plan to at least contain the danger posed by Tristan. They arranged with another seer family in the area for Tristan to be kept as a prisoner in a special magic room within their house. So, they arranged for a trap to capture Tristan, hoping that since that Maerdern and the rest of his followers had left the area they would be far away and not sense the magic being used by the Jaimesons. They sent a message to Tristan asking him to meet them at a public park not far from the Jaimesons' house and immediately adjacent to the home of their friends. They informed him in the note that they might have some information after all and that they wanted to talk to him.

At the park, they set up a containment area into which Tristan could enter, but which he could not leave. It was a power known only to a few of the seer families. So, they knew Tristan would not suspect what was to happen.

When Tristan arrived at the park, the Jaimesons successfully entrapped him, according to the plan. Mr. Jaimeson then used a power on him that put him in a trance-like state, which was also a power that was largely unknown to most seers. Once he was in the trance-like state, Mrs. Jaimeson led Tristan over to the house of her friends. She then led Tristan to the basement and placed him in a room that was blocked off and locked with magic, like a magic jail cell.

When Tristan came out of the trance-like state that the Jaimesons put him into, the other seer family informed Mr. Jaimeson, who made his way over to the house to talk with Tristan. When Mr. Jaimeson arrived, he found Tristan sitting in the corner of the cell with his head in his hands and looking down. When Tristan heard Mr. Jaimeson come into the room, he lifted his head up and looked directly into Mr. Jaimeson's eyes. It looked to Mr. Jaimeson as if Tristan had been crying because he had red, puffy eyes, and the corners of his eyes looked raw as if he had been wiping tears away. Mr. Jaimeson felt sympathy for Tristan, but he knew he had to be careful and not be fooled by Tristan's appearance as a victim and not as a potential enemy.

Tristan was the first to speak, "Mr. Jaimeson, why are you holding me here?"

"Tristan," said Mr. Jaimeson sternly, "you know exactly why you are here. We know that your story that you are simply seeking information from us about your birth parents is a false one contrived to get you close to us. We also know that you work for Maerdern and that he sent you to spy on us."

Tristan stared at Mr. Jaimeson, stunned that Mr. Jaimeson was aware that Tristan had been sent by Maerdern to spy on them. But he still wasn't willing to give up his cover. Perhaps it was a test, he thought. Perhaps they don't know for sure, and they are just trying to trick me into revealing something, thought Tristan. So, he would be careful not to be tricked into giving something away. At the same time, Tristan chuckled quietly to himself because Maerdern did not share information about his plans, so Tristan didn't know very much.

Mr. Jaimeson looked at Tristan sharply and said to him, "Tristan, Mrs. Jaimeson and I are very powerful seers. You should not cross us. You are at our mercy, and you would be best advised to cooperate with us. I'm sure you realize that you are our prisoner. But you should also know that you are also under our protection. Maerdern will not be able to get to you here. He won't be able to even find you. But, I doubt that if he knew where you were, he would even try to rescue you."

Tristan kept his face emotionless, trying not to give away any information to Mr. Jaimeson about how he felt. He did know that Maerdern would not actually try to save him. But the greater risk was that Maerdern might try to find Tristan and punish him for having failed his mission. So, Tristan hoped that Mr. Jaimeson was being truthful about the protection of the Jaimesons. Still, Tristan thought he should maintain his silence since he didn't know whether or not he could trust the Jaimesons. They could be lying to him to get information.

Mr. Jaimeson interpreted Tristan's silence as a decision not to cooperate. That was fine, he thought. He and his wife would eventually obtain information from Tristan. For now, it was enough that they had stopped him from accomplishing whatever mission the evil seer had assigned to him.

As Mr. Jaimeson turned to leave, he stated, "I'll be back. In the meantime, think about what I have said. You really do not want to have us as your enemies. You would be surprised at what my wife and I have the power to do. Don't make us show you." He then left Tristan on his own in his cell.

The Jaimesons were kind people, so they made sure that Tristan would be a comfortable prisoner and would not be in fear for his safety.

They also made sure that Tristan did not have contact with the other family whose house he was at, so that he wouldn't have an opportunity to try to convince them to let him go. Food was provided to Tristan at each mealtime by passing it through the magic barrier. The family hosting Tristan did not speak to him but provided him with reading material to keep him from becoming bored. They also provided him with a radio and a television so that he could entertain himself.

With Tristan as their prisoner, the Jaimesons continued to think they might be able to obtain information about Maerdern's plans by interrogating Tristan. They might use a truth spell on him, which was yet another magic ability that very few seers knew even existed, let alone had the knowledge to use. They might later try some additional spells on Tristan, to try to turn him from his allegiance to Maerdern. But they knew that even with the use of that magic, they still might not be able to trust Tristan fully.

The Jaimesons knew that they would have to consider carefully whether to use these types of magic because they were not generally known to seers. As well-protected secrets of the small number of the most powerful seer families, they had to be careful not to expose their existence to Maerdern or any of his followers. If the Jaimesons were to use these techniques on a follower of Maerdern, they could possibly unintentionally reveal to Maerdern that such magic existed. For everyone's safety, the less Maerdern knew about it, the safer all seers would be — as well as the norms.

Tristan wasn't happy to have been trapped by the Jaimesons. But he realized that it was far better for him to be held captive by this nice family than it would be to go back to Maerdern and report his failure. So, he thought, it might be in his best interests to be a prisoner for a while. He believed that to maintain his status as a prisoner, he would have to pretend he had information about Maerdern's plans but that he was reluctant to provide it. The better he played out that strategy, the longer he could be held captive and the longer he would be protected by the Jaimeson family.

Chapter 24

After a good night's sleep following her wand ceremony, Emaleen felt much like her old self, except that she also felt more powerful, energetic, and alert. She felt ready for the training that her aunt had said right after the wand ceremony would from now on be more intensive and that would start immediately after the wand ceremony.

Her aunt also warned her niece that the training would be in longer sessions and would be a lot more challenging. It would also include an education on the values of ethical seers, new skills, and some challenges. Aunt Zeraida had many, many more challenges to put Emaleen through. Emaleen would have very little free time for many weeks to come. It was important that her full focus was on her training.

Zeraida also informed her niece that instead of returning to school in the fall, Emaleen would be homeschooled. Emaleen would have her traditional schooling lessons first thing in the morning and then for the rest of the day, she would be training. She was excited about not returning to the school but also very nervous. She knew her aunt's standards and expectations about her school work would be high.

Emaleen was also nervous about the intensive seer training that her aunt had described. And, although she was excited to be learning all about magic, she was also used to having a lot of free time to do what she wished. The dedication of all of her time to training and the lack of free time would be an adjustment for Emaleen.

She was also wondering what the training would involve. Would it be too difficult? Would she be able to learn everything that she needed to learn? She also wondered what would happen if she did not turn out to be very good at magic. The "what-ifs" were very troubling to her.

On the first morning after Emaleen's wand ceremony, Aunt Zeraida started her training immediately after breakfast. Although Emaleen expected that the training would be upstairs, Aunt Zeraida led her niece into the family room and had her sit down on her meditation mat.

"Emaleen," started Aunt Zeraida. "It's important for you to learn a code of conduct for seers and some history of the seers. The powers that you are about to learn are so great that you have to be very responsible and careful. You have to be ethical, and you must do only good for others. You must not use your powers solely for your own purposes."

Aunt Zeraida continued, "I've known you since you were a baby, and I feel that I can trust you. But it's important that you take this very seriously and that you follow all of the rules that I'm going to explain to you in the course of your training. You must also not try anything on your own until I let you know that you are ready. If you do, you may risk harm to others or yourself."

Emaleen nodded, looking at her aunt attentively. With a pleased look, Aunt Zeraida continued, "Also, it's important for you to remember what I told you when I first informed you that you are a seer. We don't just wave a wand and then something happens without any other effort on our part. There are forces and rules of nature that determine all the events that happen in this world. Some of these you can learn from the schooling of the norms. Some of them are known only to the seers. Also, as seers, we are a part of this complex system of nature. It's through the use of these forces and rules of nature that we make events happen."

Aunt Zeraida paused for a moment, in deep thought, staring off into space, barely moving or breathing. Emaleen stared at her aunt, quietly wondering what her aunt was thinking.

After she had finished thinking, Aunt Zeraida said, "Emaleen, I have been debating when to talk to you more about the danger that you are in. I had wanted to wait and give you more time to adjust to all of the new information that has been practically bombarding you. I know it's a lot to take in — to realize that you are not just an ordinary young girl, but that you have special powers. It's also difficult to learn that you are in some danger even if you know that you're protected by many different people."

Emaleen took in a deep breath with a sigh and then gulped. Then she nodded her head. It had been a lot to take in, she thought. And it worried her that there was even more that she would have to adjust to.

"Aunt Zeraida," said Emaleen. "I think I'd rather learn about it all now and not have to wait to learn information a little at a time. It's stressful knowing that there's more going on that I don't know about."

"You're right," answered Aunt Zeraida. "I will tell you more if you promise to listen closely. And, if it becomes too much, I want you to tell me, and I will stop. If so, I can start again after you've had some more time to adjust."

"That sounds good," remarked Emaleen smiling. "Thank you."

"But first, I'm going to start with some background information and go from there," said Aunt Zeraida. "As I mentioned before, you are a seer. You are a seer because both of your parents are seers. There are not as many of us these days as there were hundreds of years ago. Over time, our numbers have dwindled as a result of seers deciding to no longer exercise magic giving us immortality, but instead allowing us to age and die the same as the norms. With the mortality of seers, the number of seers depends upon more seers being born than seers dying. But the number of new seers has dwindled due to marriages with norms because when a seer marries a norm, the children are usually norms with no seer talents and abilities — but that's not always the case. There have also been some seer families who did not pass down the seer training and knowledge to their next generations."

"Will I have to marry another seer when I grow up?" asked Emaleen. She hoped not. What if with so few seers left, there were no young men worth marrying, she wondered. What if she couldn't find love?

"Of course not," replied Aunt Zeraida. "There is no rule that says you have to marry a seer. I hope you do, though, since you will probably pass along a lot of power to your children, if you have any. But you have a long time before you have to make decisions about marriage. After all, you are only eleven years old. So, for now, don't worry." Emaleen was relieved. But her relief was shortly followed by worry and concern as she started to think about the reality that she currently lived under.

Emaleen then asked, "I don't mean to be impatient, but can you talk now about why I am in danger? You told me about a bad man named Maerdern. I would like to know why he is a danger to me."

Aunt Zeraida sighed and answered, "There is a seer named Maerdern, who wants to dominate all the other seers. He wants to rule over all of us and make us do evil things. He's been researching the various seer families and looking for a young seer with great powers to recruit as his apprentice. He is hoping to use the powers of the apprentice to boost his own powers. He is not the most powerful seer there is, and he is looking for any way he can to make himself more powerful. But don't underestimate him because he is not an extremely powerful seer, Emaleen. His ambitions are really strong, and he is willing to do anything to succeed. That makes him very dangerous."

"Why don't you just make him disappear, Aunt Zeraida?" asked Emaleen. "Wouldn't that be the best way to deal with him? Then it would be all over with, and we could live in safety and not have to worry anymore."

Aunt Zeraida sighed and then looked Emaleen straight in the eye and replied, "There is a difference between right and wrong. I believe the right way to do this is to do everything we can to cause Maerdern to fail in his efforts. Using our powers against him in a way that would hurt him physically should, in my opinion, be used only as a last resort."

Her aunt's answer disappointed Emaleen. She would rather someone do something to take care of Maerdern now, in a permanent way, so that he could not hurt anyone now or ever again. The way this was working out, Maerdern was just being given an opportunity to gain more power. And, the more time they waited, the harder it would be to defeat him, thought Emaleen. Also, she thought, the sooner they defeated Maerdern, the sooner she could go back to being just a kid and living a normal life.

Zeraida watched Emaleen carefully and felt that she could read her niece's thoughts. She could tell that Emaleen was upset.

"I, too, wish just a little that we could just vanish Maerdern," asserted Aunt Zeraida. "It would make my life easier, too. But I feel very strongly that it is wrong, and I could not live with myself if I caused such harm, even if Maerdern has bad intentions toward us. There are better and more ethical ways of dealing with the problem of Maerdern than hurting him. We will use one of those other ways."

Zeraida thought, Emaleen would not want to know how it feels to be forced to do something to hurt someone. No matter what the justification, hurting another person is a life-changing moment. The damage that it does to a person never goes away even if it may lessen some over time. Zeraida had personal experience with such matters; unfortunately, as a result of self-defense. She also had friends who had returned from military duty in war zones and learned from them about the trauma caused to them by the violence that they had witnessed or had to personally engage in. She would not wish that trauma on Emaleen. There would have to be another way. She knew, though, that they would have to be prepared to engage in violence just in case there were no other peaceful options.

"Isn't there another way we can stop him?" questioned Emaleen hopefully. "Can we have him put in jail or something?"

Zeraida answered, "The norms would not put him in jail. They don't even know about seers. Plus, Maerdern hasn't broken any laws of the norms yet, as far as I know. So, we could not seek to have him prosecuted under the norms' laws. Also, we seers are not organized, so we do not have laws nor do we have any courts or jails of our own. It would also be hard to trap him and imprison him since he is always accompanied by numerous followers who protect him. At the moment, we would be seriously outnumbered if we were to attempt to approach him and his followers. It would be very dangerous."

"But —," said Zeraida slowly, "there are some other ways we can fight him and beat him without harming him. But we need the other seers to help us with that. We need to have an alliance with the other seers, and we have not yet been able to convince the other seers of the danger that he poses. Many of them believe he is not skilled enough to pose a threat, so they won't align with us and act."

Emaleen sighed with disappointment. She couldn't believe that the other seers with all of their wisdom and powers, could not *see* the danger that Maerdern posed to all of them — not just Emaleen.

"Can I help you try to unite the other seers?" asked Emaleen. She wanted to take action instead of just continuing to hide out.

"Yes, I expect that some day you will help us unite the other seers so that we can battle Maerdern," answered Aunt Zeraida. "At least, that's my hope. But to do so, you have to be able to come out from hiding, and we just can't do that yet. You must be patient, and you must train and become as powerful as you can before we can allow you to take this risk. We all know that in the meantime, Maerdern is going to become even more powerful, but if we act too soon, before you are ready, we will definitely put you in danger and we will most likely fail."

There was silence for several minutes as Emaleen reflected on what her aunt had said, and Zeraida was now lost deep in her own thoughts. Aunt Zeraida was thinking about her own suspicions that Maerdern may be the least of her niece's problems, and that there were possibly even greater dangers for her niece to face. Maerdern was just the immediate risk that they had to deal with. But Zeraida didn't think the time was right to discuss her concerns with her niece. She also hoped that she was wrong and that when they defeated Maerdern, the danger to her niece would be finally over. Given the possibility that her suspicions of greater danger may be wrong, there was no point in worrying Emaleen. So, Zeraida tried to put these thoughts of out her mind. When Zeraida was able to shake away her own troubled thoughts, she decided the best thing to do now was to change the topic.

"There is one last ethical matter to talk about right now," said Zeraida. "Once you have powers that are developed, you will need to decide the extent to which you want to be helpful to norms. Many seers watch out for and help the norms that are around them, preventing disasters from befalling them, or preventing the norms from hurting one another in wars or other conflicts. But the extent to which a seer helps the norms depends upon the individual values of the particular seer, the powers held by the seer, and the individual seer's view of what a seer should be doing. Some seers don't interfere with the lives of the norms at all, whether positively or negatively. These seers use their powers only to make their own lives more comfortable or to practice their skills to build their own powers and self-esteems.

"What should I do?" asked Emaleen.

"You can do what you wish with respect to the norms as long as you don't harm them. I hope, though, that you will consider helping them," answered Zeraida.

Emaleen then sat and thought about what her aunt had said about helping the norms. She liked the idea of helping others, but she wasn't really sure what she could do to help or what she should do. But maybe she should focus first on the Maerdern problem and her own safety, she thought.

Chapter 25

"Now, it's time for more serious training," announced Aunt Zeraida. "We will start with something simple that is actually very powerful magic that can be used on a much greater scale than how we are going to use it today. It was used by ancient seers to assist in the creation of some very large monuments and structures that still stand today that have scientists baffled as to how they were created. We seers know how these mysterious structures were created, but we keep it secret so we do not expose the existence of seers to the norms."

Emaleen looked at her aunt with amazement. She could think of several different ancient wonders that she had learned about on various educational television stations, for which the method of construction was unknown. She wanted to ask her aunt which structures she was referring to, but she didn't want to interrupt what her aunt was about to teach her, so she decided to remain quiet and ask later.

Zeraida looked at her niece with a smile and directed, "We will also need to go upstairs to do this. And, I have a surprise for you." Emaleen followed her aunt up the stairs to the hall outside her room.

"I made you your own secret magic workroom, like mine and your uncle's," said Zeraida. "You will need to use this room to practice your magic skills so that other seers cannot sense your use of magic."

Emaleen's eyes widened, and she looked at her aunt with a surprised and excited look. She couldn't believe that she was getting her own private workroom.

"I designed the floors and ceiling," explained Aunt Zeraida, "so that they would conceal the use of magic. And, I added some items that I thought you would need to start with. But what you put in the room is up to you. You should spend some time thinking about what you want to have in your room, and I will obtain it for you."

"Thanks so much! Can I see it now?" asked Emaleen happily.

Aunt Zeraida showed Emaleen the steps necessary to open the door to her room. Emaleen followed her aunt's instructions carefully, and a door then appeared. Emaleen opened the door and went inside, holding it open for her aunt to follow her. Aunt Zeraida followed her niece into the room.

Once in the room, Emaleen looked around. The walls, ceiling, and floor were very similar to her aunt's room. But otherwise, the room was bare, except for one couch, two end tables, two meditating rugs, and a table sitting against one wall, which had shelves from the top of the table to the top of the wall. The rugs looked like the ones that Skye and Emaleen had been using in the family room downstairs, but they were slightly different.

Aunt Zeraida watched her niece carefully for her reaction. She hoped her niece liked the room. She had tried only to put the bare necessities in the room and to leave options open for her niece to customize her room to meet her own tastes.

"If you don't like something that is already in here," said Aunt Zeraida, "just let me know. We will remove it and get you something different. I just didn't want you to start off with an empty room."

"I love it all!" exclaimed Emaleen. "I don't know what else I could want yet, but I will think about it and let you know if I think of anything. I really love that I will have my own room to work in."

Aunt Zeraida noticed that she still had her niece's attention despite her niece's wonder over her new magic workroom, so she continued, "I'm glad you like your room. But we need to get to work immediately. See that vase over on the end table?" asked Zeraida.

"Yes," replied Emaleen. There was a cream-colored vase over on one of the tables. Painted on the vase were three long stem roses of different colors — red, white, and pink. The stems of the roses were intertwined. Each rose had just three leaves on its stem.

Zeraida then said, "For your first magic lessons, you will need to move that vase from the table on which it sits over to the table on the other side of the couch. You may not use your hands to do this. This will probably take you about a week to master. I'm going to explain to you the forces involved that you will use to make this move. From

176

there, you will learn by yourself, step-by-step, how to do this task. You will see that although the moving of the vase seems like such a minor task, it is actually a fairly complicated one. At first, you might wonder whether going through all of these steps is worth it, given the small result you will see. But over time, as you become more practiced, these multiple steps will become automatic and more efficient. You will also use these beginning tasks as the building blocks for others that you will learn. So, although the task seems simple, it's actually very important for your training."

Next, Zeraida described each of the forces that were involved, including the forces that allowed the vase to exist in this world; the force of gravity that held the vase on the table upon which it had been placed; the invisible forces in the air that could neither be seen nor felt but which, among other purposes, could be used to set objects upon and for them to travel across; the forces needed to move an object from a stationary position and into motion; the forces needed to stop an object in motion; and the forces needed to set an object down. It took Zeraida the entire morning to teach her niece about each of these forces and to provide a demonstration of each.

Although Zeraida taught Emaleen about all the forces involved, she left for her niece the puzzle of how to put them all together to move the vase. She would leave it to her niece to figure how to move the vase on her own. Zeraida knew that in figuring out this puzzle herself, Emaleen would learn more from the simple task assigned. She would have a deeper understanding of the various forces, and she would figure out new uses for them. The forces also were ones that Zeraida knew her niece could practice with, on her own, without danger.

Zeraida also gave Emaleen a journal to make notes in as she learned by experimenting with the forces. The journal was very large, with many pages, and had a leather cover and metal fasteners to open and close the book. On the leather cover was an ornate raised carving of a Celtic knot. At the upper edge of the book's cover was a carved engraving of Emaleen's name. Below that was a picture of a Peregrine falcon and a picture of a Bengal cat. Emaleen ran her hand over the carvings and found them to be smooth. Then she looked up to her aunt with questioning eyes.

"The pictures on the cover symbolize your special gifts and talents that are unique to you. As you discover more of these, the book cover will display a new picture as a symbol," explained Aunt Zeraida in response to Emaleen's clear, but unspoken, question.

Aunt Zeraida continued, "This book is for recording what you learn as you experiment with magic. You should record all of your observations, no matter how insignificant they may at first appear. You should read through this at least once a week from beginning to end. You never know when something you observed early on may have significance to you later when you have a larger knowledge base. Also, when you make your observations, be sure to use all of your senses, including how you physically feel at the time."

"Now, I'm going to leave you to your studies," announced Aunt Zeraida. "Take your time, and don't get discouraged if it takes you a little while. As you learn, you will find that you will learn at a faster pace over time. The first time can be very difficult and feel slow. But it will get easier. If you need help, come find me," said Zeraida. Then she turned and exited Emaleen's workroom.

After her aunt had left, Emaleen sat on the couch in silence for several minutes not sure exactly what to do. Her aunt had gone through a lot, and Emaleen was afraid that she would forget what her aunt had shared with her. She stared into space for several minutes without knowing what to do, and then she decided to open her new journal and make notes of what her aunt had taught her.

Emaleen started by listing the various forces that her aunt had taught her. She then made making diagrams of what each forces did. For each force, she wrote down as many of the instructions her aunt had provided to her as she could remember. Then she went to find her aunt so she could review with her some of the points that she was not sure about.

When Emaleen reached her aunt and showed her the journal, Zeraida praised her for taking such great notes and told her that she was off to a good start. Aunt Zeraida gladly answered her niece's questions, filling in where Emaleen had forgotten the instructions. But for those parts that Emaleen had to figure out for herself, Zeraida smiled and let her niece know that these were answers that she could not provide.

After having completed her notes, Emaleen wandered back off to her workroom. She sat on her meditating rug and began to meditate. Emaleen tried to clear her mind and relax. She wasn't sure what to do first. But she knew that she needed to have a clear mind and be relaxed.

She meditated quietly for about twenty minutes before she returned to the vase challenge. When she did, she sat staring at the vase for a while, thinking carefully. She realized that she needed to start small and work toward the bigger parts of the task. The first thing she thought she needed to do was to raise the vase off of the table. She knew that there were at least two forces that she needed to manipulate to make that happen.

She picked one of the forces and tried to affect it. When she did, she felt a vibrating through the air, but the vase did not move.

Emaleen sighed and made more notes. She noted everything she did and what she observed. It seemed to Emaleen that her practices were not going very well. But she kept in mind her aunt's advice that it might take a while before she succeeded, and she tried not to let a feeling of discouragement affect her. Emaleen kept her efforts up and after a time, she was able to raise the vase off of the table. It did not raise up very high — just about one inch — but it was off the table.

As soon as Emaleen noticed that the vase had raised off of the table, she screamed with excitement and amazement, and the vase instantly came crashing down, landing with a loud thump on the table followed by a loud cracking noise. Emaleen gasped in surprise and then stood up in wonder and amazement at what she had accomplished. She couldn't believe that she had made the vase rise off of the table.

When her aunt had explained it all to her, Emaleen surprisingly had not questioned or even wondered at the possibility that anyone could do something like this. All her life, she had presumed that moving an item with your own mind was something that was just not possible. But now she had actually done it herself, and she was not only amazed and filled with wonder, but she felt a strangely satisfying sense of empowerment.

Emaleen then left the workroom and rushed down the stairs to see her aunt. She couldn't wait to tell her aunt about her success with the vase.

Aunt Zeraida could hear her niece coming and rushed out to meet her in the family room. She sensed that something important had happened and had a huge smile on her face, which displayed both her excitement and her pride in her niece. She sensed her niece's use of power from the way her niece was so excited.

"I just raised the vase!" exclaimed Emaleen as she saw her aunt. "Unfortunately, though, I think I broke it because it dropped and then I heard a crack sound."

Her aunt laughed softly and said, "Well, I should have known better than to use a vase. I'll have to give you something more durable for the next time. I'm not worried about the vase, though. It was not valuable."

Her aunt continued, "You must have lost your concentration for it to fall and break like that. But you have made great progress just by lifting the vase up off of the table. I think, however, this is enough for now. When you start learning, you might want to start in small steps. As you go along, you will accomplish greater things in shorter periods of time and with a smaller and smaller amount of your personal energy. But right now, this small step probably took a lot of energy. You should rest some and then do something fun. Tomorrow is another day."

Emaleen nodded and then skipped off. She ran over to the phone and called Skye to ask her over to play. Skye was excited to hear from her friend and eagerly agreed to come over as soon as she could. Skye couldn't wait to hear what her friend had been up to. She also couldn't wait to play with Belenus and go on an adventure with Emaleen. Skye had worked hard for the day at her own studies and was ready for some fun.

Aunt Zeraida was relieved that Emaleen had so quickly learned the first step of the challenge that she had provided. At the same time, Aunt Zeraida was concerned because she had a feeling that her niece would need to develop her powers more quickly than the normal period of training for a seer. She feared that Emaleen would need to have all of her powers very soon, for her own protection. However, Aunt Zeraida did not want to rush the training more than was absolutely necessary. For as long as she could, Aunt Zeraida would do her best to protect her niece so that she could have proper training as a seer without rushing.

Before Skye arrived, Emaleen sat down with her book and recorded her observations and thoughts about what she had learned when she raised the vase from the table. She also wrote down her thoughts on how to accomplish the next step, which was to transfer the vase across the air to a position immediately over the other table. Emaleen had many thoughts; so many that she could scarcely write fast enough to record them all.

She also thought she should continue with her work today until she made her own decision that she was ready to quit. She could have Skye there to help her. So, she asked her aunt if she could continue working, and her aunt agreed that Emaleen could work further until she decided for herself to rest. But her aunt asked her to be careful not to overdo her training.

Chapter 26

A couple of weeks had gone by since Maerdern had sent Tristan on the mission to the Jaimeson house. But Maerdern had not heard anything from him. So, Maerdern assumed that either Tristan had failed or that he was unable to contact his leader because he had befriended the family and was afraid of making them suspicious. Either way, Tristan had not returned with any magic books for Maerdern. Whether or not Tristan was still on track to obtain such books, Maerdern considered his efforts a failure because the follower had missed his deadline.

Maerdern didn't bother concerning himself with whether Tristan was in any danger or not. To Maerdern, Tristan was unimportant and expendable. So whether anything might have happened to Tristan was of no matter to Maerdern. All that mattered to Maerdern was that he did not have any magic books.

Maerdern had been growing more and more impatient waiting for Tristan. As a result, Maerdern felt that it was now necessary to move forward with his next plan. In furtherance of that plan, Maerdern had spent the last week in the same town in which the Andarsans lived. But he was hidden away in a secret location, and only his followers knew that he was there. It was Maerdern's view that the Andarsans were the most powerful of all of the seer families.

He had previously wanted to work his way through the lesser families first, gaining access to their books and personal knowledge, and by so doing, building his power before he approached the Andarsans. But since he had grown impatient, Maerdern decided to take a significant risk and see if he could gain some of the knowledge held by the Andarsan family for himself. However, despite his growing impatience, Maerdern knew that he needed to plan very carefully and think his moves through before each and every action.

So, Maerdern had some of his followers pose as a new family that had just moved into town. This new family called themselves the

Smiths. The Smiths moved into a large home in the Andarsan's neighborhood that Maerdern had conveniently caused to become vacant. Maerdern had used some of the vast sums of money that he had extorted from his followers to purchase the house from the current occupants for a price significantly higher than its current value.

The Smiths were a young couple with a baby girl, who did not display any signs of having any significant seer talents and skills. The Smiths were friendly and approachable, despite their hidden leaning toward evil. They were always casually, but neatly, dressed. They were soft-spoken and well-mannered. Maerdern was certain that they would blend into the neighborhood and could gather intelligence about the Andarsans without anyone suspecting them. Nothing about them would indicate that they were followers of a pernicious leader.

As directed by Maerdern, the Smiths moved into their new home with a new nanny provided by Maerdern to give them the time to spy on his behalf without worrying about childcare. Then, Maerdern waited in town for the Smiths to do their work. He had decided not to leave, as he had done with Tristan, but to stay and to oversee the work of his spies.

As soon as they had moved into the house, the Smiths started befriending some of the neighbors by inviting them over for dinner. After providing their guests with food and drink, the Smiths carefully and methodically gained information about the Andarsans by acting genuinely interested in the neighbors and asking lots of questions about the various families who lived in the neighborhood. They were careful to ask about all of the families so that they did not look suspiciously interested only in one family. They tried to appear as if they were merely interested in making new friends and not as if they were nosy neighbors.

In a short time, the Smiths determined who the gossips were and how to get them to share information without much effort. As a result, the Smiths learned a lot about the Andarsans. In fact, they had discovered that eleven or twelve years ago, Seanna Andarsan had been pregnant and close to her due date when she had taken a trip and returned no longer pregnant and without a child. When she returned, her husband had quietly told the neighbors that while they were away, Mrs. Andarsan had gone into labor but that the child had not survived.

The Smiths also learned that the Andarsans went on frequent, unannounced trips to locations only they knew about. The neighbors often gossiped about the couple and these mysterious trips, but no one was able to guess where they had gone. The Andarsans enjoyed their privacy and, thus, shared little about themselves to their neighbors.

After a couple of weeks of integrating themselves into the Andarsan neighborhood, the Smiths secretly met with Maerdern to share all that they had learned about the family. Maerdern listened carefully and took notes in case there might be some information that did not seem important to him now that might turn out to be important later on. He was particularly interested and curious about Seanna Andarsan's pregnancy loss, and he was carefully contemplating whether the story was true or whether there might be an Andarsan child somewhere out in the world.

When he heard the Smiths' report, Maerdern stated, "Go back to your home and continue to learn as much as you can about the Andarsans. Also, keep an eye out for any new departures by them. If you discover that they are about to make a trip, you are to contact my tracker spy. Here is his contact information. He will follow them and report back to me once he learns the purpose of their trip."

The Smiths nodded in agreement. Maerdern then ordered, "You will also keep an eye out for patterns in the Andarsans' daily activities. For instance, you will watch to see if they have a certain day and time that they leave the home together and how long they typically stay out of the house when they do leave together." That information, thought Maerdern, could come in handy if he decided to break into the Andarsans' home to locate any books showing unique magical arts known to that family. Then Maerdern looked sternly at the couple to communicate to them his expectation that they not fail their mission.

"We will do as you order, Maerdern," vowed Mr. Smith. "We will keep a close eye on them and report to you any new information that we discover. If necessary, we will at some point try to gain entry into the Andarsans' home and snoop around for information. But we promise to be careful not to give ourselves away before we have learned whatever secrets they have that we can discern just from our spying on them." Mr. Smith watched Maerdern's face closely as he spoke to him. He was terrified of Maerdern and wanted to be careful that he did not say anything that would upset his leader and cause the evil seer to turn on Mr. Smith and his wife, and especially their young child.

After the Smiths had left, Maerdern started to ponder the story of Mrs. Andarsan's lost pregnancy. He debated in his mind whether there might be a child out there, or whether it was, in fact, true that the child had died. Eleven or twelve years was a long time ago, and Maerdern couldn't think of a reason that the Andarsan family could have had to hide a child that long ago. Certainly, he thought, they could not have predicted so long ago that Maerdern would now be looking for a young apprentice. He didn't think any seers had premonition powers that strong.

So, it seemed more likely to him than not that it was, in fact, true that Mrs. Andarsan's baby had not survived the birth. And, it would be a waste of his time to search for such a child only to find out that the story was true. At the same time, if it wasn't true and there was a child out there, that child could be the powerful apprentice that Maerdern was looking for — or if the child did not become his apprentice, that child could instead be a formidable enemy. Still, Maerdern would need to wait and see what additional information turned up about the Andarsans before he could determine what, if anything, he would need to do.

Chapter 27

Although the Andarsans were careful to keep their private lives secret and not the common knowledge of their neighbors, they were not antisocial in the least. Over the years, they had carefully formed their own relationships and alliances with their neighbors.

What they lacked in openness, they made up for in their generosity and kindness of heart. When a neighbor faced hardship, the Andarsans were frequently there to lend a helping hand. They had helped with sick children, babysat for tired parents, loaned money, and even once hosted a family whose home had been damaged by fire. Their neighbors generally liked them.

So when the Smiths had moved in and invited everyone but the Andarsans over to their house, the neighbors noticed. They started to gossip about why the Andarsan couple had not been invited over and how the Smiths seemed to have an interest in them. The neighbors had noticed this interest in the Andarsans despite the Smiths' attempts to try to appear interested in everyone. Unfortunately, the neighbors only noticed after they had shared all the various pieces of information that they had learned about the family over the years.

Mrs. Boyland was the first neighbor to visit Mrs. Andarsan to make her aware of the Smiths and their inquisitive nature. She stopped by the Andarsan house one afternoon with a container of homemade cookies and had a visit with Mrs. Andarsan.

Mrs. Boyland said, "I hate to trouble you, but I wanted to make you aware that our new neighbors down the street, have been asking all of the other neighbors about you. It seems that they are trying to gather personal information about you and your husband." When Seanna Andarsan heard about the Smiths from Mrs. Boyland, she was careful to conceal any reaction to the information.

Seanna replied, "I'm glad you stopped by. We've all been busy lately, and it has been difficult to get together. It's really good to see you. I hope all is well."

Seanna continued, "Thanks for letting me know about the Smiths. But I think they are just bored people with nothing else to do but gossip. I never see either of them leave the house for an outside job."

At the same time, Seanna quietly took notice of the interest of the Smiths. She needed to figure out who they were and why they were so interested in her husband and herself. So, she feigned a friendly interest in the Smiths and asked Mrs. Boyland some questions.

"They seem like a friendly couple, though," continued Seanna. "Do you know anything about them? Do they have jobs outside the home, or do they work at home?"

"You know . . .," replied Mrs. Boyland. "I don't know anything about them. That is so odd, too. They have invited us to dinner several times now." Unfortunately, Mrs. Boyland did not have any information to share about the Smiths because the Smiths had asked so many questions of their guests that the guests themselves did not have any opportunity to ask questions about the Smiths and the Smiths did not volunteer any information.

As she thought about it while trying to conceal her concern, Mrs. Andarsan became concerned that the Smiths very well might be spies planted by Maerdern. She needed to speak with her husband right away. But she didn't want to alert her neighbor to the concern. So, she changed the subject and then chatted with her several more minutes, after which she made an excuse to Mrs. Boyland to end the visit.

After Mrs. Boyland had left, Mrs. Andarsan found her husband in his workshop to inform him of what she had learned about the Smiths. Mrs. Andarsan's greatest fear was that the Smiths might have discovered the existence or even the possibility of the existence of Emaleen, their daughter. She and her husband had taken great pains to protect their daughter and to keep her hidden. They hadn't even seen their daughter since she was about a week old when they had left her in the care of Zeraida, her sister. Mrs. Andarsan was longing to see her daughter, but she was afraid that if she and her husband made the trip out to see their daughter that they would reveal her existence and all the care they had taken to keep their daughter safe would become pointless.

Although they had not visited Emaleen, they did, however, make some trips out to remote locations to send messages to Zeraida by carrier pigeon. This required the Andarsans to fly across the ocean from their home in England to a rural part of the United States. They varied the exact locations to which they flew, to hide their tracks. Most often, though, the Andarsans traveled to Kentucky, which was not very close to Emaleen's home in upstate New York, but was close enough for the carrier pigeons to find Zeraida and far enough to prevent anyone who might be following them from discovering Emaleen's whereabouts.

Now, with the Smiths watching them, Mrs. Andarsan was concerned about even flying to the United States. She was certain that the Smiths must be spies of Maerdern, and that they would likely follow the Andarsans should they make any trips.

Seanna also had missed Emaleen desperately and thought about her every day. She felt like a terrible mother for not being with her daughter and helping to raise her and watch her grow. At the same time, she shivered when she thought of the possibility of Emaleen being forced to be an apprentice for Maerdern. She couldn't bear the thought of her one and only child being forced to use her talents and gifts for evil purposes and the harm that would cause Emaleen. And, although she didn't know for sure what Maerdern's plans were, she was sure that they involved a gross and cruel misuse of his seer powers. Mrs. Andarsan would not see her daughter bound to such evil, and she would do what she had to do to protect her, even if it meant that Mrs. Andarsan had to sacrifice her own relationship with her daughter.

Mrs. Andarsan was also a little angry with the other powerful seer families. She and her husband had met with them some time ago, to warn them about Maerdern and to attempt to get them all to work together to prevent him from gaining power. Although they tried their best to lobby the other families, ultimately, the families refused to unite and work together. And their refusal to unite was based mainly upon an unwillingness for the seers to follow anyone. She understood that seers were strong-willed and didn't like to be told what to do, but the refusal to unite to fight evil, for this reason, was foolish, Seanna thought.

It was frustrating for the Andarsans, who not only could see the great danger that Maerdern posed but felt the danger personally as he was a threat to their very own child. That threat had also forced them to put their daughter into hiding. If only the other seer families would have united and fought Maerdern early on, the Andarsans could now be with their daughter.

After mulling over these thoughts, Mrs. Andarsan needed a few minutes to compose herself – to pull herself together so that she could be strong to face whatever might be coming. When she finally approached her husband, Mannix, he could tell by the look on her face that something was very wrong. He suspected that the problem was related to the Smiths, whom Mannix had already heard about himself. He, too, had been concerned about the excessive interest that the Smiths seemed to have in him and his wife.

He did not want to worry his wife, but Mannix was sure that the Smiths must be followers of Maerdern. He had been giving the situation some thought and was not quite sure what to do yet, but he was convinced that they should not panic, and they should not take reckless actions that might reveal their daughter's existence and location.

Seanna Andarsan informed her husband, "Mrs. Boyland was just here. She said that the Smith family seems to be taking an interest in us, and they have been gathering information about us from the neighbors."

"I just heard about that, too," replied Mannix Andarsan. "We need to find out if the Smiths are spies for Maerdern. We need to check into this possibility, but we also need to be careful not to make any rash decisions."

"Do you think we should warn Zeraida?" asked Seanna.

"No, we can't do that with the Smiths spying on us," said Mannix.

"We can't just sit here and do nothing, though, can we?" asked Seanna in frustration.

"We should spy on the Smiths. And, we should verify that they are indeed spying on us. We should also vary our normal routine so that our actions are unpredictable and do not fall into any pattern," suggested Mannix.

"Those are all good ideas," agreed Seanna.

Mr. Andarsan then thought of a plan. He would meet with his old friend, Sam Cavanaugh, who was technically, his guardian, and who had grown up with him. Mannix hadn't had a need for his protection services anymore since he was quite powerful himself and there had been peace among the seers for hundreds of years. However, Mr. Cavanaugh respected his traditional role of guardian, even though to some the role of the guardian did not seem significant for an adult seer. Mr. Cavanaugh, therefore, kept in touch with Mr. Andarsan, ready at all times to serve him in whatever way would best serve the seer if the need arose.

Mr. Andarsan, in turn, respected Mr. Cavanaugh for his commitment to his role as a guardian and considered him a close, personal friend whom he could trust for anything. Mr. Andarsan knew that Mr. Cavanaugh could be counted on to help the Andarsans and to keep their secrets confidential.

Mr. Andarsan's plan was to have his friend watch out for any persons following him if he decided to go on a small drive. If a spy did follow him, Mannix would know for sure that it would not be safe to take a trip for the purpose of warning Zeraida.

So, Mannix informed his wife of the plan, and then he called Mr. Cavanaugh to ask if he was available to get together in a public place. They arranged to meet at the library, in one of the meeting rooms, instead of Mr. Cavanaugh's house.

Later, the two met at the library at the designated time and place. Mr. Cavanaugh had taken pains to arrive early at the library so that he was already in the room. The men had planned the early arrival so the spy, if any, would not be able to detect the purpose of the meeting or learn about Mr. Cavanaugh. After learning about the Smith situation, the guardian readily agreed to assist Mannix. So, the two arranged for Mr. Cavanaugh to park just around the corner at the end of the Andarsans' street the next day, and to watch for anyone following Mannix when he pulled out of his driveway and drove down the street.

The next day, Mr. Cavanaugh drove his vehicle to the agreed upon place and sat there waiting for his friend to leave the house. At about 10 a.m., Mr. Andarsan came out his front door and got into his car and drove south toward the other end of the street, away from his guardian. As Mannix reached the end of the road and turned right, a driver in a car on a neighbor's driveway pulled out of the driveway and headed in his direction, and turned right after him.

Mr. Cavanaugh waited a few seconds and followed the neighbor's car. He followed far behind the other car, watching the driver take the route that Mr. Andarsan had planned out. It was immediately obvious to Mr. Cavanaugh that Mr. Andarsan was being followed. And, as he passed the driveway from which the car had pulled out, Mr. Cavanaugh made note of the fact that the driveway belonged to the Smiths. Clearly, the Smiths were actively spying on the Andarsans. After a short while, Mr. Cavanaugh turned his car around and returned to his home. When he arrived home, he sent a text to Mr. Andarsan with a coded message that was the agreed upon signal to let Mr. Andarsan know that he had been followed on his drive.

Later that day, Mr. Cavanaugh left his house again and drove to the airport to catch a flight to the United States. The purpose of his journey was to send a message to Zeraida to let her know to be extra vigilant for the possibility that Maerdern might learn about Emaleen. Later, when he returned from that trip, he would meet with the Andarsans to discuss the possibility of them fooling the Smiths and losing them so that they could make a secret trip to visit their daughter without risking discovery by Maerdern.

Chapter 28

It was a Saturday morning a couple of weeks after Emaleen had started to learn how to use her special powers to move a vase sitting upon one table on one side of the room to a table on the other side of the room. She had mastered that task much quicker than her aunt had expected her to and had quickly moved on to learn more complicated tasks. She had also learned more from the vase moving lessons than Zeraida had expected her to. So, she was making excellent progress.

Emaleen was so successful with her lessons because she was paying close attention to what her aunt was teaching and what she was doing. She had also found her own experiments to conduct and after clearing them with her aunt, she worked on them on her own and made her own discoveries.

Emaleen worked long into each day with greater dedication than was usually seen in a child of her age. As a result, Emaleen was learning at a much faster rate than what would normally be expected for a seer in training. She was also learning the most valuable lesson of all — that the best lesson a person can learn is how to teach oneself. Being able to teach oneself how to do anything is empowering, and a person with such an ability can accomplish anything.

Early that morning, before Emaleen and Morvin were awake, Aunt Zeraida had received a message from Mr. Cavanaugh. It was a message that she had been dreading. It stated that Maerdern might be closer to becoming aware of Emaleen, but it was not certain. It also informed Aunt Zeraida that she should keep extra vigilant and that they should prepare emergency relocation plans.

After she had read the message, Aunt Zeraida breathed a deep breath. She tried to regulate and reduce the stress that she was suddenly feeling. When she felt more composed, she quickly made a bacon, egg and toast breakfast with coffee for Morvin. She brought the breakfast upstairs so that she could wake Morvin and discuss this concerning news with him.

Morvin was a heavy sleeper and generally difficult to awaken. But Zeraida knew that bringing breakfast with some coffee to him would help him wake up.

As soon as Zeraida got a response from Morvin, she gave him the breakfast and coffee. Morvin sipped some coffee then Zeraida handed him the note. After he had finished reading it, he set it down in front of him. He sighed and looked at Zeraida.

"I think we need to keep this secret from Emaleen," suggested Zeraida. "She needs to focus on her training right now. Her best defense is to learn her seer skills well."

"I agree that she needs to keep training," said Morvin. "But we should also take some precautions. She should not be outside at any time by herself. We need to keep a careful watch over her."

"We should speed up her training too, just in case we might have to face Maerdern sooner than we might think," suggested Zeraida.

"That's a good idea," agreed Morvin. "She should start learning some defensive techniques first. Then, when she has those mastered, we should start training Emaleen on the attack skills."

Morvin continued, "We will also need to put our backup plan into place to make sure Emaleen is protected. I'll talk to Mr. Earl and Mr. Stewart for help. Then, as we have discussed previously, I am going to leave to prepare for our backup plan. You may not see me for a little while. But you know how to find me if there is trouble."

Zeraida nodded quietly. She would miss her husband. She was also worried about not having him around to help protect Emaleen. But she knew his trip was necessary and essential to their safety and their niece's. They needed to put the backup plan in place so that they could use it at a moment's notice, if needed.

Morvin finished his breakfast and then left the house. Later, he returned to the house and went upstairs to get the suitcase that his wife had prepared in advance in case the need should arise. He then kissed his wife, headed out the front door and drove away with Mr. Earl, who was outside waiting for him.

Zeraida then went downstairs to prepare a nice breakfast for Emaleen. She liked to cook for her loved ones when she was stressed. It calmed to her to know that her family was well fed and well cared for. So, she made homemade biscuits, bacon, eggs, and fresh squeezed orange juice. She also put out some jam that she had made recently.

When Emaleen awoke, the first thing she noticed was the smell of baking and sweet jam in the air. She dressed quickly and ran downstairs to find that breakfast was actually an elaborate home-cooked feast. She was pleased because she loved when her aunt made a special meal. But she also knew that although her aunt loved to cook and often made a big breakfast, she only made them on two different occasions. One occasion was when they were celebrating. But Emaleen couldn't think of a reason for a celebration. The other was when her aunt was worried about something.

Emaleen was concerned, but first, she enjoyed the breakfast. She grabbed a handful of small biscuits and put them on a small plate and spread a generous amount of the strawberry jam. As she prepared her biscuits, she breathed in the smell of the buttery biscuits and the sweet strawberry jam and smiled. Emaleen then began to eat the warm biscuits with jam, and she felt peace and happiness. After a few bites of the biscuits, she placed a couple of pieces of hickory-smoked bacon on her plate and poured some orange juice into her glass. The bacon was crisp and sweet tasting, and crunched loudly in her mouth.

Zeraida, in contrast, ate very little but watched Emaleen eat. She had too much on her mind to eat. But it comforted her to see her niece enjoy the meal so much. When she was finished, Emaleen thanked her aunt for the delicious meal. Zeraida then suggested that they go into the family room and sit and relax for a while and have a chat.

Once they were seated, Zeraida said, "Emaleen, I don't want to worry you, but it's necessary to make a change in your training for a little while. You are doing so well with your lessons. But it's important to change direction and start training you on some defensive techniques. As you know, your uncle and I have been monitoring a situation with Maerdern, the seer who abuses his powers and who may wish to try to use your powers for his own bad purposes. We believe that there is no immediate need for you to have to defend yourself. But we have to make sure that you are prepared in case. Please understand, though, that you are not alone. We are here for you, and we are taking all the precautions that we can. You also have a whole family of guardians to help you."

Emaleen was quiet for a moment and then she shared her concerns, saying, "Aunt Zeraida, I am worried. You are too, and you can't really hide it. I may be younger than you, but I do know you and I can see that you are very worried."

"I'm so sorry," answered Zeraida. "I'd really like to shelter you from all of this and to allow you to have a normal and carefree childhood. But you aren't a normal child. You have the potential to have extremely powerful abilities. There will be, and there are, those people in the world who will try to use you and your powers for bad purposes. You'll need to be able to recognize those people for who they are so that you will be able to defend yourself, and stand up for the right thing to do and against evil. Even if you did not have special powers, you would still need to watch out for those who would influence you to do bad things. It's just even more of an issue for you because you do have these powers."

"I understand. I am ready to learn," stated Emaleen with certainty. Then she asked, "Will we be working here or in my workroom upstairs?"

Aunt Zeraida responded, "You will need to work in your workroom as a precaution. These skills create some waves, but they aren't that powerful. I don't think a seer outside this house would be able to sense them, but we need to be careful."

"Please get your journal," instructed Aunt Zeraida. "You will need to take notes as you do with your normal lessons. You may also need to study your notes to memorize the lessons. The skills to protect yourself are so critical that you must know them and be able to perform them without having to think about it."

Emaleen ran up to her room to get her journal. She was eager to get started. It made her nervous that she might need to defend herself against an evil person, and she wanted to get her training started as soon as possible to help her feel safe again. At the moment, she felt vulnerable and at risk, and it made her very uncomfortable and afraid. She knew her aunt, uncle, and guardians would protect her, but she was still worried.

When Emaleen came out of her room, she saw her aunt in the hall. Her aunt signaled for her niece to open the door to the workroom. Once both were inside Emaleen's workroom, Aunt Zeraida started giving Emaleen instructions.

The lessons were slightly different from the earlier ones. Unlike the earlier lessons, in which Emaleen had to discover much of what she was to learn on her own after some basic instructions, in these lessons, Aunt Zeraida gave her niece very specific and direct instructions. She also stopped periodically to make sure that her niece had taken accurate notes so that Emaleen could later study the notes after she was finished working with her aunt.

Aunt Zeraida started by explaining the different types of protection abilities and showed how they fit into categories. She said that she would teach the different abilities by category because the skills in each category shared some common steps. By teaching this way, Aunt Zeraida felt that she could most efficiently teach a group of skills and Emaleen would be more likely to remember a greater number of them.

The first group that Zeraida taught would allow Emaleen to escape or hide herself. These were the easiest to learn. They provided a quick way to create protection that would work in just about any difficult situation.

Emaleen listened intently and took careful notes. When it came time to practice the first ability, Emaleen failed at her first several tries. But she did not give up. She kept trying and when she finally succeeded she felt proud and powerful. Her aunt was also pleased that her niece had not given up. It was a good start to her training in defensive magic.

After learning the first skill, Emaleen progressed through each of the additional skills in that same category. She worked hard on each one, concentrating carefully and making her best efforts to perfect each skill as quickly as she could. The young seer understood the importance of these skills to her safety. She knew that they were necessary for her protection. Aunt Zeraida was surprised and pleased with the speed at which Emaleen was learning and succeeding with each ability.

Chapter 29

Once Emaleen had demonstrated success with each skill in the first category, Zeraida decided that it was time for a break. By that time, it was also almost time for lunch.

Zeraida knew that Emaleen had demonstrated the skills but was not yet proficient at them. But she also knew that what they had done for the morning was physically demanding. So, Zeraida instructed Emaleen to take a rest, even a nap, while she started to make lunch.

Emaleen left her workroom and went downstairs. She then went into the family room and lay down on the couch. Within minutes, she fell fast asleep. The lessons had been intense and packed with a lot of information. There had also been extensive practice for each skill with repetition. As a result, Emaleen was exhausted.

Although the work had made her tired, Emaleen was relieved to know that she had some skills that she could use if she found herself in danger. So, she slept peacefully and deeply.

Zeraida heard Emaleen's snoring all the way out in the kitchen. So, she made some sandwiches, wrapped them in plastic and placed them in the refrigerator so that they would be ready when Emaleen woke from her nap. And then she let her niece sleep as long as she wanted. She thought back to her own training and remembered how tired she was at times, but she had not needed to learn as much in a morning as her niece had learned today. So, Zeraida understood that it was necessary for Emaleen to rest.

After Emaleen woke from her nap, she ate the lunch that her aunt had made for her. She ate in silence as she was thinking about all that she had learned. She hoped that she could remember it all and would be able to use the skills without issue if an emergency arose. Emaleen thought she should do as her aunt suggested and review her notes as if she was studying for a test and wanted an "A." She knew that it was possible that her life might depend upon how well she knew the skills. She hoped, though, that she would never have to use them.

When Emaleen was finished with her lunch, Aunt Zeraida asked her to go back up to her workroom to continue her studies. Aunt Zeraida knew that it would be a lot for one day, but the circumstances required that Emaleen learn as much as she possibly could as quickly as she possibly could.

The skills that Emaleen learned in the afternoon were in a new category of magic that could be used to block an enemy from being able to approach. They required the use of Emaleen's wand. And one involved the creation of an energy field around a seer that acts as a force field to keep persons away. The skills were all very powerful, and the practice of them was very tiring for Emaleen.

Aunt Zeraida next addressed a couple of skills in the blocking category before stopping for the day. She had noticed that Emaleen was becoming exhausted again. And, although it was important for her niece to learn how to protect herself as soon as possible, Zeraida knew that if she went too fast with her instruction that it could be dangerous. It might overtax Emaleen and cause her to become ill, or might cause her to make a mistake in practicing the harder skills that could harm her. So, Zeraida knew she must be careful and not push for too much too soon.

In any event, Emaleen was learning what Zeraida gave her faster than her aunt had expected. And since she had already learned some basic protection skills, Emaleen had, at least, some ability to protect herself. Because of her niece's progress, Zeraida decided that it would be best to stop teaching new skills for a little while and have her niece spend time just practicing the skills taught today to ensure that Emaleen had learned the skills well and could use them easily should a need unfortunately arise.

After the lessons were finished for the day, Zeraida asked Emaleen to join her in the family room. Once the two sat down, Zeraida informed her niece that her uncle had left for another trip, this time with Mr. Earl and Shaolin. Zeraida stated that she was not certain how long they would be away.

"Where have they gone?" asked Emaleen.

"They have gone to do some important business for us," answered Aunt Zeraida.

"Are we safe with Mr. Earl and Uncle gone?" asked Emaleen.

Aunt Zeraida responded, "Yes, we will be safe. I can protect you. But we will need to take extra precautions. When you play outside, I will need to be with you." Fortunately, it was summer vacation and in the fall she would be homeschooled, so there was no need for Emaleen to walk to and from school, thought Zeraida.

Zeraida added, "You will also need to have your wand on you at all times. You should wear it in its bracelet form. You need to be ready at all times for anything."

Emaleen nodded and then Aunt Zeraida stated, "The good news is that Skye and her family are moving in with us for a while. They will need to be here to provide you with extra security to keep you safe. They will be here later today. I will be setting up a bed for Skye in your room. It will be like a sleepover."

Emaleen cheered when she heard that her friend was coming. She had not had a sleepover with Skye for quite a while, and now she was going to have a very long one. She began to think of all of the fun that they would have and the activities that they could engage in.

"You might want to clean up your room and make some drawer space for Skye so she has somewhere to put her clothes. She shouldn't have to live out of a suitcase," suggested Zeraida. "I'm going to freshen up the guest room for Skye's parents while you clean your room. We need to hurry because they will be here soon and we will want them to feel at home right away."

"Also, Emaleen —," started Zeraida, "you will still need to continue your lessons when Skye is here. So, it won't be all fun and games all the time. We must be sure that you have all of your defense skills learned as soon as possible. This is for your protection as well as Skye's, by the way, especially now that she is coming to stay with us to help protect you."

An hour later, Skye arrived with her family. She ran upstairs with her suitcase and joined Emaleen in her room. Emaleen helped her friend unpack and settle in. The girls laughed and giggled loudly.

Zeraida let Emaleen have the rest of the day off so that she and Skye could arrange the room to their liking and then relax and have some fun playing. She knew the girls needed time to themselves.

Skye's parents, Mr. and Mrs. Stewart, settled into the guest room fairly quickly and then went out to join Zeraida in the kitchen for a cup of tea. The adults all sat and discussed the situation and a security strategy while the girls played upstairs.

Zeraida was relieved to have the Stewarts there to help her, especially since her husband, Morvin, had left earlier that morning. The three agreed to set up some security measures that would not be noticed by the girls and to keep everything as calm and normal as possible for as long as possible. They also developed a system of signals that they could use to warn one another if any of them sensed any danger whatsoever.

The Stewarts also had photos of Maerdern and at least twenty of his followers, and had already studied them so that they would be able to recognize any of those people if they came close. Zeraida flipped through each of the photos and studied them carefully. She suggested that they keep the photos away from the girls but that they bring them out periodically when the girls were asleep to go through them. They would refresh their memories so that they would always be alert and able to identify a follower.

Chapter 30

Maerdern had still not yet succeeded in learning any secrets from any of the seer families. It seemed that all of the families that he had approached thus far had figured out that he was up to something, and they all were being extra cautious. He assumed that for the Jaimesons.

Further, Maerdern's spy who had been trying to access the home of the fourth-ranked family, the Watsons, had returned and had reported that the Watson family had fought back against the spy's attempts to befriend the family and gain access to their house. The spy that Maerdern sent to steal secrets from the Watson family found himself unable to even approach the family. It seemed as if the family had expected Maerdern to send someone and they were ready.

Maerdern was not yet ready to give up — he would actually never give up. What he needed, he thought, was a different approach. Perhaps he should focus on the slightly less powerful families and learn all that he could from them. He could then use those skills and information to help him take the information he sought from the three most powerful families. He also had a new idea for centralizing the power of his group.

So, Maerdern gathered together his followers, which were now about thirty in number. He informed them that his plans were going along well, which was a lie, and that he would be establishing an official headquarters. He would also be forming a chain of command and rewarding his most loyal and successful followers with leadership titles. Maerdern would also be providing rewards for successful completion of missions. He would also not tolerate failed missions.

"When we have successfully achieved our goal of dominating the other seers, and I become their rightful ruler, there will be rewards for all of you who have remained with me and served me well," promised Maerdern to his followers. "When we have control over all of the seers, we will demand taxes from them in exchange for providing them with protection and for the privilege of being ruled by us. But I will only favor those of you who have worked hard to help us succeed."

"Right now, I am going to appoint Lanus Aimsley as my second-in-command," continued Maerdern. "But he may not remain my second unless he continues to be my top performer. Any of you could actually bump Lanus from his spot. There are also some other titles that I plan to award, which will fall under Lanus. The more you contribute, the higher the rank I will give you. The higher the rank in our organization, the greater your rewards will be. What I will value most among the contributions you may make is the contribution of money to fund our operations and information about powerful types of magic."

When he heard his name and new role as second-in-command to Maerdern, Lanus, a forty-four-year-old man with black hair and brown eyes, beamed with pride. He also felt a surge as he realized that he was being awarded a great deal of power and favor. He would not let Maerdern down. He would work even harder, and he would push the followers below him to do the same. And, no one would be permitted to steal his rank from him. He would take whatever actions he needed to prevent anyone else from rising any higher than him.

Lanus would also make sure that he continued to feed Maerdern's ego, which he had been doing for a long time now. Lanus had assessed his leader early on and had realized that Maerdern actually had some self-esteem issues of his own and that Lanus could play to that weakness. He had complimented Maerdern excessively so that Maerdern became addicted to the positive feedback he provided. Maerdern had fallen into Lanus' trap and had become dependent upon his good words. Lanus was exactly where he wanted to be — as the second-in-command.

Maerdern went on further, "Tomorrow, I will provide you all with an address for our new headquarters. I want each of you to bring all of the magic books that you have in your own possession. We will store these in our library, and we will use them to consolidate the powers of our entire group. Each of you will also bring the sum of money that I request from you and that money will be used to fund our operations. You may, of course, bring more money than I request and I will remember those of you who do so when I give out the rewards in the future. Some of you will choose to move into my headquarters so that you are prepared to serve me immediately upon my command. I will not require anyone to move into the headquarters, but I will look more favorably upon those that do."

They all listened carefully to Maerdern's proclamations. Most of them were very ambitious and hoped to earn a high rank and power in the organization. So, they were very interested in learning how best to please their leader. Maerdern had selected this group well. Many of these people would do just about anything for money, power, or both.

After he had finished his speech to them, Maerdern dismissed all of his followers with instructions for them to return by nine o'clock the next morning with their books and their money, when he would then give them new assignments. He also informed them that anyone who was late or did not bring what was required would be punished.

After his followers had left, Maerdern sat quietly reflecting upon this plan. It was to gather all of the magic information that he could from his followers into his own library and assign a few select inner-circle members of the organization to the task of cataloging the magic skills. Maerdern would then go through the list and identify magic that he did not already know. Then he would teach himself the magic he was missing. He would keep the books locked up so that the rest of his followers could not learn from them and become as powerful or more powerful than him.

He would then use the information from his followers' books to gain further information about magic from other families who were not members of his organization. He would start with some families with less power than the three most powerful families. These less powerful families, he thought, might not be on guard and would, therefore, not be actively involved in protecting their books. It should be easy to steal their books, he thought.

As Maerdern gathered information about magic, he expected that he would become more and more powerful. Once Maerdern had gathered as much information as he could from the other families, he would then once again attempt to steal magic from the three most powerful families. When he was powerful enough, he expected to try to obtain additional magic by force. But he knew to do so he must first be sure that he was powerful enough to challenge the families.

All the while, Maerdern would continue to seek an apprentice. He would send one of his followers out to research Mrs. Andarsan's pregnancy to see if she had, in fact, lost that pregnancy years ago or whether she might have a child in hiding. Maerdern suspected that there was no such child, but he would leave no stone unturned in his quest for ultimate power. He would send his most clever, most powerful follower out to pick up the trail that Mrs. Andarsan had followed when she was pregnant and allegedly lost the child, to determine the truth.

Once he was finished thinking over his plans, Maerdern made the arrangements for his new headquarters, which were to be located in the same town that the Andarsans lived in. Maerdern had this notion that the Andarsans would be key, in some way, to him achieving his plans of dominating over all of the seers and becoming their leader.

The house that he selected was a large country estate that was three stories high and was one of the largest, if not the largest, house in town. It also had many acres of land upon which a barn, several storage sheds, and an in-ground pool were situated.

The house was located on the edge of town in a somewhat remote area. It had been vacant for many years, and Maerdern had tried to keep his purchase of it secret. It was set off far from the road and was hidden from view by trees and a hill that were in front of the house. Maerdern hoped that his occupancy of the house could remain a secret or, at least, that it was far enough outside of town that his activities would not gain notice.

Maerdern arranged for the remodeling of the house so that it included a luxurious bedroom for himself and a separate, yet much smaller room for his second-in-command. Maerdern and Lanus would also have the highest quality meals and full, unlimited access to the pool.

All of the other followers were to be given shared bedrooms in which they would sleep on cots. The rooms for the other followers varied in their level of comfort and privileges in the household, including the quality of the meals they would get and whether they would have pool privileges.

It was Maerdern's plan to match the comfort of the quarters to the rank of each follower. The lowest members would have the most basic privileges, including a cot with a thin, coarse blanket and the right to a very simple meal of soup and bread. The higher ranked members could have nicer beds and access to the pool. They could also have more luxurious meals.

Chapter 31

Maerdern had thought that his headquarters would be secret. But, he did not take into account the gossip that occurs in a small town. Very shortly after he moved in and set up the house, the news spread in the community that a strange man had moved into the largest house in town and had many other unrelated persons move in with him.

There were many different theories circulating about Maerdern and his reasons for moving into the large house with his followers. Most of the theories revolved around Maerdern's group being a cult of some sort. And, it wasn't long before the news was known throughout the community. So, it wasn't long before the Andarsans learned about the new headquarters.

The Andarsans had mixed feelings about Maerdern moving into a house in their community. On one hand, it would allow them to keep an eye on the evil seer and perhaps place a spy in his household. On the other hand, they assumed correctly that Maerdern would be keeping an even closer eye on them than he had before. That meant that it would be difficult for them to make any trips without Maerdern and his followers noticing.

And, of course, Maerdern's vicinity made it almost impossible for the Andarsans to risk a trip to meet their daughter. It was heartbreaking for them since they had sacrificed so much to keep their daughter safe and they wanted nothing more than to meet her and explain to her why they had done what they did. They had hoped soon to be able to secret themselves away unnoticed and reunite with their daughter. They wanted to hug and talk to their daughter. But Maerdern's move made that impossible.

Until circumstances changed, the Andarsans would have to content themselves with doing as much as they possibly could to thwart any plans made by Maerdern. To do that, they needed information about what the evil seer was doing. They would need a spy inside his household. They already had a spy keeping watch on him outside the household and following him wherever he went. But they would obtain more information if they had a spy right inside the house that he had just set up as a headquarters.

Their opportunity to place a spy in Maerdern's household came soon after he set it up. That's when Maerdern posted an advertisement in the local newspaper seeking a housekeeper.

The Andarsans secretly sent word through their friend, Mr. Cavanaugh, to a guardian family that they were friends with. They asked the family to send to Maerdern, as a job applicant, a guardian who was not already a protector for a seer. They also needed the person to be someone who Maerdern would not be likely to know was a guardian. This person would be sent to apply for the housekeeper position to keep an eye on Maerdern from inside the house.

The guardian family, the Reids, actually sent two family members: a male named Thomas, who was twenty-two years old, and a female named Eugenia, who was twenty-eight years old. They were brother and sister. The Reids sent two persons to increase the chances that one of the family members would be hired.

The Andarsans' plan worked perfectly. In fact, although Maerdern had advertised only one position with the household, he ended up hiring both Thomas and Eugenia, which was even better than the Andarsans could have hoped for. The two of them, both on the household staff, could gather so much more information than just one could have. Thomas would be able to access places that Eugenia couldn't access and vice versa. Thomas was hired as a driver and a groundskeeper while Eugenia was hired to clean. Thomas would get to see wherever Maerdern traveled to, and Eugenia would be able to access all areas of the house.

The Andarsans knew that the difficulty of their plan would be for Thomas and Eugenia to pass information to them without Maerdern or any of his followers catching on. But they thought that they would just have to figure that out later. What was important to them right then was that they had planted some spies in Maerdern's household. Those spies would need to work in the household for a while and build Maerdern's trust before they could really start to dig for information. But they would also have to be careful not to become too involved in the household so that they would be unable to leave easily or they would become involved in matters that they did not feel comfortable with. It was a delicate balance that would be hard for the two to navigate. In any event, for a while, they would just have to observe carefully and pick up whatever information they could that way.

Eugenia was the first to discover helpful information after she had started her new position. Eugenia had access to all of the rooms in the house for cleaning purposes except for one room that was always locked. The locked room had made Eugenia very curious. She felt that there must be something very secret in that room if the maid could never get in to clean it. But she knew she could not steal the keys and let herself in the room. If she were to do that and she was caught, it could be very dangerous for her. She had to wait for a time when she was invited.

Her patience finally paid off while she was cleaning the room next to the mystery room. While she was cleaning, she heard a loud explosion, followed immediately by a strong smell of gas. She ran over to the door and knocked repeatedly and loudly. When no one answered her frantic knocks, Eugenia yelled out, asking if anyone needed any help and was hurt. Still no one answered, so Eugenia just stood there waiting.

Her waiting was rewarded because, after several minutes, Maerdern came to the door and opened it. He saw the concerned look on Eugenia's face and immediately informed her that nothing was wrong. He told Eugenia that he had just had an accident and made a large mess that was going to be difficult to clean up, but he was unhurt. Eugenia offered to clean up whatever mess was inside the room.

Maerdern hesitated for a moment because he did not want anyone in the room. It was where he had located all the magic books he had collected, and it was where he was practicing magic that he was learning from the books. He didn't want any other seers to be learning the magic or knowing what Maerdern was learning. But he decided to let Eugenia in to clean since he couldn't work in such a mess. Also, since she wasn't a seer, she probably wouldn't know what the books were, anyway. She would probably just think they were antique books that Maerdern was collecting as an investment. So Maerdern allowed Eugenia to enter the room and then he left the room while she began to clean. He would return and restart his work when the mess was cleaned up.

"Don't let anyone in here," Maerdern warned Eugenia sternly. "And don't touch any of my books. They are very valuable and not replaceable. When you are done, lock the door behind you."

Eugenia nodded and then looked around the room. She gasped with surprise when she noticed that there was a grayish powder all over the floor and the furniture. The powder was on just about everything except it was not on any of the books. Somehow, the books had escaped the disaster.

"This is probably going to take me hours," Eugenia called over her shoulder to Maerdern. She wanted to buy as much time as possible to allow her to do the cleaning and still have time to look around. It's too bad, she thought, that she wasn't a seer so that she could clean up quickly using magic. Maerdern was a fool, she thought, not to have used his own magic to clean this up. Either that or he was lazy. But his flaw was to her advantage since it was getting her into this room.

"I suggest you get started right away then and be quick," demanded Maerdern sternly. "I want this room back within the hour." Maerdern exited the room.

Eugenia looked around some more and realized that she was going to need more than the broom that she had in her hands to clean up this mess. So she turned to leave the room to get a vacuum. Since she wasn't sure whether she would be locked out if she closed the door behind her, Eugenia propped the door open with a chair and then hurried to get the vacuum, which was in a closet down the hall.

When Eugenia returned to the room, she shut the door behind her. She put a chair under the doorknob so that should anyone try to get into the room, the door would appear stuck and it would provide her with warning that someone was coming. She did not want to be surprised by Maerdern returning before she expected him.

Then Eugenia turned the vacuum on so that it would sound like she was working. While the vacuum was running, Eugenia surveyed the room. On three walls were bookcases that started on the floor and rose all the way up to the ceiling. Only one bookshelf had any books on it, though, and there were about fifty by Eugenia's rough count.

In the middle of the room was a desk. But the desk was covered in the grayish powder. So, Eugenia brought her vacuum and cleaned the powder off of the desk to reveal what was on it. Under all of that powder was a magic book that was opened to a page on wands and that explained how to disguise a wand as another object so that it could be carried around without the norms realizing that the seer had a wand. Most seers that Eugenia knew already knew how to accomplish that magic, so it did not impress her. She chuckled to herself, though, because it seemed to Eugenia that the explosion must have been caused by Maerdern practicing the magic of changing a wand into another object, and it looked as if he had failed what was actually a simple task. Maerdern was not very bright, thought Eugenia, who usually did not like to think badly of people.

Eugenia next shifted her focus to the drawers in the desk. There might be something more useful inside the desk, she thought. So, she started to pull one drawer out at a time. The first drawer only contained paper, pens, and pencils. The second drawer, however, contained a worn leather book about the size of a paperback novel. Eugenia pulled the book out of the drawer and flipped it open. On the first page was a notation indicating that the book was the diary of Maerdern. Eugenia flipped through the pages generally and noticed that there were many pages of writing. She put the book down momentarily while she vacuumed the chair so that she could sit down on it. Then she sat on the chair and read the diary, skimming it quickly to gain as much information from it as possible. She needed to hurry and finish her spying before Maerdern returned.

The diary was all about Maerdern's ideas to obtain as much magic knowledge as possible so that he could become the leader of all the seers. It contained lists of the various seer families and the names of the family members, and the guardian families and names of the family members. Eugenia did not know the names of all of the seers, but some of the seers that she knew were not on the list, such as Mrs. Andarsan's sister, Zeraida. Some of the seer family names were starred, which Eugenia interpreted to mean that they were targets of Maerdern. She also noticed that her family's name was not on the list of guardians, which was fortunate.

Maerdern's journal also set out his plans for how he would obtain the magic, which included stealing it from other families by force. There was also a section of the book about his suspicions about Mrs. Andarsan's alleged pregnancy loss and his suspicion that the child had actually survived. The book described Maerdern's efforts thus far to investigate. To Eugenia's relief, Maerdern had not yet figured out that Emaleen was alive and was potentially a very powerful seer. But Maerdern had hired a private investigator, who was investigating and had not yet reported his findings. Eugenia made note of this diary and hoped that she would be able to return to this room to read it periodically so she could keep track of Maerdern's investigation.

After flipping through the book and skimming it quickly, Eugenia pulled a small camera out of her pocket and took pictures of each page of the book. She would somehow send these photos over to the Andarsans.

When she had finished copying it, Eugenia put the book back in the desk and checked the third drawer. This drawer contained financial information showing how much money Maerdern had in his organization's bank accounts as well as the sources of his income and donations from his members. Eugenia was surprised to see that

Maerdern had amassed £500,000 and was currently bringing in donations from his members of about £30,000 a week. The records also showed Maerdern's monthly outlays for the expenses of the house. Eugenia returned the financial records to the drawer she had found them in, careful to stack them in the same order that they had been in before she had removed them in case Maerdern may be keeping track of the arrangement of the items in the drawer.

She then returned to her cleaning efforts while continuing to look around the room. She dusted the books, and as she took each book down from the shelf, she flipped through it quickly, reading the titles of the magic skills on each page. She was looking for any magic that looked unusual or that might be a danger for Maerdern to have.

Although she was not a seer herself, she had been around seers long enough to know the types of magic that were of general, ordinary use and the types that could be dangerous in the hands of an evil seer. She had perused through about twenty of the books before she felt that any further time spent searching through them was too risky. So, she stopped looking through the books and just dusted them on the shelves. But from what she had seen, Maerdern did not yet have any information about magic that posed a threat to the other seers.

As she dusted, she continued to observe everything in the room. She noted a closet and some end tables next to some comfortable leather chairs. The closet interested Eugenia, but she was afraid to stop her work and risk the possibility of getting caught by Maerdern.

It would also be a great idea, she thought, to unjam the door in case he returned. If Maerdern had returned before she was ready, she did have an explanation for the door jam, but it would be better if there were no door jam for her to explain. She did not want to arouse any suspicion, particularly since she had discovered a good source of information, and she did not want to lose her access. But, more importantly, she did not want to put herself in danger.

As Eugenia continued to vacuum, she glanced around at the various books on the shelves. The books were all old looking, and each had a name on the spine that appeared to be the last name of a seer family. Eugenia realized immediately that these were the hereditary magic books of various families.

Maerdern must be gathering these and practicing to increase his magic skills, she thought. What if she were to take some of them, she wondered? She considered doing so but then realized that Maerdern might miss them and if he suspected her, that could put her in danger.

Eugenia had just finished and was turning off the vacuum and winding up the cord when Maerdern returned. He immediately motioned for Eugenia to leave the room, and she complied quickly. Maerdern didn't seem to suspect that Eugenia had been snooping in his secret library. Eugenia kept herself calm and as normal as possible to avoid causing him to become suspicious as she quickly left the room to return to her other cleaning duties.

Maerdern suddenly shouted out after her, "Please come back in here, Eugenia!"

Eugenia froze with fear. She was afraid that Maerdern might be suspicious. But she slowly turned and returned to the room, acting as if everything was normal.

"I'd like you to come in here and clean once a week, on Fridays," ordered Maerdern bluntly. "I will let you in." Eugenia smiled. This would allow her to keep tabs on what Maerdern was doing.

"Yes, sir," replied Eugenia. She then curtsied slightly, a move that inflated Maerdern's ego further. It was a smart move on her part. Then she left the room.

Chapter 32

Skye and Emaleen were enjoying Skye's stay at Emaleen's house. It was like a continuous slumber party at night. The girls were often tired, though, because they weren't sleeping well. They were often up all night giggling, playing games, and using their computers.

By day, Emaleen continued her magic studies with Zeraida. After practicing many different types of defensive magic and becoming comfortable with them, Emaleen started to learn some offensive magic, studying some very specific attacks that could be used against an enemy. But none of the offensive attacks were of a type that could cause a fatality or a serious permanent injury. They were all simply intended to inconvenience and potentially delay an opponent.

Emaleen was also learning counter-magic skills, which were ways to halt or reverse magic that another seer might use against her or others. For Emaleen to study these types of magic, Zeraida had to cast some magic against Emaleen so that she would have magic to counter.

None of the magic that Zeraida cast was powerful enough to harm her niece. She used just enough so that her niece could sense the magic as it came at her, which was necessary to be able to counter it.

Zeraida also slowed the training, carefully teaching Emaleen techniques and advancing to the next skill only after she was sure that her niece had mastered the technique. When it was time for Emaleen to learn to counter more powerful magic, Zeraida had her cast a powerful defensive magic that created a force field of protection that resembled a blue bubble. That way, Emaleen could have a powerful magic to counter, but with little risk that the powerful magic would harm Emaleen if she failed. Zeraida was an expert teacher, who had taught many family members, including her own sister, Seanna Andarsan. So, Zeraida knew how to train safely.

Skye had also been training with her mother, Angelina Stewart. Skye had been learning the history of the guardians along with the value system and ethics of the guardians. Mrs. Stewart had also been teaching Skye about the various types of abilities and powers that a guardian had.

Angelina instructed Skye, "Even though the guardians do not have magic like the seers they protect, guardians have certain talents and abilities that the seers do not. For instance, a guardian will typically serve as an extra pair of eyes and ears for his or her seer, but the eyes and ears of the guardian sense more than a normal person or a seer would."

Mrs. Stewart continued, "A guardian typically has an intuitive ability that allows the guardian to assess people, including their motivations and intentions, and use these assessments to interpret what they see and hear. Thus, a guardian does not see and hear anything just at its face value but is often able to derive a deeper real meaning. A guardian who observes carefully can detect attempts by any person to fool and deceive the seer who the guardian is protecting."

Skye listened carefully to her mom and then commented, "It sounds like a guardian is a seer for the seer, in some ways."

"Yes, you might say that," responded her mother. "The guardian sees in a different way than the seer, though. Guardians have an intuitive sense about people."

"A guardian also comes to know his or her seer very well," explained Mrs. Stewart further, "so that the guardian is also able to assess the seer. A guardian can often sense a seer's own internal vulnerabilities, such as fear, unhappiness, and self-doubt, and can help his or her seer overcome them so that these feelings do not create a danger to the welfare of the seer."

"Is that all we do?" asked Skye. "Do we only size other people up and try to figure them out?"

"No," answered Mrs. Stewart. "A guardian is also a security guard of sorts. A guardian can sense danger that may be approaching a seer, such as another seer with malice for the seer that the guardian protects, or norms that may be a risk to the physical security of the seer. A guardian can provide a warning, or in the case of a physical security risk, a guardian has great strength and training that allow him or her to engage in hand-to-hand physical combat to protect the seer."

Angelina Stewart worked hard to train her daughter in all these skills as quickly as possible as she feared that Skye might need these skills in the very near future to protect Emaleen. Skye was happy to train because she loved Emaleen and wanted to be prepared to protect her should danger arise.

Despite all of the hard training, however, both of the girls still had time for fun. Angelina and Zeraida felt that it was important for them to have an outlet to relieve any stress that they might be feeling. After all, they were children, and although they could not be protected from the reality that Emaleen could be in personal danger, it was important to protect the children from being afraid and feeling anxiety as much as possible. It was also not good for any person, especially children, to have excessive stress and anxiety without any means to relieve them.

So, there were special projects and some special outings to balance out all of the serious hard work and worries. One such trip involved going to an amusement park with a water park, for the day, with the girls and ladies wearing disguises. Another trip was a visit to a unique elevated walkway up in the trees at a museum in the Adirondacks.

But Angelina and Zeraida kept the outings somewhat limited in number. Outings were a risk since being in public limited how the seers could respond with their magic. Also, there were so many people around that it could be difficult for the guardians to detect dangers against Emaleen. At the same time, a public outing could potentially limit the risk since there were so many people around that Maerdern himself might be concerned about revealing his magic or they might be able to lose Maerdern easily in the crowd. Also, they had not yet had any indication that Maerdern had any knowledge about Emaleen or her location. In any event, they still needed to be very careful.

Mrs. Stewart also used the outings as teaching tools. She would pull her daughter aside and ask her to observe people and provide her intuitive assessment of them. She would assist by pointing out details that Skye missed. Skye needed as much practice as possible to be able to read people to determine their intentions so that she could protect Emaleen. Skye would need to be an expert at reading people.

During this time, Emaleen was also learning the traditional lessons that she would normally be learning, in addition to the defensive and offensive magic used to protect herself. For instance, she was learning about the world and the forces of nature and how she could, after the right training, affect the forces of nature, such as making it rain in a small area. She was also learning how to use such powers responsibly to assist humankind and not only upon a simple whim.

Zeraida had allowed her niece to start exploring her library and reading the family magic books. Emaleen was practicing her magic more and more often in her aunt's special room under her aunt's close supervision because the magic she was practicing was complicated and risky. Zeraida also wanted her books to remain in her own workroom.

There were some books that Zeraida had specifically asked Emaleen not to work with yet. They were books full of bad types of magic that Zeraida had been keeping only for the purpose of keeping the magic they contained away from people like Maerdern, who would use it for evil purposes. It was the kind of magic for which it was difficult to imagine a good purpose. So, there was no reason for Emaleen to learn any of it at this time. But it was important for Emaleen to know about the existence of such magic and the importance of keeping it from getting into the wrong hands. Zeraida informed her niece that there might be a time in the future that she would have to learn that magic — just in case. So, Emaleen was allowed to review those books, but not use the magic in them.

When Emaleen had worked her way through her aunt's library, Zeraida planned to have her work in her uncle's library. She wanted Emaleen to have all the potential powers that she could have so that her niece could protect herself and protect the future of all the seers. The other seers did not know it yet, but Emaleen was very important to the well-being of all of them. Zeraida would need to school her well.

Emaleen was also learning how to heal people and animals of their ills. She had discovered by accident recently that one of her gems gave her the power to heal wounds. When she had been practicing her magic one day, Belenus had come inside the house through the cat door that had been recently built for him. He approached Emaleen and held out one of his paws to show a cut on it. Emaleen took his paw into her hand, and as she did so, she noticed that one of her gems was glowing. She closed her eyes and concentrated hard and imagined Belenus' cut healing. When she opened her eyes, the cut was gone. It was as if she knew how to heal by instinct alone.

When Belenus realized that his pain was gone, he started purring softly and rubbing himself against Emaleen's legs. He loved her very much.

When Emaleen reported this new discovery to her aunt, she learned that there were limits to the healing power. She would only be able to heal when the wound or injury was one that would eventually heal, like sprains, cuts, broken bones, and infections. The magic she used resulted in a speedier healing, by helping expedite the body's natural healing process. Emaleen could not heal any injury or illness that a person's body could not eventually cure on its own, such as cancer. She also could not restore life to a person who had died.

Many weeks had gone by since Emaleen's training had become so intense and Skye and her family had moved into the house. The summer would soon be coming to a close and school would be beginning again. Emaleen already knew that she would not be going back to school but would be homeschooling with Aunt Zeraida instead. Aunt Zeraida had started to get the school material together and had ordered books online, and it seemed like school books were arriving on a daily basis. It seemed like Aunt Zeraida expected Emaleen to be doing a lot of reading and studying.

Emaleen didn't know if Skye would be returning to school or if she, too, would be homeschooled. She would need to ask Skye about that soon. She hoped that Skye would be homeschooling with her.

Chapter 33

One morning in early fall, Angelina and Zeraida arranged a camping trip for a few days for the ladies and the girls to one of the small islands in Blue Mountain Lake, which they traveled to by canoe. When they left for their trip, it was a beautiful day with only a few white, fluffy clouds in the sky and an air temperature of about eighty degrees Fahrenheit. It was unseasonably warm. The water was cool, but not cold, and the sunlight reflected off of small ripples in the lake.

The trip was intended, in part, as a relaxing break, but it also had a training purpose. Recently, thought Emaleen, everything that they did had some training purpose. But it was fine with Emaleen. She was learning vast amounts of material in a short time, and she was enjoying the lessons and increasing her magic abilities. She was excited to see what she would be learning today and couldn't wait to get to the island.

She also enjoyed the field trips, such as this trip to the island, even if it wasn't completely recreational. Today, she was especially looking forward to camping, which they had not done in a while.

The ladies used two different canoes to travel across the lake to the island. Mother and daughter were in one canoe and aunt and niece in the other. The lake was about twelve hundred acres in all and was surrounded by mountains and lots of pine trees along the shore. There was a slight breeze, but the water was mostly still with small ripples that day as the ladies paddled the canoes.

Once on the island, the ladies and girls checked to see if anyone else was on the small island, but they found it to be empty. Then they unloaded their supplies from the canoes and set up their campsite with two tents around the fire pit.

When they were finished setting up, Zeraida said to Emaleen, "We are going to be practicing some special magic while on the island over the next few days. One skill we will practice will be a defensive magic that will involve placing a blue bubble around the entire island to shield it from view and prevent anyone from entering."

Zeraida had chosen the island because the shield was a very powerful magic, the casting of which would create large vibrations that could normally be felt far away by other seers. But a large body of water also tended to absorb the vibrations so that they could not be felt beyond the island. So, an island was a perfect place for her niece to exercise this kind of magic.

This particular island was also far away from any main road that may run along the shore of the lake. It was also near a section of the lake where most of the homes on the shore were summer camps. Since it was early fall, these homes would likely be vacant. Thus, there were unlikely to be any observers who might see their actions on the island.

Zeraida started her instruction by saying to Emaleen, "We are going to start making the magic blue bubble around the island by painting many of a certain kind of rock blue and placing the blue rocks around the perimeter of the island."

Holding up one of the rocks as a sample, Zeraida said to her niece, "Here is one of those rocks. I would like you and Skye to collect these rocks and put them in a pile right here."

"Skye!" called Emaleen excitedly. "We're going to create a magic blue bubble. Would you like to help me?"

"Yes," answered Skye with excitement. "How?"

"Come with me and I will show you," requested Emaleen.

Emaleen asked her aunt, "How many rocks do we need?"

Her aunt answered, "It depends upon the sizes and shapes of what you collect. You collect them and put them here, and I will let you know when we have enough."

The girls ran off together to gather rocks. Emaleen showed Skye the kind of rock that was necessary. Then the two girls gathered up a lot of rocks in their hands and carried them in batches to the spot that Zeraida had indicated. After about thirty rocks had been placed in the pile, Aunt Zeraida let them know there were enough.

Then, Aunt Zeraida brought out some blue paint and paint brushes and asked, "Who would like to paint?"

The girls jumped up and down with excitement, shouting, "I do! I do!"

"Paint each rock blue on all sides. First, paint the tops and then when the tops dry, we will turn the rocks over and paint all of the bottoms," instructed Zeraida.

"Can we paint designs on the rocks?" asked Emaleen hopefully.

"Not today," replied Zeraida. "These rocks must be uniformly painted blue so that the magic works correctly. But tomorrow, we can have an art class if you girls would like to express your creativity."

"That would be fun," remarked Skye. Emaleen nodded her head in agreement. The girls then began to paint the tops of the rocks and were finished in about a half hour. Once the girls had painted the tops, Aunt Zeraida suggested they take a break while the rocks dried.

"Why don't you girls have a swim?" said Mrs. Stewart. It was very hot, and the girls needed to cool off a little. They agreed and ran off to swim. They had their swimsuits on under their clothes, so it didn't take them long to get into the water. The water was cold but bearable.

"Stay close to the shore, where we can see you," instructed Mrs. Stewart.

"Okay," shouted back the girls.

While the girls swam, Zeraida used some mild magic to cause some light winds to blow over the top of the rocks to dry them more quickly. When the rocks were dry, Zeraida flipped them over, and she and Angelina began to paint the other sides. They could have called the girls back, but the two women had decided to let the girls swim just a little while longer.

After they had finished painting the other sides, Zeraida caused wind to blow over them again, drying them more quickly. When they were dry, the rocks were all uniformly a dark blue color. Aunt Zeraida called the girls back from their swimming so that they could help set up the rocks for the magic.

When the girls had returned from swimming and had put swimming cover-ups on, Zeraida directed, "Girls, we are going to need to place these rocks around the edge of the island. You will need to put them close to the shore, but not in the water. When we are done, they will form one big circle around the island."

"The rocks should be about this far apart from each other," Aunt Zeraida informed them, holding her arms out to her sides to show the correct distance between the rocks.

Mrs. Stewart suggested, "Let's split into two teams and go in opposite directions. When we meet back up, we will have closed the circle."

"That's a good idea," commented Aunt Zeraida. "Emaleen, you are on my team, and Skye you are on your mom's team."

The ladies proceeded to lay the rocks around the island. When they met up again on the other side of the island, the circle was complete.

"Now, please come with me to the center of the island," requested Aunt Zeraida when the teams met up.

They all walked together to the center of the island. In the center, they found a fire pit. Zeraida asked the girls to gather some twigs and brush to start a fire and then some larger sticks and pieces of wood.

Once the girls had gathered a fairly large pile of twigs and brush, Zeraida arranged them in the center of the fire pit. Then she lit them and then blew gently on the sparking pile. Once a flame started, Zeraida slowly started putting larger twigs and branches on the fire and then finally some large pieces of wood. When the fire was going fairly well and not in danger of extinguishing, Aunt Zeraida said she would be right back.

When Zeraida returned, she was holding a small metal pot. She placed the pot in the middle of the fire.

"Emaleen," called Aunt Zeraida. "Wave your wand over the pot. And while you do that, think of stirring the contents of the pot, like you would mix together the ingredients for a cake."

Emaleen turned her bracelet back into a wand and then waved the wand over the pot as her aunt instructed. Moments later, the pot began to smoke and then a blue flame arose from it. Emaleen also noticed a light earthy and fruity scent that seemed to be coming from the strangely burning pot.

"What's in the pot?" asked Skye curiously. Emaleen wanted to know, too, but Skye had spoken first. So, Emaleen waited patiently and let her friend ask the questions.

"The pot contains blueberry seed oil and blue cypress wood oil, and a secret ingredient, which were all made into a blue powder using a recipe known only to seers," answered Zeraida.

"What does the blue flame do?" asked Skye, rapidly firing out her questions. "How is the fire blue? What is happening inside the pot?"

Aunt Zeraida laughed softly and commented, "So many questions, Skye. You usually are so quiet. But I like it. You should ask me questions. You need to learn, too. And, when you ask questions, your questions may also help Emaleen learn more."

Aunt Zeraida continued, "The blue flame is not hot, but is cool to the touch. The blue flame is also technically not a flame. It's a chemical reaction between the three substances together with the power generated from Emaleen's wand. It results in a flickering release of gas that resembles a flame."

"When the magic is invoked," Zeraida continued, "a person out on the lake sees only water where the island should be. And, the border created by the rocks is so thick that it covers the entire island without the rocks having to be on the very edges of the island. The magic also prevents any person from approaching the island because the magic creates powerful currents that pull watercraft away from the island."

"Let's show the girls how this works," suggested Zeraida to Angelina. "Can you take them out on the canoe and show them how the island is invisible? After you've been gone for about a couple of minutes, I will extinguish the blue flame, and the island will reappear and then you may return."

Mrs. Stewart agreed and took the girls out in the canoes. Once they were a short distance away from the shore, the girls noticed that it seemed as if the island had suddenly vanished. Wow, thought Emaleen.

She couldn't believe that there was magic that could make an entire island disappear.

After sitting out in the water for a couple of minutes, the girls saw the island suddenly appear again. Mrs. Stewart then brought the girls back to the island and they returned to find Zeraida.

"We're going to use this island for some other magic lessons, Emaleen," stated Aunt Zeraida when Emaleen returned. "Before we do that, though, I am going to restart the blue flame and make this island invisible again so that the norms can't see what we are doing."

Over the course of the next several days, Emaleen learned other skills such as moving clouds to make it rain in a small location, making it snow in the fall when it was still quite warm out, creating a natural thick fog, and moving out the clouds to reveal a clear blue sky.

As Emaleen learned these skills, she thought about how learning how to create snow could have been useful during the school year. If she had learned that magic last year, she might have created some snowstorms simply for the purpose of forcing the school to declare a snow day. But upon further thought, she was sure that her aunt would not approve of her using magic abilities for such purposes. Her aunt certainly would think it an abuse of the power.

Emaleen and Skye also learned some survival skills, such as making shelters out of tree branches, fishing, and cooking on a campfire. Hopefully, Emaleen would never have to rely on these skills for her safety and survival, but it was Zeraida's view that it was very important for her niece to learn these skills. It might be necessary at some point in the future for her to have these survival skills.

She also learned from her aunt about different herbs and plants that could be used for healing and general medicinal purposes. Aunt Zeraida wanted Emaleen to be as self-sufficient as possible.

When they had finished the various training activities, they extinguished the blue flame and gathered the blue rocks. Then they dug a big hole and buried them. They did not want anyone to find the rocks. When they had finished, they packed up and returned home.

Chapter 34

Maerdern's efforts to obtain magic books of seer families was finally starting to pay off since he had recently switched tactics and had decided to target a family much less powerful than one of the three most powerful. He had chosen to focus on obtaining magic from the family that he believed to be the seventh most powerful family.

This family was among the families that had shared information about Maerdern and were supposed to be keeping a watch out for him. But when Maerdern arrived in their town, he found that they had foolishly left their home locked, but otherwise unattended and unprotected by magic. They had decided to go on vacation and had not heeded the warnings of the other seer families who warned that homes should be secured and protected so that Maerdern could not gain access. So, Maerdern was able to have two of his helpers destroy the door by manual force and break into the house with ease.

Once inside the house, Maerdern entered the family's library and started searching through their books. Maerdern did not see any magic books containing rare secrets, which he thought were often kept together in a special type of book. All he saw, at first, were books that contained information about those magic secrets that were more commonly known to seers.

But still, the library did contain information about magic that Maerdern did not know, but the magic was not rare or very powerful. Maerdern determined the content of each book by the title of the book only. He did not take the time to actually read through or even skim any of the books. Maerdern just directed his followers to load the books he felt were of interest into boxes and carry them out of the house to be brought to his library.

Little did Maerdern realize there actually were some books in that library that contained rare magic of the type that Maerdern was looking for. But these magic skills were hidden in books about very ordinary magic of little interest to Maerdern such as how to clean a house with little physical effort. Not having been raised by seers, Maerdern did not know that some of the families hid their best magic in the ordinary books to protect it from intruders.

Maerdern also explored around the rest of the house, looking for other useful items since he was already there. Looking around, Maerdern noted that there were a lot of valuables around. He could use some more money, he thought, to fund his operations. It was very expensive to pay for his followers' care, including lodging, meals, and travel. The current weekly donations from his members were just barely enough to keep up with the weekly expenses of the membership.

At some point, rationalized Maerdern, this seer family would be paying him taxes when he became their leader. It made sense to him that the family should now contribute. So, he ordered his followers to gather up some of the valuables so that they could be sold and the money used for funding his operations. They gathered up silver, electronics, and cash that they found.

After gathering the books and valuables from the house, Maerdern and his followers left to return to their headquarters. Once there, the followers unloaded the books into the library. When they were finished, Maerdern directed the followers to take the valuables — other than the cash, which Maerdern pocketed — to a pawn shop to sell the items.

Maerdern then resumed his work of going through the books and looking for magic that would be useful for accomplishing his plan of dominating the seers. The evil seer ignored any magic that would be useful to humankind or that would be of general beneficial use since he cared only about conquering the other seers. He was not interested in any magic that would not serve his own specific, selfish purposes.

He worked day and night reading the new magic volumes, stopping only occasionally for short naps. Maerdern did not get a good night's sleep for at least two weeks. Often, during this time, he found magic that was generally useful to his efforts, but he did not find any magic that was of such an extraordinary power that it would give him a great advantage. But he kept reading on, hoping that he would discover some magic that could be so useful. In any event, there could be no dispute that his power was growing as he read through the books he had newly obtained and practiced the many magic skills he found explained in them.

When he reached the last of the books, he was encouraged by the magic he found in the first few pages of that book. Those pages provided instruction on magic that could be used in a fight, both offensively and defensively. The book also explained how to break down doors and break locks with magic. Maerdern did not have many of these skills already himself so that magic was very useful to him. The magic could particularly be useful for Maerdern in breaking into other seer homes and stealing additional magic.

Maerdern practiced the new magic skills in this last book many times, slowly becoming more and more powerful. After he was confident that he had sufficient skills in this new magic, he felt ready to approach and hold his own against a family that was more aware of his efforts to steal magic and who would put up a fight. So, Maerdern started to form a plan for obtaining more powerful magic from one of the three most powerful families, by force. His plan involved the one powerful family, besides the Andarsans, who he had not tried yet, and he decided to confront them directly himself instead of sending a follower.

This particular family was the Caravagio family, and they lived in Rome, Italy, on the outskirts of the city. That family included two parents and two grown children who had not yet left their parents' home. All of them were very powerful seers. They would be difficult opponents for Maerdern.

Chapter 35

When Maerdern arrived in Rome with his two followers, Baldolf and Rycroft, he was impressed by the beauty of the city. From the airport, he took a taxi cab to the hotel where he would be staying. It, too, was on the outskirts of the city like the home of the Caravagio family. In fact, his hotel was within walking distance of the home.

The taxi ride from the airport to the hotel was very different from any other trips he had taken before. It seemed to Maerdern like he was riding around in circles, and that he rode across the Tiber River multiple times until he arrived at the hotel. The taxi drove around numerous beautiful piazzas, containing beautiful fountains, sculptures, and fine works of architecture.

Maerdern noticed the beauty of the art that he passed, but he was primarily thinking about the upcoming fight with the Caravagio family. So, he did not fully appreciate all of what there was to see in this beautiful, historic city.

Once he arrived at the hotel, Maerdern asked his personal guards not disturb him. He then settled into his room and spent the rest of the day there. He needed time to think and focus on his plans. It was crucial that his efforts against this family be successful. He needed the additional magic for his larger objective.

Maerdern also needed a victory. He knew that his followers had been carefully watching his efforts and gossiping amongst themselves. He needed to keep his powerful hold over his followers intact. There could be no doubt amongst his followers of his ability to succeed and dominate the seers or his overall mission may fail. So, he needed a success to report to them, and he needed it soon.

The next day, Maerdern sent his two followers out to spy on the Caravagio household. When they came back, they reported that the entire family was at the house. Maerdern knew that he was not yet powerful enough to take on an entire seer family, especially one of the three most powerful seer families. He would need to wait until the time was right to attack. So he waited at the hotel for the ideal time to approach the Caravagio house, when he would have the best chance of success. Each day he continued to send out the followers so that they could report to him how many of the family members were at home that day. He would make his move when less than the entire family was present.

Several days into his trip, his followers came back and reported that only Mrs. Caravagio was at home. They told him the other family members had left the house and that it appeared to them that the others would be gone for a while. So, Maerdern walked over to the house to confront Mrs. Caravagio with Rycroft and Baldolf.

When he arrived at the house, as reported, only Mrs. Caravagio was home. He directed Rycroft to knock on the door. When Mrs. Caravagio answered, Rycroft pushed his way into the house. Then, Maerdern and Baldolf went into the house right after Rycroft.

"Mrs. Caravagio," began Maerdern. "We would like to see your family's library of seer books. We suggest that you let us review your books and do not give us any trouble. If you wish to fight, we are prepared to win. So, you would be smart to comply without resistance."

Mrs. Caravagio, a thirty-two-year-old woman with black hair and emerald green eyes, looked at the men for a few minutes and thought about what she was going to do. She knew that she could defend herself, but she was not sure just how much power these men had. But if she gave in and allowed them to access to the family's library, she would be putting all of the seers in great danger. The Caravagios had some very significant rare and dangerous spells that should not be allowed to come into Maerdern's hands.

But she also knew that their library did not contain all of the books held by the family. After word had passed around to the top seer families that some books had been taken from the household of one of the other seer families, the Caravagios had carefully gone through their books and removed the most dangerous books from their library along with the journals of each of the family members. These books were moved to a hidden location within the home that could only be found and accessed by a member of the family.

Still, Mrs. Caravagio realized that if she gave in too easily, Maerdern and his followers might suspect that she might be hiding other books. So, she decided to try to use evasive tactics first. Maybe she could outsmart them.

"I don't want any trouble," she spoke carefully. "But the library has been in my family for many generations, and it is only for the use of my family. My husband has never permitted outsiders inside our library. He is due home soon, and he is very powerful. You should leave now before he gets home."

Maerdern narrowed his eyes and looked carefully at Mrs. Caravagio. It was his impression that she was bluffing about her husband coming home soon. But even so, Maerdern was prepared to face Mr. Caravagio, too, because he could not turn back. Viewing this family's magic books was too important for him to give up so easily.

"Step aside," ordered Maerdern with a snarl, "or I will be forced to use my magic to move you. If I have to do that, you won't be very happy. I guarantee you that." Maerdern pulled out his necklace with the seer trapped inside so that it lay on top of his shirt and Mrs. Caravagio could see it.

Mrs. Caravagio refused to step aside and let Maerdern by her. Instead, she waved her arms and caused her wand to appear. She then waved her wand and created a blue force field in front of her that formed a wall that blocked Maerdern and his followers from her.

Maerdern could see the wall in front of him, blocking his farther travel down the hall to the library. He shot out a bolt of energy to break the force field that Mrs. Caravagio had created, but he failed. His energy bolt was simply absorbed by the defensive shield, causing it to become even stronger. This took Maerdern by surprise but also intrigued him because he had not heard of such a technique before. He definitely wanted to learn how that magic worked so that he could use it himself.

Recently, Maerdern had learned some magic that allowed him to weaken the magic of another seer unless that seer knew the defensive technique to counter it. So, Maerdern tried that against Mrs. Caravagio next. But she knew that magic as well and quickly countered it. Mrs. Caravagio, thus, did not grow weaker. Strangely, though, it seemed as if she became a little stronger.

"She's tough," thought Maerdern. He would not give up, however. This was also good practice for him, and he was also learning the existence of some interesting magic that he could learn and use to become more powerful if he could figure out how to cast it.

Maerdern then moved his wand from side to side. The effect was to move the force field to the side a little, changing the angle at the same time so that the field was not perfectly parallel to Mrs. Caravagio. Maerdern was thrilled that he was able to affect the force field but disappointed that it did not work well enough for him to be able to slip by to get to the library. The effect was also only temporary as Mrs. Caravagio widened the actual size of the force field and curved it around to close the gap to the wall of the hallway.

Since he had suspected that the battle with the Caravagio family would be a difficult one, Maerdern had developed a backup plan. It was simple, and there was a significant chance that it would not work, but he thought he might try it anyway.

So, Maerdern signaled to Rycroft for him to employ the backup plan. Rycroft nodded and turned to leave. He walked out of the house and into the backyard. He then looked for an open window or another opening in the house. There were no open windows on the back of the house, and all the windows were locked so Rycroft could not force them open. He was about to break a window when he noticed a small pet door in the kitchen door on the back of the house.

Rycroft approached the pet door and then reached into a backpack that he was carrying. He pulled out a small white mouse with a pink nose, named Pinky, from a small cage that he had in his backpack. The mouse was a pet owned by Maerdern, who had been hand-feeding it for some time. The mouse would often sit atop of Maerdern's shoulder while he walked around the house, and Maerdern would feed the mouse rewards for staying on his shoulder. But today the mouse had a mission. Today, he would be assisting with the battle — little did Pinky know.

Rycroft gently ran his finger down Pinky's back and fed him a treat. Then Rycroft raised the pet door, and while holding Pinky gently in his hand, put his hand through the door until he reached the kitchen floor. Then he placed Pinky down on the floor. After he had retrieved his hand from the door, he blew on a whistle to signal to Maerdern that Pinky was inside the house.

From his place in the hall, blocked off by Mrs. Caravagio's force field, Maerdern closed his eyes and cleared his mind, and connected with Pinky. He gently willed Pinky to find the woman.

Pinky ran through the house, looking this way and that. He could smell food in the kitchen, and it was difficult for him to walk past the pantry without stopping and attempting to enter it for a little snack. But Pinky resisted that urge to stop for a snack because Maerdern was gently willing him to run quickly through the house to accomplish his mission. Since Maerdern was uncertain of the layout of the house, he was not able to direct his pet. So, Pinky had to find his own way.

Pinky ran in out and out of several rooms on his tiny little feet until he finally located Mrs. Caravagio. Pinky then climbed on top of her foot and grabbed onto her pant leg and started to run up her leg. Mrs. Caravagio instantly started screaming and waving her arms around, shaking them up and down in a panic. She then reached down to swat away the little mouse, sending the poor little creature flying through the air. Fortunately for Pinky, he landed on a soft dog's bed in the corner, and he was unhurt.

When she had become distracted by Pinky, Mrs. Caravagio had dropped her wand, and her force field disappeared. When the force field dissipated, Maerdern pushed past the woman to search for the family library. By the time Mrs. Caravagio had recovered from her shock and had refocused, it was too late.

"Secure her," Maerdern bellowed at Baldolf as he walked to the library.

Baldolf, following behind Maerdern, walked up to Mrs. Caravagio, kicked her wand far away from her and pulled her arms behind her back. He led her to a chair in the kitchen and tied her to the chair. Baldolf hoped that Mrs. Caravagio's source of power was solely from her wand and that she would not be able to use magic to escape the restraints he placed on her.

By this time, Maerdern had found the library and was already searching through the Caravagios' magic books. The Caravagio library was larger than the previous library that he had broken into. The library had two walls filled with floor-to-ceiling bookshelves. The books on the shelves were also much older than those in the other library. Some of the books were so old, and their covers were so worn, that it seemed to Maerdern that the books might fall apart as he flipped through the pages. There must be something useful here, he thought.

However, to his disappointment, from Maerdern's first perusal through the shelves, although there were at least one hundred books in all, it did not seem to him that the Caravagio library contained any books that contained extraordinarily powerful and rare magic. As he had previously, Maerdern initially based his conclusion on the book titles on the spines of the books.

But Maerdern eventually did try, this time, to methodically, but quickly, read through each book looking for magic that he did not already know instead of basing his judgment solely on the titles of the books. But there were so many books that he would not expect to be able to examine them all in a short time period.

Even though he could not find what he was looking for, he did find some new magic that he thought would be helpful for him to learn. As Maerdern inspected the books, he stacked in a pile those books that contained magic that he had not yet learned. In all, he had found ten such books when he decided that it would be best if he departed — before someone else came home.

Maerdern knew he should not stay much longer. He did not know when the rest of the Caravagio family was due to return, and he knew that he could not fight them all. It was also not his magic that had defeated Mrs. Caravagio. He knew that he had only defeated Mrs. Caravagio by cheating and with a little luck. And, he did not have a good backup plan for defeating the entire family at once.

So, Maerdern had his two followers pack the ten books in the backpacks that they had brought with them so that they could leave. But right before they left, Maerdern decided to take another ten books — just in case. He mostly picked the books randomly, but he tried to pick the books that were on the older side. He thought these might give him the best chance of finding some unexpected, powerful magic.

Maerdern then willed Pinky to return to him. When the mouse did, Rycroft scooped him up and returned him to the cage in his backpack. Pinky was disappointed to go back into his cage. Aside from being tossed through the air, Pinky had enjoyed his small period of freedom at the Caravagios' house. He squeaked loudly in annoyance. Maerdern used his will to quiet Pinky. He promised him a nice big piece of cheese when they arrived back at the hotel. So, Pinky settled himself down quietly in his cage and had a nap.

Chapter 36

To avoid a return confrontation with the Caravagio family, Maerdern left the city of Rome immediately after he returned to his hotel room. When he arrived back at his headquarters, he placed the twenty new magic books in his library. He then locked himself in the library with orders for his followers not to disturb him. He spent the next week locked away in his library with the new books.

Maerdern wanted to start his studies with the first ten books that he had searched through while at the Caravagio house. He knew these contained certain magic skills that he wanted to spend his time to learn immediately. But he knew that he needed to survey the magic available.

So, he started by skimming through each book to discover the kinds of magic detailed in the book and adding the magic to the catalog that he had created. One by one, he went through each of the other books. His plan was to create a priority list of the magic from the most important for him to learn to the least important. By making such a list, he planned to learn the most significant and powerful magic first.

He had been getting very impatient to get his plan for dominating all of the seers underway. To do so, he needed to learn as much as possible as fast as possible, and he had felt as if he would never obtain the necessary knowledge. So, although he wished to be thorough and learn each magic skill well, he also worked in haste, working as quickly as possible.

After surveying the ten books he had purposefully selected at the Caravagio house to list the magic that they contained, Maerdern started to go through the additional random ten. In the first of these books, he was excited and surprised to find magic that would allow one seer to compel the will of a seer weaker in power. That could be very useful, he thought, in obtaining additional followers or perhaps an apprentice. It was similar to the power that Maerdern had to will animals to do something. But this magic was different and likely even more useful. The books also contained magic for affecting the weather, making oneself appear more charismatic to others, avoiding the effect of magic on oneself cast by a seer with less power, creating fires, reading the minds of other seers, and an assortment of other types of magic that Maerdern might find useful in a battle against another seer.

Many of these magic skills were very interesting to Maerdern, but he thought that the most useful skill for him might be the one to compel the will of another seer. So, Maerdern immediately focused his work on that magic, reading the pages of the book, for that magic, multiple times and studying the instructions.

When he was ready to practice the magic, he chose the least powerful seer among his followers. He had that person, a man in his early twenties, called to his library.

When the follower arrived, Maerdern cast the magic on him to will the man to scratch his head. The follower scratched his head. Then Maerdern willed him to jump up and down and make clucking noises as if he were a chicken. The unfortunate man did all of these actions with a shocked look on his face because he did not know why he was acting so silly. He even apologized to Maerdern.

It was clear to Maerdern that this magic had worked, and he was satisfied. So, he dismissed the follower.

Maerdern continued to work through all of the magic books. Although he had first started the work in haste and without working carefully and deliberately, he was now practicing each magic skill, fully and methodically. He worked long hours each day, rarely stopping for meals and breaks. He had always been ambitious in his dreams, but his dedication to hard work and his thoroughness in his studies was new. With these two new attitudes, he was even more dangerous to Emaleen and her group than before.

While he had secluded himself inside his library and devoted his time entirely to training, he left his number two, Lanus Aimsley, in charge of managing his followers. Lanus managed them well, sending them out on various missions to further Maerdern's plans. But while managing the followers as Maerdern's second, Lanus, was setting his own groundwork for the day that he would overthrow Maerdern and take over the empire that his boss was building. Maerdern's followers were all very afraid of Lanus and followed him without question.

Lanus was creating loyalty to him among his boss' followers to prepare for the takeover he planned. But although Maerdern was absorbed in his own training and was not paying attention to this organization, the timing was not yet right for Lanus to invoke his takeover bid. He was continuing to bide his time, carefully planning and waiting for the right time to invoke the plan.

As he increased his own training regime, Maerdern started to rely more and more on Lanus to take over the day-to-day management of the followers. He also entrusted to Lanus the management of the organization's finances. His trust of Lanus promised to lead to the downfall of Maerdern's leadership over his own organization if he didn't start to pay attention. The more the leader trusted Lanus, the more he inadvertently set his second up to overthrow him.

Chapter 37

It was mid-October when Maerdern finally found some magic that he thought would be useful in solving the mystery of whether or not Mrs. Andarsan had a child out in the world somewhere. Maerdern had discovered this magic in one of the books that he had obtained from the powerful Caravagio family. The magic skill was located in the very last book from the Caravagio house that Maerdern reviewed. He had not noticed it when he went through the books the first time to catalog the magic in them because it was between two pages that were stuck together. In fact, he almost missed the magic entirely.

Maerdern had practiced the magic using the trees of other families to verify its accuracy in providing information before preparing to use it for the Andarsan family. It was now time for Maerdern to use it to pursue his true goal.

Maerdern took out the family trees that he had prepared for each of the seer families. He searched through them until he found the tree for the Andarsans. He laid the Andarsan family tree down on his desk. Then he pulled a sheet of paper out of one of the desk drawers. Onto that sheet of paper, he copied the Andarsan family tree. Maerdern's copy of the Andarsan family tree did not include Emaleen or Aunt Zeraida or Uncle Morvin because his original did not include them.

Then Maerdern took out his wand and a bag of black glittering dust. He poured the dust onto the paper containing the Andarsan family tree. He closed his eyes and waved the wand over the paper and the black dust. The dust began to swirl around. Some of the black dust began to stick to the paper.

Eventually, the dust stopped swirling around on the paper. Then Maerdern leaned over and blew the dust off of the page. When the dust cleared, he could see that there was a new addition to the tree. It stated "Emaleen" under the Andarsans with Emaleen's date of birth.

When Maerdern saw this, his eyes opened wide in astonishment. His own private investigator had failed to turn up any information about whether Mrs. Andarsan had lost her child or not. Maerdern had conducted the magic now simply to verify that there was nothing to be discovered. He was expecting not to discover anything, so he was amazed to have learned the Andarsans' long-held secret.

Now, he would need to set about finding Emaleen. If the Andarsans were hiding her, there must be a good reason. And he thought that their good reason for hiding her might be proof that Emaleen had, or would have, the type of powers that he was looking for in an apprentice.

Maerdern was so surprised to see Emaleen's name on the family tree that it almost escaped his notice that two other names had also appeared on the tree. The name "Zeraida" appeared next to Mrs. Andarsan's name as a sister. The name "Morvin Barsan" appeared next to Zeraida's name as her husband. He had not been aware that Mrs. Andarsan had a sister.

It was a fair bet, Maerdern thought, that the girl was living with Zeraida Barsan, wherever it was that she lived. Maerdern's next step would be to figure out where it was that Zeraida and her husband were living. He would then travel to their house for what was in his mind a long overdue visit.

But he wondered how he would find her. He was pretty sure that Mrs. Andarsan wouldn't tell him. He was also sure that she wouldn't be foolish enough to visit her sister and lead Maerdern's followers right to the girl.

Maerdern looked up at the books in his library and tapped his chin while he thought carefully. There had to be some magic that would help him, he thought.

He sat there for a while, thinking. He pulled out his notebook, too, and went through the list of skills. There was magic that would allow a seer to follow the trail of a person, but for that to work there must be a known starting point for the person from which the trail could be followed and the trail had to be fresh. After more than ten years, even if the magic would work to track an infant in the womb, Emaleen's trail was likely way too cold for it to work.

He could not come up with any other magic that could help him find someone when there was no trail to start with. Zeraida could be anywhere in the world, and he wasn't sure how he would find her.

Since he couldn't think of a way to locate Zeraida and he was very impatient to act upon his new information and find Emaleen as soon as possible, Maerdern sent for his number two follower, Lanus Aimsley. Maerdern opened the door to his library and asked the assistant that he had stationed at a desk right outside it to message Lanus the request that he appear at the library for a meeting with Maerdern.

Maerdern decided to ask Lanus if he knew magic for locating a person. If not, they could try to use the private detective again. But Maerdern was hoping that there was magic so that he could find Zeraida faster.

When Lanus arrived, Maerdern didn't disclose the real reason that he called Lanus to the meeting. Instead, Maerdern pretended that his purpose was to test Lanus' knowledge. Maerdern didn't want to let Lanus know that Maerdern didn't himself know the answer to the question that he wanted to ask Lanus.

So Maerdern stated, "Lanus, you are my second-in-command. I selected you as my second out of all of my other followers because of your great skill and leadership potential. I have a challenge for you to test your knowledge. If you succeed, I will provide you with a reward."

"Here is the scenario," continued Maerdern. "You need to find someone using magic. You do not have any starting point or trail for the person. You just need to find that person's current location."

Lanus smiled as he listened. He knew that Maerdern didn't know the answer to the question but was treating the matter as if he was testing him so he wouldn't know that Maerdern did not know. He was a lot smarter than his boss realized. However, he went along with the test because it suited his purposes at the moment to be Maerdern's second-in-command. To maintain his position as second, he must play the role of a follower who feared and respected his leader.

If Lanus let on that he knew that Maerdern was somewhat incompetent, Maerdern might perceive Lanus as a threat, and he might remove him from his position as second-in-command. If he were removed, that would thwart his plans of replacing his boss as the leader in the near future. Before Lanus could act to replace Maerdern, he needed to solidify his position in the organization so that he would be seen as the natural successor. Lanus also needed to wait until the organization was on solid ground and was not so loosely formed that Maerdern's vacancy from the leadership position would result in the demise of the organization itself.

"I think I might know how to do this," said Lanus. "I will give it a try. But I can't guarantee that it will work, though. Sometimes, people don't want to be found. And, some seers have magic that prevents them from being found."

Lanus actually happened to know how to do the magic but pretended to be doubtful as if he were being tested. Maerdern was satisfied that his ruse had worked and that he not only was going to obtain information about how to use magic to find a person but that Lanus was going to do the magic and locate Zeraida for him. Maerdern chuckled to himself and thought that Lanus was a fool.

"The name is Zeraida Barsan," stated Maerdern.

"I need a map of the world that is flat," said Lanus.

Maerdern went into one of the library's closets in the library and pulled out a flat world map and handed it to Lanus, who rolled the map out on the desk. The family tree was no longer on the desk because Maerdern had removed it while he was talking and placed it inside of one of the desk drawers. Once the map was rolled out, Lanus got out his wand and said the name Zeraida Barsan and pointed his wand at the map. The northeastern part of the United States lit up as if light was shining on it.

"Now, I need a flat map of the United States," said Lanus.

Maerdern retrieved this too from his closet and handed it to Lanus, who unfolded this map and placed it on top of the world map. Once again he said the name Zeraida Barsan, and pointed his wand at the map. This time, the state of New York lit up.

"Do you have a map of New York State?" asked Lanus.

"No, I don't," answered Maerdern. There hadn't been a need for him to have one. It was fortunate that he had a world map and a map of the United States.

"Let's go on the Internet and see if we can get an address for Zeraida," suggested Lanus. "If not, then we will print a map of New York State and use this technique to narrow down Zeraida's location."

Maerdern brought out his laptop, which he stored on one of the shelves of the bookshelf. When he searched the Internet for a New York address for Zeraida, he was unable to find an address. So, he printed out a map of New York State.

Lanus placed the state map on top of the others. He again said Zeraida's name and waved the wand over the map. An area on the map that appeared to be in the region of the Adirondack mountains lit up. So they printed out a map of the Adirondack area and repeated the technique. The area around a lake in the Adirondacks lit up on the map. Maerdern felt that this was a sufficiently narrowed location for him to be able to travel to the location and track Zeraida from there.

"Thank you, Lanus," said Maerdern enthusiastically. "I will have a reward prepared for you very soon."

"You're welcome, Maerdern," said Lanus, bowing slightly.

"I'm going on a trip," announced Maerdern. "I will be bringing two followers with me. I'm leaving you in charge here while I'm gone. Now, I'm going to go pack. Set up a meeting for tomorrow morning with all of our followers so that we can let them know that you will be in charge temporarily while I am away."

"I'll have them ready first thing in the morning," agreed Lanus.

Maerdern led Lanus out of the library. He then turned and spoke to the assistant who was sitting outside the library door at his desk and asked him to arrange a flight to Albany, NY for tomorrow or as soon as possible after that.

Eugenia, who was cleaning nearby, overheard Maerdern arranging his trip. Eugenia knew that she needed to get a message to Mrs. Andarsan as soon as possible, but she couldn't leave for many more hours when her cleaning shift was over. She knew if she left any sooner, they would suspect her and she would not only lose her access to the house as a spy, but she might be in danger for her personal safety. So, right after her shift was over, she arranged for a message to be sent to Mrs. Andarsan using the secret method that they had arranged.

Seanna Andarsan did not get the message until late the next morning after Maerdern was already on a plane headed to Albany in New York State. She tried to call her sister to warn her, but no one answered the phone at the Barsans' house, and the call did not go to an answering machine. So, as a backup, she arranged for a message to be sent by pigeon through Mr. Cavanaugh.

Mr. and Mrs. Andarsan also left their home immediately to drive to the airport. There they purchased tickets for the first available flight to New York, which would cause them to arrive on a flight ending in Albany the day after Maerdern's arrival.

Hopefully, Mrs. Andarsan thought, they would arrive soon enough. She was also not concerned about being followed since Maerdern now knew about Emaleen and where she was. It was now more important for them to join their daughter in case their daughter needed help fighting Maerdern.

Maerdern arrived in Albany, New York in the afternoon the day after he discovered Emaleen's existence and general location. When he arrived in Albany, he rented a car, and he and his followers traveled north to the Adirondacks. He wasn't sure exactly where he was going, but he knew that direction would, at least, bring him closer to Emaleen.

With a follower driving and Maerdern sitting in the back seat with maps, the rogue seer thought out a plan. His general plan was that he would start by arriving in the lake area in which he suspected Emaleen lived and finding the office where the local land records were kept to see if he could find any properties that were owned by the Barsan family. He looked up on his phone the location of the office with the property records in the county in which the lake was located. He then directed his driver to set the GPS device to the correct address.

The driver drove up the Adirondack Northway, which is the name of the highway that runs from Albany up to Canada, even though the highway goes south as well as north. Along the way, Maerdern noticed that some of the trees were leafless, and those with leaves left had red, orange, or yellow leaves. If Maerdern weren't so focused on his mission of locating Emaleen even he would have been impressed by the natural beauty of the trees surrounding the highway and on the mountain tops that could also be viewed from the highway as they drove farther and farther north into the Adirondack region. But he was too focused on his mission to absorb the beauty that surrounded him on all sides.

When he finally arrived at the local records office for the county in which he thought Emaleen resided, he asked for some assistance in looking up the property records. It was not long before he located records for a property owned by the Barsan Family Trust. Maerdern suspected that this must be the correct location for Zeraida, given the name of the trust.

So, after he left the office, he searched the property on his phone and viewed a satellite image of it. It was hard to see the house and its surrounding yard in the satellite image because there were many very tall trees surrounding the house and providing it with some camouflage. He also looked on a map-making program on his phone and checked out the area.

It was getting late in the day, and Maerdern was tired from his long journey to the United States from England. He decided to check into the hotel that had been arranged for him and find some nourishment and get some rest. He expected that his arrival at Emaleen's house would result in a battle. So, he needed to be well rested to ensure his best chance of success. He instructed the driver to drive him to the hotel. Once he arrived, he ate an early dinner and went to sleep.

The next morning, Maerdern was awake early. He was too excited and nervous about this mission to eat much for breakfast, but he had a piece of bacon and a small glass of orange juice at the hotel breakfast bar. His two followers, Baldolf and Rycroft, both ate hearty meals and took a long time finishing their breakfast, which was greatly annoying to Maerdern, who had wanted to go over to Emaleen's house as soon as possible.

After breakfast, Maerdern went back up to the room and spent some time meditating and clearing his thoughts. He was getting ready for a powerful magic encounter. He would need all of his inner strength and focus to win this battle. He did not know much about Zeraida or her husband, so he had no idea what to expect from them. In particular, he did not know how powerful she and her husband could be. This was of great concern to him.

When he was finished with his meditation and focusing, he called together his two followers, Baldolf and Rycroft, for a meeting. He explained to them the object of the mission and their roles in it. He did not want either follower jumping in and interfering. Maerdern did not want them to do anything that might impede him.

Also, although Maerdern did not share this with his followers, he simply wanted to handle the matter himself so that he could have the credit for the success. He did not want either follower having any chance of being responsible for the success of the mission.

After he had completed his meeting with his two followers, Maerdern left the hotel to start his drive to the Barsan residence. By this time, it was late in the day.

Chapter 38

Skye and Emaleen were playing outside on the day after Maerdern had flown to Albany. Zeraida and Angelina were outside too, keeping watch. Mr. Stewart was away on a trip and was expected back shortly.

Zeraida had not received the warning message from Mrs. Andarsan yet. So, none of them knew that Maerdern was on his way.

Although it was almost the end of October, the weather was still warm. It was about seventy degrees outside, which was very unusual for this time of year. And there was not one cloud in the sky. The girls had completed their homeschooling for the day and were enjoying their free time.

The women were sitting on the porch swing sipping lemonade, talking quietly, and rocking back and forth. It was so calming and relaxing that the ladies could have fallen asleep but for their duty to keep a close eye on the girls.

Suddenly, a strange feeling overcame Skye. She felt goosebumps form all over her body. It felt to her as if every nerve ending in her body had awakened. Skye's guardian necklace also started to glow and become warm. She knew immediately what the problem was because her mother had described it to her exactly. She knew she must act quickly.

Skye shouted, "Everyone inside, now!" Her mother had instructed her to order everyone into the house if she had any warning of danger whatsoever. Skye had never felt before what she was feeling now, and so she was glad that her mother had described it so well.

Emaleen looked up in surprise as did the adults. Then they all did as Skye had commanded. They ran into the house quickly.

Aunt Zeraida locked the door behind them and directed them all into the family room, which was an interior room. From there, they would not be visible from the windows and being in an interior room meant that they would not be as susceptible to magic being cast at them from outside the house.

Once inside the family room, Mrs. Stewart turned to Skye and asked her if she had sensed danger. Skye nodded without saying a word. She was now shivering uncontrollably.

Mrs. Stewart looked with sympathy and compassion at her daughter and hugged her tightly, hoping that she might calm her. She was concerned for her daughter but it was also important for Skye to recover herself and keep her focus and calm so that she could think clearly.

After Skye had stopped shaking, Mrs. Stewart asked her daughter gently, "Can you tell us about what you sensed?"

"Yes," answered Skye, speaking quickly. "There is someone coming. He has bad intentions against Emaleen. I can feel his evilness. His heart is dark. He will not stop until he finds her. He knows about her, and he knows what she looks like. He has a picture of her in his head. He knows where we are."

"Is he alone or are there others?" asked Mrs. Stewart.

"There are two others. And, they will do anything to help their master," said Skye.

"Thank you, my dear. It will be all right," promised Mrs. Stewart.

Angelina and Zeraida looked at each other for a few seconds without saying a word. They knew it must be Maerdern.

Zeraida reached over and hugged Emaleen to reassure her. Then she whispered to her niece, "It will be fine. We have a plan. Stay calm and keep your focus."

Zeraida then held her finger up to her lips, signaling both girls to be quiet. Both girls and the two women became quiet. Zeraida and Angelina stood still, listening for any sounds that they could potentially hear from outside the house.

It was quiet for at least ten minutes. Skye's internal radar had been much stronger than Zeraida or Angelina had expected it to be. That was helpful because that gave them plenty of warning.

"Emaleen, use your mind to will Belenus to come over here. You will need him to be with you," whispered Zeraida. "We will need him with us in case we have to move away fast. We don't want to leave him behind."

Emaleen did as Zeraida instructed and Belenus appeared almost instantly. He laid himself down at Emaleen's feet and waited there patiently and quietly for further direction from her.

Aunt Zeraida had a very effective emergency plan in place, but she wanted to wait to be sure that Maerdern or his followers or both would actually appear and take action against them before she enacted her plan. So, they continued to wait there in silence.

As they waited, Zeraida quietly instructed them that, upon her signal, they would all form a circle, holding hands with Belenus in the middle. But they would need to wait until Zeraida's signal. In the meantime, she had them all stand in a circle just in case.

Zeraida did not want to rush away and reveal the unusual way in which she had planned to escape because it was a power known only to a few seer families and she did not want Maerdern to know that it existed. She also wanted to see whether they might successfully fool Maerdern or if they could not, Zeraida wanted him to reveal some of his powers. But they would be ready to disappear in a flash if needed. It would also be a chance for Emaleen to have some practice with her defense skills with Zeraida by her side. If Emaleen's magic were to fail, Zeraida would take over. Aunt Zeraida would be very careful, though, not to risk their safety. Nothing would be worth risking their safety. Still, they did need to know what Maerdern was capable of.

It was silent for several minutes more and then suddenly there was a bang at the front door, and the house shook. From the family room, they could hear the door being blown off of its hinges and falling to the ground, and the three men climbing over the door into the house.

Aunt Zeraida sent a signal to Emaleen. In response, Emaleen raised and lowered her left hand quickly. The motion caused the bracelet to slide off of her arm and turn into the wand. The jewels on the wand caught the light and glowed. She could feel a surge of power run through her as she held her wand ready.

Emaleen looked over and saw her aunt holding her wand as well. Her heart was pounding so hard that she thought she could almost hear it. She had practiced magic for quite some time now, but she had never had an opportunity to put it to use for real. She hoped that she would be able to keep her focus and perform the magic that she had learned without any difficulty.

On Zeraida's signal, Emaleen evoked one of the protection skills that Zeraida had taught her. She made herself, Skye, Mrs. Stewart, and Aunt Zeraida invisible from view. They were still standing in the same place, but they were not visible to the human eye.

Zeraida had informed Emaleen that this skill was a first line of defense. Sometimes, she had explained, the enemy would simply leave, not realizing that the target was actually there. And, unlike many of the other skills, this particular skill did not generate any waves of energy that could be detected by an average seer. That would give them time to evacuate with less urgency and be able to bring some supplies along with them. But, it depended upon the enemy not being able to sense them and not having the skills to counter the invisibility.

As the two girls and women stood there under a cloak of invisibility, they watched as Maerdern and two of his followers, Baldolf and Rycroft, walked through the doorway of the family room and stood just inside the room looking around. They barely dared to breathe as the men stood there. After only a few seconds, which seemed to them like an eternity, the men turned and left the room.

Chapter 39

They could all hear footsteps as the men walked through the house looking for the occupants, particularly Emaleen. From these sounds, she knew that the men walked into the kitchen, guest room, bedrooms, bathrooms, and even the attic upstairs.

In some of the rooms, the men stopped for a while. Each time, following a brief silence, loud noises that sounded as if furniture was being dragged across the floor and drawers were being opened and then slammed shut, made their way down to the females.

It was seemed to Emaleen that the men were searching through the family's possessions. But from the angry sounding shouts, it appeared that they were unsuccessful. They also did not find Aunt Zeraida's or Emaleen's secret rooms since Emaleen did not hear the sound usually made by the door. She also knew that these rooms were designed so that no one but the owner could enter them or even become aware that the rooms existed in the first place.

Emaleen could hear the men talking upstairs as she listened very carefully. She had trouble making out the exact words being spoken, but it sounded to her as if there was one man who was ordering the others around. His shouts sounded increasingly angry as they searched. The man's voice also sounded evil, and it made her shake with fear.

After several minutes upstairs tearing through the rooms, the men descended the stairs, stomping loudly on the steps. Then they walked into the family room and discussed their next steps in hushed voices. From the words she could hear, it sounded to Emaleen as if they weren't sure where to search next.

Maerdern was convinced that the family was home. They had to be in the house, he thought. But why hadn't they found them, he wondered. Perhaps his men weren't searching thoroughly enough, the evil seer thought further.

So, he barked to his men, "They have to be here. I expect you to find them now or there will be serious consequences that will be worse than anything you can possibly imagine." Maerdern knew, however, that he could threaten these men all he wanted but if the Barsans weren't there, it was pointless. Still, a little threat would make them search harder, he mused.

Thinking the matter through for a few minutes, it occurred to Maerdern that perhaps the Barsans were actually in the house, but were using magic that the family was versed in, but he was not. But then he remembered an invisibility technique. He had also learned, recently, that there was magic that could counter invisibility.

So, he raised up his wand, which had only two gems affixed to it, when it should have had at least three. He waved the wand around him in alternating directions. As he did so, he shouted out loud for the benefit of anyone who might hear him, "Hiding from me will not help you. I will find you. And, when I do, I will make sure you are extra sorry for hiding from me."

Maerdern was about to give up trying to find them with his magic to counter invisibility because it seemed to him that he had waved the wand all around and still had not achieved his goal. But just then, to his surprise, Emaleen, Skye, Zeraida, and Angelina appeared right in front of him.

Emaleen had felt a strange sensation when Maerdern had been waving his wand. Now, she could tell by the expression on Maerdern's face that she was no longer invisible. He must have countered my magic, she thought.

She would have to remember what it had felt like when she felt Maerdern's magic, she thought. Her aunt had shown her how it felt when a seer nearby had cast magic so that Emaleen would recognize the feeling. That was a gentle vibration. But this was different. It was somehow icky and gave her that creepy feeling that she felt when someone invaded her personal space. In a sense, she guessed that someone countering her magic was the same as invading her personal space, so it seemed logical to her that when an evil man such as Maerdern cast magic around her, it would cause her a creepy feeling.

Zeraida, too, knew that they were no longer invisible. She had felt Maerdern's magic, and she knew from her own personal experience the kind of magic that evil seer had cast. Zeraida knew that it would be pointless to counter Maerdern's magic and make them invisible again because Maerdern could not now be fooled. Clearly, he knew they were there. But Zeraida had prepared for this event and so signaled her niece to do additional magic.

Emaleen held up her wand and concentrated. The tip of her wand gave off a blue glow that quickly grew into a clear, blue bubble that wrapped around the females. She felt a sense of relief because she knew it was an energy field that protected against any person approaching the people inside it. In fact, any person who approached would bump up against it and would be unable to push past it since it was stronger than the strength of any human. However, Emaleen also knew that the energy field could be broken by magic, but only by a seer who knew how to. She hoped Maerdern didn't have that knowledge.

In signaling her niece to cast this magic, Zeraida was counting on Maerdern not having the knowledge necessary to break the field. But if he did, Zeraida was prepared — she had trained Emaleen to address that possibility as well.

Maerdern, in fact, did not know the magic for breaking Emaleen's energy field. But he did not want to make that known to his targets or his followers, who were under the impression that Maerdern was all-powerful. So, he stood there thinking about his next move.

After several moments, Maerdern came up with a plan. He would try to distract them the same way that he had distracted Mrs. Caravagio, he thought. Pinky, his pet mouse, was in his bag. He would let Pinky out and see if the presence of the mouse might spook the ladies and make them lose their concentration and, as a result, cause them to drop the magic force field.

So, he leaned forward. Then he closed his eyes and concentrated and willed Pinky to come out of the bag and approach the ladies. The mouse climbed out of the bag and slid down Maerdern's slanted back to reach the floor. The little mouse walked over to the ladies, squeaking loudly at them as he did so.

Pinky was hoping to scare the ladies and make them lose their concentration as Mrs. Caravagio had. The mouse remembered that his role in the attack on the Caravagio home had earned him dessert privileges for a month. He would not forget that privilege and hoped that he could be successful now in case he might get rewarded again.

Pinky's efforts didn't have the effect he intended. Emaleen's concentration stayed on her magic, and the bubble remained in place, unaffected. She was instantly thankful for her extensive training in ignoring distractions, compliments of Aunt Zeraida and Belenus. Aunt Zeraida, who was even more skilled, was also not distracted.

Belenus, however, did focus on Pinky. He crouched down on the floor, rested his head on his front paws, and wiggled his behind. Emaleen knew from her research on cats that Belenus was preparing to pounce at Pinky, and she knew she didn't need that distraction. So, while careful not to break her concentration on her magic, she willed Belenus to stop. Belenus meowed in annoyance but complied.

Maerdern let out a disappointed sigh. He had not considered that Pinky would not be able to get beyond the force field. In the Caravagio situation, Pinky had entered through a back door. Here, Pinky was just as blocked from reaching the women and girls as Maerdern and his men were, since the targets were encased in a bubble.

"Emaleen!" Maerdern called out loudly. "I know your mother. She is alive and well, and she wants to see you. If you come with me, I will take you to see her." Maybe he could either convince her to join him or he could bully her into doing so, he thought.

"I know about my mother, and I know all about you," retorted Emaleen with a look of defiance and tone that demonstrated an attitude. "You are nothing but a stranger to me, and you are evil. I will never go with you. I want nothing to do with you! Go away!"

Maerdern shook with anger at Emaleen's response. He was not used to anyone talking to him that way and defying him. All of his followers were scared of him and did as he bid without any disrespect. The girl must be taught a lesson, he thought.

"Emaleen," continued Maerdern. "Do you see this necklace that I have around my neck? Do you see the man inside the bottle? Do you know how he got there?"

Maerdern paused for a moment watching for Emaleen's reaction. He searched her face for evidence of her fear. But Emaleen just stood there with her face clear of any reaction. Maerdern could not believe what he was seeing. He had expected the girl to be frightened, but she was standing there cool and relaxed. What he didn't know was that she was terrified, but she wouldn't let Maerdern see it. She was also determined to win against this awful man.

"Emaleen," said Maerdern with an evil snarl. Then he said, rambling wildly, "I could put you in that bottle. Or I could put your cat in that bottle. I could put your friend in the bottle. I could pretty much do whatever I want."

Emaleen stared directly at Maerdern with a defiant look in her eyes as if communicating to him that she would not give up and would not back down. The evil seer wasn't used to such defiance, so the girl's challenge made him violently angry causing his body to shake visibly.

Maerdern shouted at Emaleen, "You are weaker than me, and I will win. You can either come along with me nicely, and I will be nice to you. Or you can come along with me the hard way, and you will live in chains."

Belenus was pacing nervously back and forth in front of Emaleen's legs. He wanted badly to hiss and snarl at the evil seer. The cat also wanted to jump on the man and bite and scratch him. He knew that Maerdern had bad intentions toward his girl, and he did not like it at all. He was so angry that all of his hairs were sticking straight up, and his tail was flicking back and forth violently. He let out some low, but still audible growls.

If it weren't for the fact that Emaleen was willing him to hold himself back, Belenus would have already been all over Maerdern, biting and scratching him fiercely. He hated Maerdern because he could sense that the man wanted to harm Emaleen. But she willed him to hold back because she did not want him to become injured and perhaps die. She loved Belenus too much to see him harmed. She and her aunt would take steps to fight without risking Belenus.

"Maerdern, you cannot harm Emaleen!" shouted Zeraida sternly. "She has all of us by her side, and we will beat you. You cannot win. You don't know all that I'm capable of. So, I suggest you leave and get out of my house now!" Zeraida waved her wand, and the man in the bottle disappeared.

"Look at your necklace," Zeraida scoffed. "I've freed the poor man in your bottle, and he is now beyond your wrath." She knew, however, that freeing the man had both advantages and disadvantages. On one hand, it weakened Maerdern. But on the other hand, it potentially created other dangers for Emaleen.

Maerdern let out a loud roar of anger. The release of the man was a loss. He had been drawing upon the man's power to increase his own. That man also was a danger to his operation because he knew too much, having been in a position to overhear Maerdern's conversations.

He knew that later he would have to send followers to search out the man so that he could try to recapture him. But he had been lucky to have trapped the man the first time, and he knew that he might not be able to do it again.

For now, he knew that he must focus his efforts on Emaleen. So, he raised his wand and shot a bolt of energy that glowed with red light and hit her blue bubble force field. The magic did not break through the bubble but bounced off of it and hit Maerdern in the chest, as well as his two followers. When the magic hit him, he instantly fell to the floor. His followers, however, had received only a mild effect because only a small portion of the energy had actually hit them. However, even though it had been minor, the followers were not pleased.

Baldolf and Rycroft, fearing that Maerdern was potentially dead and that they would be harmed by an angry Zeraida, ran out of the room and out of the house without him. They had never been hit by magic before, and they did not want ever to get hit by it again. So, running away seemed the best course of action.

Once outside, the two men discussed what to do. If Maerdern was, in fact, dead, they were free. If their leader was not yet dead but was at risk of being harmed further by Zeraida, it was of no concern to the men because their leader was truly cruel and as such they had no love for him. So, they decided the best action they could take was to stay outside and see how the evil man fared in his battle.

As a result of being hit by the rebounded magic, Maerdern was stunned and did not move. But after a few minutes, he slowly rose from the floor and stood to face his enemies. He realized at once that he had shot himself with his own magic, but he still blamed Emaleen and Zeraida. He was not the type of person who took responsibility for his own actions. There was always someone else that he could blame.

His next move was to throw compulsion magic at Emaleen to try to force the girl to leave the circle of protection and join him. Although Maerdern was successful in casting the magic, his effort was weak and ineffective because he had lost some of his power when Zeraida had released the mysterious man in the bottle. So, the inclination that Emaleen felt to join Maerdern was minimal at best, and it was easy for her to disregard it and stay where she was.

Zeraida felt the compulsion as well, and she was shocked that Maerdern knew the magic to produce it. It was a relatively rare form of magic that was known only to a few families, and it was an example of the kind of magic that the most powerful seer families were trying to keep from him. The fact that Maerdern knew this magic could indicate that he had other rare abilities as well, thought Zeraida. He might be even more dangerous than she had supposed him to be.

Suddenly, Zeraida knew that she needed to take quick action to end this battle immediately. If she were to allow it to continue, they might lose, and a loss to Maerdern would come with severe costs. She could not risk her niece's safety any further. So, she threw out magic to put Maerdern into a deep sleep from which he would not arise for several hours. The magic hit her target square in the chest. He was just recovering from his fall and from absorbing the energy bolt that he had accidentally shot at himself. So he was not prepared for Zeraida's magic and, as a result, he was not able to counter the spell. He quickly fell to the floor and drifted off into a deep, deep sleep.

Then Zeraida used magic to lift Maerdern up and float him through the air and out of the house. Once he was outside, Zeraida dumped him onto the ground in front of the house. When he hit the ground, his body made a satisfying thud that all of them heard from inside the house. Zeraida then used magic to fix the door and lock it.

Once Maerdern was gone, Pinky decided he should try to sneak off quietly. He turned and started to scurry toward the door. However, he was stopped by Belenus, who put his paw down on Pinky's tail, trapping him. Pinky squeaked loudly and tried to pull his tail out. But he was unable to escape the cat's grip.

Emaleen noticed and asked Belenus not to harm Pinky. Perhaps they should take Pinky with them, she thought. He seemed like a harmless little mouse. He might make a very good pet and certainly she and Skye would treat him better than Maerdern did, she thought.

Aunt Zeraida asked Emaleen, Skye, and Mrs. Stewart to each pack a small suitcase and meet her downstairs in the family room in less than ten minutes. Zeraida informed them all that they would be moving to a new house in a new location as soon as possible. They should pack only their most essential items because the new house was well stocked and already contained what they would need.

"Please pack light," requested Zeraida, "but please do pack your most favorite items that you feel you cannot live comfortably without. But don't worry so much about clothes. We have plenty of new clothes for everyone at the new location. Right now we need to hurry. The magic that I used should keep Maerdern asleep for at least a couple of hours, but we cannot be sure that he doesn't have enough power to bring himself out of his slumber earlier than that."

"When he wakes up, he probably will not feel all that well," added Zeraida with a self-satisfied smile. Everyone chuckled heartily before they started the packing.

Emaleen ran upstairs and collected her laptop computer, her phone, some favorite books, and some of her favorite clothing items and packed these away in a small suitcase. She also retrieved her cloak from the closet in her room and put it on. She then ran downstairs and gathered together some of Belenus' favorite toys. She also found a small plastic box in which to carry Pinky to a new home. This might make a good carrier for Pinky if she added air holes, she thought, and so she did so. After gathering all that she felt would be necessary, Emaleen took her suitcase to the family room and waited for the others.

When everyone was gathered together in the family room, Zeraida asked them all to form a circle, with their suitcases inside the circle. They each placed their suitcases in the center as instructed by Zeraida, but Emaleen also put Pinky in the box and placed it in the center.

Then, Zeraida asked Emaleen to put Belenus in the center of the circle and for everyone to hold hands and close their eyes and to keep them closed until she told them that they could open them again. Zeraida also asked them to stay as still as possible.

They closed their eyes after all had joined their hands. Emaleen felt powerful vibrations around her as Zeraida cast magic. But she kept her eyes closed and remained still. Then, she heard a swoosh sound.

Right after they closed their eyes and Zeraida had started the magic, Mr. and Mrs. Andarsan ran into the room and shouted their daughter's name. They were just in time to see the ladies disappear. Although they were sad to have missed their daughter, they were very relieved to see that she was unharmed.

Chapter 40

"You can open your eyes now," announced Zeraida after the magic had been completely cast.

When they opened their eyes, they found themselves inside an unfamiliar room. Standing in front of them were Uncle Morvin and Mr. Stewart, who both looked surprised at first at the sudden appearance of the girls and ladies but then they smiled joyfully. Emaleen then ran up to hug her uncle while Skye hugged her father.

After she stepped back from her uncle, Emaleen glanced around and discovered that they were in a room with rugs and couches and a fireplace. It must be a family room, thought Emaleen.

"We are on an island in the St. Lawrence River, in an area known as the Thousand Islands," explained Zeraida. "Maerdern shouldn't be able to find us here. There are over eighteen hundred islands in this river. And this is a safe, secret home that we have kept prepared for the event that we would have to flee our Adirondack home."

"Aunt Zeraida, how did we get here?" asked Emaleen softly in a slightly shaky voice. She still felt a little shaken and stunned by the appearance of Maerdern and the magic battle that had occurred.

"When your uncle and I were married, the wedding rings we exchanged contained matching gems. The gems have a special property that gives them the tendency to want to be together when they are apart. All I did was tap into that property so that the rings would bring us here. When we created the circle, that allowed us all to travel together, along with anything inside our circle. This magic is ancient and is only known by very, very few seers. But I'm glad that we were able to transport ourselves without Maerdern observing us. He should not know about this power."

"I thought I heard a woman's voice right before we left," commented Emaleen.

"Yes, I believe it was your mother, and I think your father was there too," replied Zeraida. "They must have come to help you but arrived just a little too late. But by the time I had heard their voices, it was too late for me to stop the magic so we just missed them, and there was nothing that I could do about it."

"Will I ever meet them?" asked Emaleen sadly.

"Yes, I believe you will . . . someday," responded Aunt Zeraida.

"Aunt Zeraida," asked Emaleen, "why didn't you kill Maerdern? If you had done that, wouldn't the danger that I am in be over?"

"I didn't kill him for at least two very important reasons," answered Zeraida. "One reason is that I'm against using our magic to hurt others, no matter how much we might feel the other person might deserve to suffer severe consequences for his or her actions."

"We have also learned from our spies," interjected Uncle Morvin, "that it isn't just Maerdern who is after you now. He has formed an organization with many followers and a leadership structure under which the followers have various degrees of rank. The second-in-command, Lanus, is actually more dangerous to you than Maerdern, which might surprise you. Maerdern has derived much of his powers from having followers and learning from them, although it would be foolish to underestimate him. But Lanus is actually much more competent and has even twice the desire to obtain power over all of the seers. So, it's better for us, for now at least, for Maerdern to stay in power until we can figure out how to defuse the entire organization."

Aunt Zeraida nodded and said, "My second reason was concern about Lanus."

"Any other questions?" asked Zeraida.

"Why did Skye tell us all to go inside?" asked Emaleen. "How could she know that Maerdern was coming?"

"She is your guardian," replied Zeraida. "One of her special talents is the ability to sense when someone who means you harm is near. But I was surprised by just how much warning Skye was able to give us. She must have some pretty strong talents to have detected Maerdern from so far away."

"Any more questions?" asked Zeraida again.

"Yes, are there any other people living on this island?" asked Emaleen.

"Mr. Earl is also here with Shaolin. But other than that, we are the only residents of this island," answered Zeraida.

"I understand that there are a lot of islands," stated Skye, jumping in. "But why are you so confident that we can't be found here and that we should feel safe to explore this island as we wish?"

Zeraida responded to Skye, "The reason why we believe this is a safe place is that this island is actually invisible and not on any map. There are also very many islands in this river, and we are on an island that is pretty far away from any large cities, towns, or villages. We also have developed at least a dozen different routes to get back to this island when someone goes out for supplies, and each route has at least one method of losing any person who may decide to follow us. Finally, because it so remote and surrounded by so much water any magic that we use here is virtually undetectable by any other seer."

Aunt Zeraida then said to her niece, "Emaleen, as I said a little earlier, we believe that someday we will be able to unite you with your mother and father. It may not be right away, though. They are both being watched carefully by Maerdern, and they are followed wherever they go. They know where we have gone, but they can't join us because they might be followed. But we will figure out a way."

Emaleen smiled and nodded at her aunt. It would be wonderful to reunite with her parents permanently, she thought. She would love to get to know them. She was also pleased that they had tried to come to her rescue. At the same time, she was disappointed to have just missed them after all the years of being apart from them.

Zeraida continued, "But you need to remain hidden for longer so that you can continue to learn as much as possible. You need to be as powerful as possible before you next meet Maerdern."

"When you are powerful enough," added Aunt Zeraida, "you can come out of hiding. You will then work with us, and other seers, to defeat Maerdern permanently. I know this is hard, but he will not stop until we defeat him. He will continue to search for knowledge about magic and to train because he wants to defeat all of us. He will become more powerful."

"But," said Zeraida, "you did a great job today casting magic to protect yourself. I am extremely proud of you. You kept your cool, and you kept your focus. You are going to make a very fine seer someday. You just need to keep working hard and learning as much as you can."

She just might even turn out to be a peerless seer, thought Aunt Zeraida. But, she knew it would be best not to share that possibility. It was her opinion that it would be best to keep her niece focused on her studies and to wait and see how she turned out than to fill Emaleen's head with dreams of being a peerless seer.

Emaleen beamed with pride. It felt wonderful to hear the compliment from her aunt. She knew her aunt loved her, and her aunt often provided praise. But after all of the stress from the day, the incredible fear that she felt earlier, and the self-doubt that she had felt at the time and pushed aside, it felt good to feel so proud of her accomplishment. She was also relieved to be away from Maerdern. He truly was an evil person, and she hoped that she never saw him again.

Zeraida continued, "That being said, Emaleen, please do not think that because we were able to escape Maerdern today that he is not all that powerful. He might not seem very powerful, but he is desperate for power, and he is very ambitious. You should never underestimate someone who is strongly determined to do something no matter what your opinion is of his or her ability. A determined person can often overcome a lack of natural talent with hard work, and in an enemy such determination can make the person a very dangerous opponent."

"Wouldn't a person with both talent and determination be even more dangerous?" asked Emaleen.

"Yes, but you have a lot of work to do," replied Aunt Zeraida with a smile. "Fortunately, although Maerdern will be back again, it will probably take him a while to find you because we will now have you hidden even better than before. We must use that time wisely and continue your training with haste. As I said, when he returns, he will be even more powerful. So, you must be prepared."

Emaleen looked sadly and nervously at her aunt. Her battle with Maerdern had been scary. She couldn't imagine coming up against him again. It worried her still more that Maerdern would be even more powerful the next time.

Aunt Zeraida and Mrs. Stewart looked sympathetically at Emaleen. Zeraida wished that she could completely shield her niece from all of this so that the poor girl would never have these experiences. But until the seers all got together and became officially organized and fought and defeated Maerdern, Zeraida knew that he would keep coming for Emaleen and that there was no way that she could prevent it. So, she would have to train Emaleen as quickly as possible and protect her as securely as she could.

"So — we have all had a really rough day," commented Mrs. Stewart. "I suggest that we all take a break and relax. Let's get something to eat and settle in. It would be nice to have a bath and a long nap and to unpack and make ourselves feel at home. We can get to work again tomorrow."

"That's a good idea," agreed Zeraida. Then she added, "Girls, you each have your own room upstairs. I think you can figure which ones and choose a room."

The girls nodded quietly and proceeded upstairs to choose a room and settle in. Once on the second floor, they noticed that there were indeed two rooms decorated for girls of their age. Each of the rooms contained a bed made up with matching sheets, pillowcases, and bedspreads, but each had different designs on the bedding. One was decorated with blue flowers, and the other was decorated with stars and moons. Skye chose the star and moon-themed room, and Emaleen picked the flower-themed room. Emaleen moved Belenus' items into her room while Skye made a space for Pinky in her room and made him a makeshift home with bedding.

Both rooms contained a desk with a laptop computer. They had hardwood floors and fluffy white area carpets in the center of the room. There were also clothes in each room, in the closets and in the dressers matching the desk and bed. It appeared to Emaleen as if someone had predicted which room each girl would choose because the clothes in each room were sized for, and suited to the fashion tastes of, the girl who chose the room.

As the girls were settling in, Zeraida unpacked in the room that Morvin had settled into. Mrs. Stewart found the guest room and discovered that her husband had already been there and unpacked. So she unpacked her things there.

After unpacking, Angelina and Zeraida met with Morvin and Jay to give them a summary of what had happened. They did not include the girls in the discussion but instead allowed them to play on their own. They needed that time just to be kids and to relieve some of the stress and anxiety that the encounter with Maerdern must have caused them, thought Zeraida.

Morvin informed the ladies that he had learned that the Jaimeson family had captured a Maerdern follower and were hoping that he might be a good source of information. He also reported that the follower had so far refused to talk.

The girls had remained upstairs after settling in their rooms. They had been too tired to do much more than lay around on the carpet in Emaleen's room and play a board game that they found on one of the shelves. But they were so tired they did not finish the game.

Zeraida noticed both girls were asleep when she came to check on them. Belenus had also fallen asleep on the carpet next to the girls. Pinky was also there, fast asleep inside his makeshift house. Zeraida did not want to wake them, so she put a blanket on each girl and slid a pillow under each girl's head. She also put the board game away for them and turned out the lights. It was better, she thought, to let them sleep because they had been through a lot this day. And sadly, Zeraida knew that there would be more trouble to come.

Thank you for reading The Peerless Seer.

If you enjoyed it, won't you please take a moment to leave a review at your favorite retailer?

Emaleen's adventures continue in

"The Peerless Seer's Gambit."

B.S. Gibbs

Creative Assistants A.R. and S.R. Gibbs

www.Emaleen.com

www.facebook/EmaleenAndarsanSeries

www.facebook/BS-Gibbs-1675139912704406

@EmaleenAndarsan

Made in the USA
San Bernardino, CA
10 October 2016